Ivy Eff

By Louise Burness

Self-published by Louise Burness through Amazon Createspace.

Cover illustration by Louise Burness, design by David Spink

www.louiseburness.info

For my wee Ma, Meg.
You've always encouraged and supported my ideas, no matter how random. Thank you.
This time, next year...

Chapter One

'I'm so sorry, Ivy, I think it's better that I'm honest with you. I just don't see things working out for us in the long term.' Will looks at me earnestly, with the expression of a budget, day time TV show, agony Uncle. He takes my hand; I withdraw it and wipe the remains of his clammy grasp on my dress.

'Just go,' I reply, wearily. I can't be bothered with the, now verging on two hour, post-mortem. My favourite show, 'Don't Tell the Bride' is on in five minutes. I laugh at the irony and think of my stunning dress hanging in the back of Mum and Dad's wardrobe. Will clearly didn't think it appropriate to tell the Bride he didn't actually want to marry her before the invites went out this week. *This week!* What the actual fuck was he thinking? How humiliating. One hundred day-time guests with a further seventy, for the evening reception. I suppose I should be grateful for small mercies, like him not calling it off on the day. I think of all the pitying glances I'd get. Wry smiles from his ex-girlfriend, who he had insisted on inviting and his best mate and best man, Johnny, who had expressed his disgust at our decision to get married in the first place. Mainly, I suspect, because he is too unpleasant to attract a partner himself, with his habitual, loud belching and collection of porn. Will's Mother, who I'm convinced has never liked me anyway, would no doubt be relieved. She gave me the considerate gift of a bleaching kit, 'for your upper lip,' and a pair of hold-in pants as a Christmas present last year. She had thoughtfully voiced her concern at the possibility of us having a female child, based on my 'hirsute problem.' I was raging mad when I got home and looked that one up in the dictionary, I can tell you.

Will and I have been together since the evening of my twenty-second birthday. I couldn't believe my luck that this gorgeous, funny man that all the girls were trying to flirt with, was interested in me. Even then, all I had wanted was to get married and have children, unlike some of my Uni friends who had dreams of travel and climbing the corporate ladder, before even entertaining the idea of settling down. I had split up with my high school boyfriend six months before I met Will and had been reluctantly planning with a few school friends to go backpacking around Asia and Australia. Will wasn't keen to wait a year for me to travel and I took that as a good sign, he saw us as serious already. I pulled out just before the flight tickets were bought and off my friends went on the chance of a lifetime trip, leaving me to wander dreamily around Habitat, picking out scatter cushions and candle holders. I think sadly of the children we had planned. One girl, one boy, with blonde curls like Will and brown eyes like me. Our bouncy, chocolate Labrador and lazy, affectionate ginger cat, our Victorian detached five-bedroom house with an endearing clutter of plastic toys in the back garden and cosy evenings watching Disney classics on the sofa, with a blanket and a huge bowl of popcorn. Ok, so my future life was based around a variety of American sitcoms but still, it was my perfect existence and now it's gone. When I say this was our plan, I now realise with sadness that Will was never very proactive in our discussions and the red flags had been there but I'd missed them.

'Just go' I yell, with a sudden surge of anger. 'Oh, and you needn't think I'm telling anyone it's all off, you can have that particular pleasure.' Will smiles wanly at me and pats my hand.

'Of course,' he whispers. 'Thing is, well, as you know, I have kind of been paying the rent until you got your new job and the first pay cheque came through so...' I look at him in disbelief. He's dumping me *and* kicking me out? I had found this flat and begged with him that we could afford it. We needed a spare room so we didn't have to move immediately after having a baby. Two even. I had lovingly restored a junk

shop find of a table and four chairs, painted every room myself on my weekends and holidays. This is *my* home.
'How can you have changed your mind so suddenly? We were fine until your fishing trip with the lads,' I trail off as it dawns on me. This Stag do was the first of three; I had joked before he left to make sure he didn't catch anything. He had looked puzzled and asked if that wasn't actually the point, and chortled when I listed: Herpes, Syphilis, Crabs.
'Hey, crab can be quite tasty, ' he'd laughed. Oh how we'd both laughed. I'd ruffled his hair like the cheeky chappie he was and sent him off to some wader-sporting ho, who had clearly thrown him a line and reeled him in, hook, line and sinker. I allow myself a bitter, congratulatory smile that I could be so utterly heartbroken and still funny. He had been distant and withdrawn since his return. I had put it down to pre-wedding jitters. I've had a few myself.
'Who is she?' I enquire, intently watching his reaction. Will starts, then smiles and gives the sigh of a smitten man.
'There isn't anyone else, Ivy, he simpers, ' I'm not the kind of man who would go out and find a replacement before I'd got rid, er, broke up with the one I'm with. I was serious about us, I just still feel so young and I know you are desperate for kids. I can't give you that right now.' A vision of his balls as a knapsack to make sure he can't give any woman that springs to my mind. I dismiss it on the grounds that he will in no way turn me into a dismembering, psycho bitch. So this is it. Eight years, a posh frock and a 'collection' of two Le Creuset casserole dishes later and I am single. I pack a few things into a Tesco bag and slam my departure and disgust behind me.

I sit in my Parents' lounge; the good one, for special guests and big events, and listen to the Grandfather clock tick away my fertility in the hallway. Mum sighs dramatically and twists an invisible string of pearls in her fingers. Dad looks awkwardly out of the patio doors at Mr. Twattington Bollocks

mowing a further tenth of an inch off his lawn. It's not his real name of course, but I have never been particularly interested in remembering his real one. He's a snob, much like my Mother actually who guffaws when he laughs and calls other men, 'old bean.'
'I have to say, we are terribly disappointed, Ivy. Aren't we, Brian?' Mum's voice trails off unexpectedly high in a hysteria that only dogs could hear. Mum's expression takes me back to my ballet recital, aged five, when I couldn't disrobe from my tutu pre-show and wet myself on stage. To be fair, Mum considers both Dad and I jointly, the family embarrassment. Dad, for his bumbling, social ineptness, me, for pretty much everything from the style of my clothes to my choice of career. I say career, but I haven't found anything I'm particularly good at that earns anything over minimum wage and prefer to sketch stuff, in my spare time. My CV has more pages than your average tabloid, with everything from sheep shearing in the Hebrides to an advertising stint as the arse end of a Highland cow. My elder sister, Evelyn (which annoyingly they insist on
pronouncing Eev-lyn and not Eva-lyn, like I do, just to annoy her) has the perfect life, with her catalogue-gorgeous three children and Doctor husband. Mum never misses a chance to inform me about all their achievements, from the extension to their six-bedroom Corstorphine home to the glowing school reports of my niece and nephews. My mother doesn't do emotions, finding them unnecessary. I know she is inwardly trying on a variety of facial expressions to use in front of the Bridge club ladies, when she has to face them for the first time since I brought shame on the family.
'Well since your Father and I bought your dress, I guess we could salvage it by turning it into some new curtains for the bathroom. First thing I thought of when I saw you in it, Ivy, wasn't it, Brian? That's the exact material I've been looking for. Shame it's on a dress.' My Father and I exchange a look.

Mine says; she's not actually my real Mother, is she? Dad's says; you get the shovel, I'll fetch the lime.
'Barbara, for goodness sake cut the girl some slack. This isn't any of her doing, you know. It's hard enough for the lassie without having a constant reminder every time she goes for a slash.' I raise my eyebrows at Dad's sudden outburst. Mum's hand flutters to her throat and with an indignant sniff she mutters that it must be time for a G&T, in the southern hemisphere, possibly.
'Would you like one, Ivy?' Mum asks over-zealously. 'Today is a cause for commiseration.' She nods her sympathy. She prefers to have an ally to enable her daytime drinking.
'No thanks. I'm going out to meet Ginny,' I mumble, desperate to escape the pea-souper of an atmosphere. Dad audibly sighs his relief and gets up for an awkward embrace.
'Look after yourself, darlin', and you know you are welcome to come home here if that's what you want to do.' He pats my shoulder gently. I smile my gratitude and leave Mother Superior inspecting herself in the over mantel mirror for a sudden increase in grey hairs. I slip out the front door into the fading Edinburgh sun.

I spot my friend through the bustling, post- work throng in our local. I fall gratefully into Ginny's outstretched arms as she rocks me back and forth to her muttered, sympathetic words.
'Twatting prick....absolute shit-stain...the worst kind of bastarding whore-meister...the single-most useless ever waste of a sperm.' She soothed me for a good minute before holding me at arm's length and examining me with a frown.
'Wimbledon starts tomorrow, my dear. I know exactly what you need.'
'Champagne and strawberries?' I enquire hopefully. She shakes her head.
'New balls, please,' she shouts jovially. Ginny is my oldest

friend, we have known each other since Nursery class. She has always had an opinion on anything and everything. Imagine my horror, aged eight, to discover that Barbie was a misogynistic view of the perfect woman; huge rack, tiny waist, a range of clothing that would make a page three girl look classy and although she may pretend to have a career, everyone knew she only had the aspiration to become Prom Queen. Ginny chose to intentionally take an apprenticeship in the male-dominated profession of plumbing, just to prove a point to our career advisor who had suggested either hairdressing (on account of the funky, dark quiff she still sports) or office work. She doesn't have a girlfriend to distract her at the moment, which means she will make me a full-time project. Ginny's view of fixing someone is similar to her view of plumbing; if you can't sort what's already there, simply order a new part. It has around a fifty percent success rate when it comes to real-life situations. It worked for my Walkman in High School, I'm not convinced about it mending my sham of an almost marriage. We order our cocktails and I nod dutifully in agreement as Ginny launches into a half hour rant about what she'd like to do to Will, ranging from prawns in his curtain rail to itching powder in his boxers. She finally exhausts her cathartic tirade by announcing,

'Of course, you wouldn't get this crap with a woman.' I splutter on my margarita as I think back to Ginny's last girlfriend, Shaz, who had cleared off whilst Ginny was out on call, stealing her entire CD collection and the cat, who she had grown attached to.

'Well, you can't stay at your parents, obviously. Your Mother will have a new man lined up for you to be married to by this weekend, just to save face. No arguments, you're staying with me.'

'Thanks, Gin,' I exhale my relief. 'Just until I get my own place, my bank manager is going to have a hairy canary if I extend my overdraft again but too bad. I don't even have my

portable telly anymore. Will decided to give it away to his niece, for her bedroom.' I give a long sigh. 'How can my life's total of possessions be measured in shoes?' I slump my head onto my arms.
'And very nice shoes they are, Ivy. If you sold all but two pairs you could probably buy yourself a rather nice 50", smart TV. '
'Naff off, Pollyanna,' I mumble to the table, 'I don't need your posi-fucking-tivity today. My life is in tatters. I can't even succeed at the one thing I thought I was doing right.'
'Well, when life gives you lemons...' I glance up at Ginny with a frown, 'squeeze them in the eyes of the feckers who are pissing you off,' she finishes. I give a hollow laugh.
'Let's get another round,' I announce, ' I need more stories about what you're going to do to Will.'
By nine o'clock, our imaginary revenge plan has included Gin and I going on my Honeymoon where I meet my real future husband, to discovering Will's new girlfriend is secretly a man. On Ginny's instruction I have had a tentative look at what's on offer out there, on the man front, while she checked out a few of the women. She made me feel better by telling me there are more straight men in the world than gay women, so statistically I'm bound to meet my real husband-to-be before she meets her wife. My phone buzzes and I look at the display, its Will. Ginny reaches across the table and rejects the call.
'He may have changed his mind,' I wail, 'Let me talk to him, please.'
'Won't hurt to make him wait overnight,' Ginny gives me a stern look and pops my phone into her jeans pocket. Too tired to have anything resembling fight in me, I down the dregs of my drink and we head out onto Lothian Road towards Ginny's self-named 'Bitchelor pad.'

I arrive at work early the next morning. I couldn't sleep

and thought I may as well get up and treat myself to breakfast and the banter of my favourite Welshman, in Taff's caff. The conversation begins as normal with Rhys, the owner, moaning about the latest tourist pointing out his eatery's intentional spelling error. Three this week, it transpires. Eventually he cocked his head to the side and announced,
'You look like shit today, Ivy. Had a rough night?'
'I've just had the arse ripped out of my world, Rhys. Why, what's your excuse?' I lower my voice and look sheepishly away, 'Will dumped me.'
'No, Oh Ivy, I'm so sorry. You know I never liked that pillock anyway, but wow! And just before your wedding. He's reached new depths this time, this is the shittest of shit things to happen.' I smile at his solidarity. He reaches over the counter and awkwardly pats my hand. 'Breakfast on the house, for Ivy,' Rhys yells to the waitresses and twenty odd commuters. 'She just got binned.'

I rush through the corridors of the call centre, avoiding eye contact, and slink into my tiny cubicle. I twist back and forth absent-mindedly in my swivel chair. The crowded office makes me hanker after the space allowance for a battery hen. I put on my headset and look at my calls list. And the winner of the first call to receive a fantastic offer to change broadband providers is... Mr. Salmond. His name makes my mind turn to thoughts of fishing, and subsequently, Will. I visualise a welly-legged couple frolicking on a boat. The mother-of-all-sharks slips silently through the calm waters towards them. The man tells the woman how he will always love her and what an exciting future they have together. The cello infused, movie theme gets louder and faster in my head. He whispers something and she giggles like one of those annoying girls you'd roll your eyes at on the bus. She's unzipping his fly, *take it out,* I urge. Let him be shark engulfed by that tiny morsel first. The shark raises her head from the water, bares

two rows of razor sharp teeth and....
'Ivy!' I drop the pen I'd been chewing thoughtfully and look up in fright.
'Mr McLeod!' My employer looms above me with a thunderous expression. 'I was just thinking about how I could increase my sales this week,' I whisper meekly. He simmers with anger and points with a chunky digit, towards his office. I trail humbly behind and sit down opposite him.
'Ivy, as you know you're on a temporary contract here at Diamond Edge. Your position as a sales person for our client companies requires you to achieve twenty-five sales per week.' Mr. McLeod looks down at a spreadsheet on his desk. 'Now you got off to a great start on week one, but your subsequent five weeks have indeed resulted in twenty-seven sales.' Well, that's fine then. I can't help wondering how the old codger has managed to get the figures so spectacularly arse-about- tit, there is no way I've made my weekly targets, but I'm saying nothing. Week one I thought I had finally found my calling. I stormed it. Every call was received with great enthusiasm and willingness to chat. Yes, they would love to save money on their phone package; they had plenty of time to chat, no urgent dental appointments or running late for the school run. I grew in confidence; strutting along the corridors saying hello to everyone I met with the mutual smiles of a winning team. Until, week two, and the seventeen people that had been off with Noro Virus returned and I discovered I had been following up their established leads to close a quick sale.
'Twenty-seven sales, *total,* in those five weeks, Ivy. What the hell happened?' Oh! I stare like a terrified deer in front of a rifle. 'Today is your six week review and as you know I only have twenty permanent positions. I was so sure you would slot nicely in to one of those but I'm afraid I am left with no choice but let you go. You just aren't a sales girl, Ivy.' Ginny's incredulous face appears in my mind's eye mouthing

the word, 'girl.'
'But, and I do like to leave things on a positive note, you gave a great interview. You managed to sell yourself enough to convince me to take a punt. I'm happy to provide a reference for a non-sales position for you.' He glances at his Rolex, 'You may as well head off now, actually. I have a lot of people to get through today. Goodbye, Ivy.'

'I need to come round, I need some stuff.' I'm aware I sound indescribably miserable and I hate the thought that Will thinks it's all because of him. He's only the icing on the cake, the cherry on top is the fact I have no idea how I'm going to fund a new flat on Jobseekers allowance. I definitely don't want the further humiliation of letting Will know that I'm jobless, as well as homeless and dumped, and give myself a mental shake.
'Erm, now isn't good for me, Ivy.' Will's reply sounds distracted. I can hear the sound of running water in the background. It stops abruptly and I hear my shower door open. I hang up and head towards my old, regular bus stop. He can get to Falkirk if he thinks he can deny me entry to my own home. Calling was only a formality; I'm perfectly within my rights to let myself in with my own key. And anyway, when Ginny had kindly unpacked my carrier bag as I lay prostrate on the sofa, she had raised an eyebrow at my emergency gathering array of two pairs of pants, a greying bra, toothpaste, tampons and one sock. The bus stops at a red light. I glance out of the window at a teenage girl smiling up at her boyfriend, placing a delicate butterfly kiss on his lips.
'Get a bloody room,' I murmur ungraciously, before tutting and nudging the elderly lady next to me, to share my scorn. She shakes her head in mutual disgust. The bus rumbles down the familiar street and with herculean effort, I push the button. I fish for my keys in my coat pocket and steer myself towards the front door before I can change my mind. I turn

my key in the lock and hear an unfamiliar woman's voice. 'That was quick, I hope you haven't forgotten the condoms,' she laughs. I round the corner from the hall and the smile freezes on her lips. Some blonde, skinny, damp-haired, woman is standing in front of me in *my* dressing gown and drinking coffee from my favourite cat mug. She must be twenty-two if she's a day. How dare he move on so quickly, in my home and with my personal things still there? She eyes me nervously, backing slowly behind the dining table to put an obstacle between us. How dare she think I would lower myself to the level of punching her lights out? She'll suffer enough, going out with Will, if what he's just done to me is anything to go by. I rally my senses and seize the upper hand.

'Oh don't worry about me, dear, I Just popped by to pick up...' my eyes search the room frantically, 'my mail. Here it is.' I flick through them. 'Bill, bill, bill, Will's credit card statement, council tax,' thank God, I have one. I clutch my only letter gratefully and head for the door. I turn back and gesture to the remaining envelopes on the table. 'Since you've replaced me in all other aspects, I'm sure you won't mind taking over my share of those.' I calmly close the door behind me and rest my head against the coolness of the frame. Prick!

I wait at the bus stop and congratulate myself on how calm I remained. Nobody else? My arse. Well she's welcome to him. I have had a very costly near miss. I slide my finger along the inside of the envelope and pull out the letter. After the week I've had it's bound to be our Honeymoon tickets ready for collection. I so deserve them after this; Gin and I can head off for two weeks in Barbados where I shall no doubt shamelessly shag many a hot young local. I unfold a reminder, disappointingly from the NHS. Your smear test is now due. Please make an appointment at your earliest convenience.

Chapter Two

It's the day of my should-have-been Hen party, on one of those glorious, freak sunny, Scottish Saturdays with just a hint of a breeze. How typical. Today was originally going to involve a picnic in Princes Street Gardens, followed by a ghost tour on the Royal Mile and culminating in a Rose Street pub crawl. This was to be my Henny for friends only so we could really let our hair down, with a more sedate one for the relatives and oldies in a couple of weeks' time. Instead, Ginny and I are swigging back weak Pimms to numb the pain of being forced to attend a barbeque in my sister's generous back garden. 'My Gerald,' our name for my sister's husband on account of her every conversation beginning with those exact words, is removing the fat from steaks like he's performing surgery. God forbid the perfect family should be tainted with an extra few calories. Mum wobbles over, kitten heels sinking into the lawn and sloshing half a glass of Pimms onto her cream cardigan.

'Gin-ny,' she says fondly, tilting her head to the side. Dad trails obediently behind and gives my friend a hearty handshake.

'Mrs. Efferson,' Ginny smiles politely, glancing around for the nearest exit. It had taken a lot of persuasion to get her to come along today, as my plus one. There's nothing as conspicuous as a furtive, lonely character skulking by the drinks table, trying to go unnoticed. Particularly one that everyone would want to interrogate, to satisfy their morbid curiosity by dissecting every detail of the tragic bride's misfortune. Ginny, by her mere presence, gives me the confidence to take on my family.

'How's your boyfriend?' Mum squeezes Ginny's arm hopefully.

'I told you, Mrs. Eff, I'm a lesbian.' Ginny smiles patiently.

'I know, dear, but I don't see what being foreign has to do

with it, unless your parents want you to marry a nice Greek fellow, hmmm?' Gin rolls her eyes and throws me a look that leaves me in no doubt that I will be paying for this later.
'Lovely place, Lesbos. That's where we went, isn't it, Brian?'
'Lindos,' mumbles Dad. Mum's not stupid; she knows the situation full well and just refuses to acknowledge it. Ginny's 'condition' can be cured once she meets the right man. This current conversation has been going on in a variety of forms since Ginny came out, just after we left high school.
'Isn't My Gerald a fantastic cook?' gushes my sister, barging into our conversation, as usual. She smoothes down her black bob and winks a brown eye at me. We look very similar, my sister and I. Although my hair is longer and I'm more tanned than she is. Of course, My Gerald makes sure none of his family so much as open the curtains without a head to toe covering of total sun block. Evelyn looks much more polished than I and oozes money from every pore.
'So how's my baby sis?' she nudges me, with less than a hint of concern. 'Just awful news, *awful,*' she reiterates for emphasis. 'Luckily, Boden has a fantastic returns policy and when I explained, they said there was absolutely no problem returning our outfits.' She exhales her relief and gives me an indulgent smile.
'Ginny,' Evelyn acknowledges, with an expression of someone who has just stepped in a dog turd. They don't get along. She still blames Gin for me throwing up in her expensive handbag aged seventeen after a bottle and a half of Blue Nun.
'Evelyn,' Ginny responds with an identical expression.
My sister grabs my arm conspiratorially and pulls me behind the marquee and out of earshot of the others.
'What the heck happened, Ivy? You must have done something pretty bad to make him change his mind at the last minute. Do you want to end up like Aunt Eleanor?' I pull my arm away in disgust at the thought. Mum's older sister, the single most unpleasant person ever born, which is saying

something, given some of my family members, sports a five o'clock shadow. Men take it bravely in turn to ask her up to a sympathy dance at weddings. Unfortunately this gives her the impression that she has a collection of suitors and the misguided assumption that she's a cross between Kate Moss and Elle MacPherson. I look around surreptitiously, expecting her to step out from the shadows; I've managed to avoid her so far today as I suspect she will have a list of tips for me on attracting a new man.

'I haven't done *anything*,' I hiss. 'He has taken it upon himself to meet some embryo and trade me in for her. As far as I was concerned, everything was just dandy. ' Evelyn's face softens slightly.

'Well, come and meet Mark. He's a Doctor at My Gerald's hospital and amazingly still single.' Really? My sister reckons that I can forget all about an eight year relationship and a cancelled wedding by being chatted up by some dull doctor? If her husband is any kind of measure, his friends will be misogynistic and full of their own self-importance. Evelyn leads me by my elbow to a small huddle of loudly chatting men.

'Oh, hello there, you must be Ivy,' smiles a surprisingly handsome gent, offering me his hand. Salt and pepper hair flatters his forty-something looks. Even though the last thing I want right now is another relationship, I would never have thought of going for an older man; grown up enough to have sown a few wild oats but with some left for me, probably financially secure and emotionally mature. His blue eyes crinkle at the corners when he smiles. On seeing my empty glass, he proffers a jug of Pimms; attentive too, I smile appreciatively as the amber liquid splashes into my glass.

'So, what do you do, Ivy?' he enquires with interest.

'I'm kind of between jobs at the moment,' I bluff. 'Latterly in sales but before that I was in, erm, advertising,' I finish lamely.

'Interesting,' he nods his approval, 'in which aspect of advertising?'
'I was in... well, it was mostly involving farming...supplies?' I stutter.
'Intriguing. I have my own advertising agency in the city centre. Are you thinking of meandering back down that path again?'
'I think so,' I reply, enjoying some proper attention for once. 'I didn't particularly enjoy the role I was in, but through negotiation with my Senior Manager, I did eventually move up into a position that I enjoyed slightly more.'
I note a twinkle of glee in Evelyn's chestnut eyes.
'Oh, be honest with the guy, Ivy. She moved from the back end of a cow to the front, after complaining to her boss about her male colleague's flatulence problem,' she gives an evil cackle.
Mr. Salt and Pepper gives a small cough and takes a sudden interest in the conversation next to him. Damn you, Evelyn, I flush. I'm not bothered about missing out on a potential beau but it could have been a much needed crack at a job. I glare at my sister's smug face, rosy with superiority.
'George? George! There you are,' a busty red-head in a low-cut, floral sundress elbows me aside. 'I shall just remove my husband from your way, shall I?' she aims a pointed look in my direction. Evelyn is pointing towards me, chatting animatedly to a large, rosaceous man, who is currently trying to fit the remains of a sausage sandwich into his mouth. No!
'Ivy, meet Mark. I've been filling him in on your latest drama. He's very sorry to hear of your sadness,' Evelyn gives a mock sympathetic pout and strokes my arm. Mark nods, chewing furiously. His lascivious gaze settles on my cleavage, I give a small, involuntary gag as he holds out a greasy hand for me to shake. I give the briefest of acknowledgments, my eyes transfixed on a dribble of ketchup on his chin and I am trapped, for over an hour. Hearing all about his 'interesting'

job as a podiatrist, as if he wasn't quite the catch enough already, he messes about with people's feet all day. Yuck! He has never been married and feels that perhaps he scares women off with his high status and gentlemanly ways. Apparently, he's a dying breed and women just don't appreciate the little things, like doors being held open for them anymore. He has joined an online dating service and has had a lot of interest. He asks me nothing about myself what-so-ever but does ask me to go out for dinner with him tonight. He has a villa in Spain and owns outright a mansion, on Burdiehouse Road. Eventually Evelyn can stand it no longer and needs an update. She *seriously* thought I'd be interested in this egotistical buffoon?
'Such a sad state of affairs,' Mark is shaking his head. Evelyn gives me a sidelong glance. 'Poor Ivy, or should I say, Sister Theresa?' he smiles graciously. Ok, I got desperate and for some reason I thought of The Sound of Music and there we have it. Unfortunately, my vows don't allow me to take up the kind offer of a date with Mark. I 'm leaving for the Highland convent in two hours and this was my last visit to my family and my final few drinks other than the occasional communion. I head off to find Ginny and leave an open mouthed Evelyn staring after me.

I lie on the sofa, in my one sock and Ginny's pyjamas, watching Jeremy Kyle. It's not my usual type of programme but it makes my life feel more normal. We are currently awaiting Jeremy to give us the results of a DNA test to see if the teenage, tracksuit-clad, bleach blond with obligatory dark roots, baby is the boyfriend's, his father's or the bloke who drives the ice cream van's. My money's on the latter. My mobile rings, I sit up and glance at it and the TV in turn for a few seconds. It's my grandfather. He wins every time.
'Hello, Granddad!' My last remaining grandparent has always been my favourite.

''Ello, Ivy, me little love, what's my girl been up to this time, eh?' his familiar, Cockney accent immediately making me feel safe and loved. Granddad, my dad's dad, now lives in Surrey but is a former East-end market trader. He used to make Evelyn and I laugh by shouting out what we were having for breakfast as if he was on his stall.
'Cocoa Pops wiv' toast and jam for Ivy, muesli and scrambled eggs for Evelyn. Last ones today, three for a paaaaand.' Sadly, Evelyn hadn't kept up too much with Granddad as she got older, Just the occasional wedding or funeral obligatory meet-up. She didn't know what she was missing.
'Oh you know, Granddad, just finished my PHD and being headhunted by NASA.'
'Again?' he laughs, 'they just won't take no for an answer.
'Well I'm probably going to have to leave Richmond soon. Every rich-bitch, twenty-one year old in town has been hammering on my door. They can't get it into their heads that I'm just not interested.' I laugh loudly; nobody can cheer me up like my Grandfather can.
'So, what you up to in real life then, girly?'
'Jeremy Kyle re-runs. You?'
'Just been down Waitrose for my messages and making a cup o' rosy, want one?'
'Oh, yes please. ' I smile at my grandfather's use of a Scottish word. He had looked most puzzled the first time we had said we'd pop out for messages and came back with groceries.
'Come down, Ivy, love. Get your head together in sunny, old Surrey. There's a new restaurant on the Quadrant you'd love. Your old Granddad could take you shopping in Kingston...'
'Oh, I'd love to but I have to find a job, you tempting, old git.' He chortles, and splutters into a coughing fit.
'Please tell me you've been back to the doctor, Granddad,' he coughs through my concern.
'Yes, Ivy, yes. Now get your arse down here. You need a proper break and you've no job to limit your stay this time.

Put the train fare on your card and I'll sort it out when you get here.'

'I'll think about it,' I give my hesitant reply as we say our goodbyes. I'd really love to go but running away won't solve anything. Anyway, the wedding won't be cancelled yet. I need to be here in case Will changes his mind. I can go and see Granddad any time. Right now, salvaging my marriage is the main concern. My biological clock is beyond ticking, it's now an incessant alarm going off in my head. I'm thirty-one next birthday. I know there's plenty of time, statistically, but I've been desperate for years. I never expected it to take seven years for Will to propose, and under duress. I falsely spoke about wanting to travel after all and since we didn't seem to be going anywhere, maybe I should. I pushed him into it, didn't I? He never wanted to get married. I left him no choice and brought it all on myself. I pick up my phone again, I promised Ginny I'd let Will contact me again, after the first time when he left no message. It's been four days now and he still hasn't called. He made the first move and probably hasn't called again as he thinks I'm not interested. I search his name in my favourites and hit call.

'Hi, this is Will; I'm probably in the pub and can't hear my phone. Leave a message and I may get back to you. If I don't, you'll know I never liked you anyway.' I start at the sound of my own laughter at the end of the recording. That seems like a whole different world now.

'Will, its Ivy. I really need a time when I can come and collect my things. Or talk, we can talk if you want. I, er, met your friend. She probably said. I wasn't too happy she was using my things, to be honest. I miss you. I miss our flat, our life. We should be getting married in five weeks. It's not too late. Anyway, give me a call. Bye.' I'm annoyed at the desperation in my voice. Really? Am I that desperate that I could push someone to marry me when they say it's not what they want? Someone who could be unfaithful to me before they even have a ring on my finger? I absent-mindedly watch the resulting fight on Jeremy Kyle as I ponder this. Eight years is a long time to waste with someone who decides they don't want to be with you after all. He needed the push either way. Most of my school friends are married with at least one child, one of them has *three*. Why was it my choice that went wrong? Maybe I do need a trip. The last place on Earth I want to be on my supposed wedding day is Edinburgh. I shall spend all this week setting up interviews and waiting for Will to call. If I have no joy by then, I'll go and visit my Granddad in Richmond.

Chapter Three

I sit in the cramped waiting room with around thirty other interviewees, all of us looking increasingly nervous at the prospect of a group interview. I detest these jolly, team player exercises with their ridiculous questions designed to portray your true self. If you were a car, what type would you be? My Grandfather's old Volvo; green, a bit rusty and prone to regular breakdowns, of course. I smile at the fact I have an answer ready; they always ask that one. The door opens with a squeak.
'Would the candidates like to come through now, please?' We follow the secretary through like obedient sheep, subconsciously forming the kind of line my primary school Headmistress would have been proud of. We take our seats in the circle and look up with anticipation at the kindly-faced woman making her way to the chair at the front of the room. This is my third interview this week. The first, a total disaster, had started off well. I was in fantastic form, shooting back answers with the occasional, humorous anecdote to boot. Mr. Stewart had clapped his hands with glee at the end.
'My gut instinct is telling me to offer you the job, Ivy. The fact you already have some Sales experience is a bonus too, but as a formality I will have to get in touch with your referees.' Mr. Stewart perched his glasses on the end of his nose, like a wise old owl, and glanced at page ten of my CV, entitled referees.
'Well bugger me! Jim McLeod,' he gives a booming laugh, 'We go back bloody years. This is wonderful, Ivy, I'm seeing him this weekend for a round of golf.' Mr. Stewart leans in toward me with a wink, 'I may have to ply him with a couple of extra malts to get him to dish the dirt on the real you,' he smiles. I'm sure that won't be necessary, my horrified, frozen smile tells him.

Interview two, personal assistant within a small group of life-

coaching consultants. So thorough in their asking of key, open questions that I spilled my troubles within two minutes and embarrassingly tearfully, to boot. The panel of three coaches shook their heads sadly at my tragic tale of woe. The poor, jilted thirty-year-old, fired from her job, had just admitted to sneaking a few ciggies after five years of quitting and teetering on the slippery slope of ending almost every day with half a bottle of Sauvignon Blanc. I didn't leave with a job, but I did leave with their brochure and an insistence to get in touch as soon as I could afford the four hundred and fifty pound fee to get my life back on track. This current interview is the last one I have before my deadline of a week to turn things around. I've promised Granddad I will stick to it; I can't go back on my word. I've heard not a peep from Will, since my garbled message. He's clearly moved on to pastures new, not that I'm calling his new bit of stuff a cow or anything. She's clearly just not very bright. How can she expect Will to stay faithful if he cheated on me, with her?
'Hello, everyone, my name is Kate McIntosh and as head of recruitment, I will be hosting our meet and greet for today. We have a rather relaxed intro for you, just a little getting-to-know-each-other chat, for the moment. As we move around the room, I'd like you to stand in turn and tell us your name, your current circumstances, followed by what you consider to be the most interesting thing about yourself.' Kate turns to the person on her right, six away from me. I smile politely, in anticipation, but my insides appear to have turned into a washing machine on fast spin. The first potential employee smiles adoringly around the room. You can tell she's just that type who loves nothing more than to talk about herself.
'Hi everyone, my name is Emma and I'm twenty-six years old. I live with my husband in our four bed-roomed, detached house in the New Town and this will be my first job since having my adorable twins. The most interesting thing about me, in my opinion,' she giggles girlishly, 'is that I won 'Come

Dine with Me,' last Christmas.' Emma does an annoying, little curtsey to her applause and sits, with a smug expression.
'How interesting, Emma,' beams Kate, 'and you?' she smiles at a nervous looking guy in his late teens, who is sweating so much his shirt has huge patches under each arm and all down his back.
'My name is Ally and I'm nineteen and a half.' Bless, oh to be young enough that the half still counts in a good way.' This is my first interview since leaving college and I like to write computer programmes in my spare time.' Ally sits quickly after blurting out his introduction. Without missing a beat the next woman stands and clears her throat importantly, 'Unaccustomed as I am to public speaking...' the whole room laughs, except me. I am in a blind panic as to what to say. Hi, my name is Ivy and until last week I had a job, a home and a fiancé. Now, I have nothing but a wedding dress that is about to become some bathroom curtains, an annoyingly perfect sister and a mother who's disappointed, but not surprised, by the mess my life has become?
Silence. I look frantically around the room as everyone looks at me expectantly. I'd completely missed the last few people; such was my desperation to find something to say that wouldn't involve them calling the nurse to bring Kate the smelling salts. I stand quickly, my chair scraping across the floor. So my life is shit, do I know anyone here? I glance around for a quick check. No, I don't. I can be whoever I want to be. I don't need to lie; they can choose to interpret what I have to say in any way they wish. Besides, it is true, or will be. I'll make sure of that. It's time to stop being the pathetic wimp I have become and reclaim my life.
'My name is Ivy,' I smile broadly, 'I am thirty years old and I'm actually not sure why I am here.' I laugh nervously at my confused audience.' I have the most amazing, warm and loving man waiting for me down in Surrey, he has been calling me all week, begging me to go and join him. The job I

really want to do isn't in a call centre, it's with the sun on my back and the breeze in my hair, sitting by the riverside, drawing the scenes before me. Also, I'm going to have a baby! I can't wait, I'm beyond excited.' I note the envious looks of some of the younger women and smiles of encouragement from the older ones. 'All my life I have dreamed about becoming a mother, and now it's going to happen.' I can't decide if I am relieved or concerned by my declaration. Am I insightful or delusional? Who cares, it felt bloody good to say it.

'My goodness, that does sound fantastic, Ivy,' Kate looks a little bewildered by my sudden announcement. 'So what are you telling us, dear?' I glance around at the sea of faces, feeling sick with anticipation, but caged by the thought of being part of yet another crowded conveyor belt of zombified calling machines. Yes, they look happy now, probably relieved to get a job at the end of this, but give it two weeks and they will hate it. I look back to Kate, I feel sick and a little dizzy, but there is an undeniable buzz of adrenaline coursing through my veins.

'I'm telling you I have a train to catch, Kate', I pick up my bag and coat. 'Thank you so much for the opportunity, good luck, everyone,' I shout behind me. I run down the stairs like the free woman I am. The stunned silence in the meet and greet is eventually broken by Kate.

'Would anyone else like to do a runner now, or shall we continue, she laughs.' I guarantee at least ten others thought about putting their hands up, right after my exit.

'Are you sure this is what you want, Ivy?' Ginny's face is a mixture of admiration and shock. When I had got back to the Bitchelor pad, I had discovered two of my cases on the doorstep, no note, no text message to say they were there, just two sad cases summarising all that I meant to Will. I tip the contents of both on to Gin's bed and separate them into two

piles, one to take to Surrey and one to store here.
'I'm positive, Ginny. I have no job, no wedding and no man to hold me back. I'm going to get my head together and then go it alone. I meant what I said at that interview, I only need a minimal input from a man to have a baby. The rest I can do on my own. Just a sample from a lab is all the commitment I want from now on where men are concerned.' Ginny gives me a small squeeze and her trademark, lopsided smile. This is one of the many things I love about my oldest friend, she never judges and always allows me to know what's best for myself, even if she does think it's not the best road to go down.
'Well, you make sure you give Bert my love. I will come down for a visit once you're settled in.' Gin nicknamed my Granddad, Bert, after watching Mary Poppins one Christmas eve when we were much younger, as she thought he sounded just like the character. He used to make us laugh by doing his own rendition on the chimney sweep rooftop dance. With no living grandparents of her own, Gin had pretty much adopted mine.
'You'd better,' I push a stray lock of hair behind my ear and survey my packing. I only need one case of summer clothes. I will go for a month and then put plan B (for baby and also for second choice) into action. It could take me up to a year to meet someone new, a couple of years to date before even mentioning kids, or risk watching him run for the hills, and then who knows how long of trying. At any stage of the relationship he could change his mind or decide it's not what he wants anymore and I'm not taking any more chances on this. I'm in control from now on.
I call Granddad to let him know I'll be on the one o'clock train and to expect me into Kings Cross around seven-thirty. I brace myself for the call to my parents and with a deep breath hit their home number. I inwardly pray that dad will answer, but no such luck.

'Efferson household, Barbara speaking.'
'Mum, hi, it's Ivy. How are you?' my stomach sinks.
'Hello, dear, how did your interview go? Good news, I trust?'
'Well, good news for me, actually, Mum. I'm going down to Granddad's house for a while to get my head together and...'
Fifteen minutes later and the phone sits cradled in my lap. Ginny brings me a coffee and a magazine, as mum continually rants on. After a further five minutes I hear a muffled shout.
'Brian? Brian! Come and talk some sense into your daughter.'
I pick up the phone again.
'Hi, Dad.'
'Hiya love, so you're off to Richmond then? Take me, take meeee!' he whispers urgently.
'Well, get packing then, by last orders, you, Granddad and I could be in the Emperor's nipple with a pint of real ale.' Dad chortles at my latest bar name. We like to come up with new and original names for pubs involving important people and body parts after remarking how many there were in London. Why stop at the Queen's arms or the King's head?
'Oh don't tempt me, Ivy. Maybe I could sneak away for a weekend between building the new greenhouse and creosoting the fence. I swear your mother is trying to kill me for the insurance money.'
'I'll be in touch, Dad, I really need to get going or I'll miss my train. I'll text you when I arrive.'
'Bye darlin', stay safe.' I marvel, for a short moment, at how my parents managed to end up together. Mum must have been normal at some point; I can't see how else dad would end up marrying her. Sure, even Evelyn had been normal once. I never really noticed her change. It's not like she went off to Uni and came back an arsehole. It was clearly a very subtle manoeuvre from being down-to-earth like Dad and I, to a crashing snob like Mum. I hear Ginny revving the engine of her work's van downstairs. I grab my case and hurry down the hallway.

We arrive at the Haymarket Station platform with only a few minutes to spare. The ticket machine queue had taken forever to move forwards. I had visions of not making this train, losing my nerve and going home. This brave, new person, embracing change, she's not the real me. It's taking every ounce of my resolve to see this current situation as an opportunity, but the realisation that home, to me, no longer exists gives me the impetus I need. I board the train and pull down the window.

'So, how are you going to cope without me for a whole month?' I smirk at Ginny.

'Oh, you know, just fine. Probably go out winching for a new bird, now I don't have your ugly mug cramping my style.'

'Ha! More likely they've been looking at me and assuming you're taken. I mean, with competition like this to contend with, I'm not surprised that nobody approaches you.'

'You're more bull-dyke than lipstick lesbian, my love,' Ginny laughs, 'but keep telling yourself that, if it makes you feel better.' Ginny's words are drowned by the guard's whistle. She grabs my head through the train window and plants a sloppy kiss on my lips. I wipe it off with the back of my hand and grimace.

'Don't go! I love you, she meant nothing to me,' I convulse with laughter as Gin runs alongside the train with the guard breathlessly picking up pace behind. The last thing I see is her flinging herself into his arms and mock sobbing into his lapel. I shake my head and offer up thanks, for my best friend. Where would I have been all these years without her hoisting me up by the big girl pants and making me laugh in the face of every disaster? I throw my case on top of the already haphazard pile in the storage compartment and settle in to watch the town and my troubles disappear.

Chapter Four

I awaken to a cacophony of birdsong, as the hyperactive parakeets descend on Granddad's garden. I look out the window to see him hanging up a new seed feeder. He senses me watching and waves up at the window. It's a beautiful day. The sun is already splitting the sky at 9am. Today, I'm going to take a long walk by the river with my sketch pad. I already feel so much more relaxed than I did this time yesterday. I wander downstairs after my shower and help myself to the jug of orange juice on the table. Granddad has set out cereal and fruit, toast in a rack and is currently grilling some bacon. I flop down into a dining chair and smile contentedly; a warm breeze and the smell of jasmine wafts through the open back door. Granddad's two cats, Archie and Dave, languish on the stone patio, raising their noses occasionally to sniff out the bacon. This trip was definitely a good idea.
'Why don't they make men like you anymore, Granddad?' I wonder aloud.
'Course they do, Ivy, love. You just haven't found one yet. You young folks look in all the wrong places, nightclubs and the like,' he tuts.
I reflect on this for a moment, he's probably right. Work was too busy to chat with anyone else and the men all seemed to either be too young, or married. I hadn't been looking anyway, just overheard this complaint from some of my single, thirty-something female colleagues. I watch Archie lazily raise his ginger head as a dragonfly whizzes by. Richmond is undoubtedly one of my favourite places in the world: the riverside, the deer park and the treasure trove of little alleys and unique, curios shops. No wonder Granddad had settled here after the hustle and bustle of the East end, although again, an entity of its own. I adored the noise, the food smells and the wonder of not knowing what was on the

next stall. Granddad and Nanny had moved here after they retired from the market trade. Years of being thrifty and planning ahead had meant they could sell up their East end town house and buy outright their beloved home, just down the Star and Garter Hill, in Ham, at the bottom end of Richmond. With its spacious garden and three bedrooms, they had lovingly redecorated their home and furnished it by scouring the local area for antiques. It was one of their joint passions and probably where I got mine from. Sadly, Nanny had died just after they had completed their beautiful home and never got to fully appreciate it. Granddad had installed a small fountain in Nanny's memory, as she had dreamed of sitting on the patio listening to the soothing sound of water. Granddad had amused us all by naming this lovely abode, 'The Back-Arse of Beyond,' as that's where he and Nanny had said they were moving to, after retirement. He had a plaque for the door and he still occasionally chuckled to see his mail addressed that way. Any new postie would knock to say how it had tickled them too.

I leave Granddad tending his rose bushes and take the scenic walk through Petersham, to the riverside. Granddad has kindly packed me a lunch in Nanny's old wicker basket. The sun beats down on my back, as I pull Nanny's straw hat onto my head, and walk past the stables and cow field. The fragrant air reminds me of carefree, childhood days; Evelyn and I running along the tow path with our bags of old bread, ready to feed the ducks and geese. To the right, the dramatic slope of Terrace Gardens, where we'd take our sledges in winter. All my favourite Christmases have been spent here in Richmond; to me the place is magical, like Narnia. I cut through the underpass which opens out onto the riverside. Colourful boats putt along the river, the breeze ruffles the trailing branches of the weeping willow trees. I remember my long-held dream of owning a houseboat on this very spot. I stop and sit on the grass on the slope by the row of pubs, and investigate my fare. There are home-baked breads and an assortment of cheeses and ham, a mixed salad, a slice of lemon drizzle cake that Granddad made himself and a bottle of chilled Chablis. Classy man, my Grandfather. I give a little chuckle and look around guiltily. Drinking alone in the middle of the day, can I do that? I notice a folded piece of paper on the bottle of the basket, I open it and read.

My darling Ivy,
It's such a thrill to have you here with me this month, please enjoy your picnic and wine. Your Nanny and I used to love our picnics on the riverside and the giggly walk home after. Raise a glass to her and enjoy your day out.
Love,
Grumpy Grampy xxx

I smile at the name we used to call him. It was a rare occasion that he was grumpy but he had told me off one day for 'falling' in the river. In truth, Evelyn had pushed me and denied it. The name had stuck for a while after that day. I pour the Chablis into the plastic wine glass and raise it to the sky.
'Cheers Nanny. Thank you for all the wonderful memories. I miss you.' I hear the scraping sound of chair legs on concrete behind me. A barman from the pub is setting up the tables for the lunchtime diners. He smiles and runs a hand through his too long black hair before disappearing back inside. I fold Granddad's note and put it in the keepsake section of my purse. I think of what I would have been doing back in Edinburgh today. Probably lounging on Ginny's sofa waiting to hear if I had got the call centre job and hoping desperately that Will would call to say he'd made a big mistake. As it happens, I haven't even brought my phone out, but left it on charge at the side of my bed. Already I've come so far. I finish my lunch and pick up my sketch pad. I outline the far

away bank and the willows trailing in the water, an inquisitive swan, keeping a cautious eye on the diners on the bank, and a sweet little family of ducklings paddling frantically to keep up with Mum. The distant murmur of chatting diners and clinking crockery, broken by the occasional honk from a goose are the only sounds. I am almost trance like when I sketch.

'Not bad at all,' I hear a soft, Irish lilt and a chuckle from behind me. I snap out of my reverie and turn to see the barman standing over me. He sits down uninvited and peers closely at my sketch. 'And to think I've been so busy putting out chairs that I missed Her Royal Highness going by on a feckin' jet ski.' He slaps his forehead and rolls his eyes. I glance at my picture in confusion. Yes, there she is, clutching her crown with one hand and skirts billowing behind her. At the bottom of the page I've written 'Fundon, by Ivy Efferson.'

'Well Ivy Efferson, I think it's a masterpiece. You just need Boris on the London Eye and the Prime Minister in a jellied eel van and you've got yourself a collection,' he laughs.

'I don't even recall doing that,' I smile, 'I was in another world there.' I hold the sketch up; it's actually not too bad.

'Conor Byrne, guv'nor of The Inebriated Leprechaun Bar.' He holds out a hand for me to shake.

'Not the easiest of pub names to say after a third of a bottle of wine.' I indicate to my bottle, 'would you care for a glass, Conor?'

'That's the whole point,' he laughs, 'it's hilarious listening to my punters try to order a cab at the end of the night. Oh, why not, I'm off duty for a few hours now and was just about to head off upstairs for my break,' he replies and takes off up the hill. He appears a moment later with a glass and flops back down.

'So Ivy Efferson, you don't sound like a Londoner, where do you hail from?' Conor enquires.

'Newington in Edinburgh,' I smile, 'just down visiting my

Grandfather till I start the boring chore of job hunting again.'
'Ahh, the dreaded job search. What's wrong with what you're doing right now, so?'
'Oh, this?' I wave a dismissive hand over my drawing, 'It's just a hobby. You can't pay the rent on a few scribbles, unfortunately,' I sigh wistfully.
'Well, maybe you're right. I'm a writer in my spare time and just waiting for that big break so I can join the rabble on the right side of the bar,' Conor raises his glass and swirls it around. 'Check the legs on that! That's a nice drop there, Ivy.'
'Oh, my Granddad chose it, he's the wine buff. I'd be sitting here with a £2.99 bottle from the offy, that's how cultured I am.' Conor chews his lip thoughtfully and looks a little nervous.
'Any chance I could take you out and educate you on fine wining and dining this evening, Ms. Efferson? I mean if you're not meeting your boyfriend, husband? ...or, er, have plans.' He trails off with a blush and looks the other way to hide it. Wow, he doesn't waste any time. We've barely spoken for five minutes and he's asking me out. He's very good looking in a roguish kind of way, a little unkempt but a lovely smile and a real naughty spark in those sky blue eyes. And he's a writer! I'm a sucker for creative types with a passion. This is what Will lacked. The only passion he had was for his games console. He lacked in a few areas to be honest. I dreamed of decorating our flat together but Will claimed he couldn't due to an old, repetitive strain injury in his Playstation thumbs. Come to think of it, we never did much together. He certainly never offered to take me out and teach me all about fine wine. He was more of a beer and shots man, really.
'Well, as friends, I guess would be ok. I'm not really looking for dates right now. I'm not in that mind-set at the moment. I *could* do with a good night out, however. So yes, I think I

could make myself free for the evening.'
'I shall be a perfect gent, I promise you, Ivy. Friends is cool by me,' he adds with a glimmer of naughtiness in his eyes.
'I'm serious, Conor, you don't want to be going there, the last thing I need is any more complications in my life.' We shake on the agreement and arrange to meet at 7pm at Richmond Station. I gather up my belongings and head for home. I notice there's a bit more of a spring in my step, on the way back. I've made a new friend and Granddad can have a guilt free dominoes night with the boys down the local too.

The afternoon passes quickly and before I know it, it's time to leave for my bus into town. I typed and deleted several texts to Will as I sat out the back with the cats and a coffee. Just to let him know I'm here, not to see if he misses me, not at all. I give up; he doesn't really need to know and probably won't care. My Grandfather had loved my sketch and told me I was wasted in sales and advertising. The truth is, I'm just crap at those two things so it's a given that I'd be better at anything else. The bus lumbers up the steep incline and turns into the gorgeous Richmond Hill streets. I sigh wistfully at what might have been. The style of these houses epitomises everything I ever wanted in my forever home. I peer nosily into the blur of windows as we go past. My gaze falls on a father teaching his young son to ride his bike without stabilisers, laughing as he falls sideways from the pavement into a hedge. I give a small giggle and the lady next to me smiles kindly.
'Do you have little ones?' she enquires.
'No, not yet, hopefully someday soon,' I shrug.
'I have a new Grandson, only three months old.' She pulls a well-thumbed picture out from her purse and hands it to me. I coo and fuss and comment on how he has her eyes. 'Seems like no time at all since my children were that age. Time passes so quickly. Don't leave it too late, dear.' She pats my

hand, pushes the bell and walks down the bus.
I stand outside Richmond station, torn between feeling indignant at the woman's innocent enough comment and laughing manically at the irony.
'Look at you laughing like a loon on your own. Have I made a big mistake taking you out this evening?' Conor puts his hands up in a mock horrified look and takes a few steps back.
'Shut up and tell me where you're taking me, to refine my Philistine palate.' Conor indicates across the road to a Tapas restaurant.
'My friend's new restaurant, the food is amazing and I get mates rates,' he winks.
'Conor, do me a favour and don't say that if you bring a proper date here. That would be one big strike against you already.' Conor raises his eyebrows and laughs, incredulously.
'Bit of a gobshite for a student wine buff, aren't you? Being a Scot I'd have thought you'd be up for a bargain.'
'I hope you're not implying that Scots are tight, you cheeky git? Strike two, for insulting your guest.'
'Jaysus, I'm bloody glad this isn't a real date, I'd feck off out the back door as soon as I'd got you seated.' We walk in to the restaurant and I slide into the chair that the waiter has pulled out for me.
'Well, just helping you out with your manners, you'll never get a girlfriend with your talk of freeloading and cultural stereotypes,' I bat back to him.
'And you won't get yourself a man if you manage to pull them up about two things by the time you cross the street,' Conor gives me a sly look over his water glass.
'Well actually, that suits me fine, since I want nothing to do with men. You lot are far too flaky and unpredictable. Life is infinitely easier as a singleton.'
'Ahhh but you need us for some things,' Conor adopts a mock serious tone, 'What are you, around 5'3"?' He gives me a

critical once over. 'Can't see you being much use at changing a light bulb, and spiders? Can you get them out on your own? I thought not.' Conor finishes with a satisfied smile on seeing the horror on my face at the mention of spiders.
'I will have you know, actually, that my housemate is better than any man at removing spiders, even the big, bitey looking ones.' I omit to tell him that I stayed at Mum and Dad's for three days when Gin was on holiday and I had a big one in my bath, back when we were roomies before.' And as for light bulbs, I manage just fine, along with plugs, fuses and unblocking drains,' I shoot back.
'So, Miss Ivy, you won't be wanting children then I assume,' Conor looks triumphant, 'Tis the one thing you super-humans just can't manage on your own yet, unless there has been some miraculous new discovery I've missed in the last hour or so. But then, I did miss her Maj on a water ski, so I could be mistaken.' The waiter interrupts us to ask if we are ready to order. I thought it was just Ginny and I that could talk solidly, forgetting all about our menus. We pick them up frantically and scan the choices.
'You go ahead and choose a wine then, Mr. Expert,' I eye Conor over the top of my menu.
'Er, we will start with a bottle of the Pinot Noir, please. Is red ok, Ivy?'
'Yes, lovely, thank you.' I am enjoying the slight discomfort on Conor's face; he talks tough but is clearly a bit out of his depth. The waiter walks off and we peruse the menu, choosing a few sharing plates between us. The Pinot Noir flows well, it transpires that Conor knows much more about cocktails than wine and confesses he had asked his restaurateur friend what would be nice, on a trip to the loo via the kitchen. I note through the fuzzy warmth of the evening that there had been no awkward silences and a lot of laughter. Conor will be a real catch for some lucky woman. I shake my head in wonder at his single status. I haven't had an

opportunity to ask about it as yet. We have discussed our past jobs, his writing (three crime thrillers so far but no agent has taken him up, as yet). We talk about Edinburgh and his short stint as a relief manager in a pub in Rose Street, and how much he loved our fair city. By eleven, we glance around and notice we are the last ones to leave. Jay, the owner and friend of Conor glances over in an amused manner at us, before tearing the bill in half with a wink.
'Cheers, mate. I owe you one,' Conor shouts across the restaurant, knocking his chair over as he stands. I wave and shout my thanks to Jay and we stumble outside into the warm, Richmond evening. Conor walks me to my bus stop outside the train station and ensures I am safely on the 371 home. I wave enthusiastically out of the window and settle down to reflect on our evening, laughing occasionally, in my inebriated state, as I remember some of Conor's quips. What a lovely guy, really good fun, warm and sweet; this evening was just what I needed. The bus pulls up alongside Granddad's street. The house is in darkness as I approach. I climb the stairs, snorting with laughter as I trip over Archie, in his favourite, precarious position on the stairs. I flop into bed and look up at the slightly swirling lampshade in the centre of the room. I find myself wondering dreamily if Conor will call again, like he said he would. It would be so good to have a friend to hang out with for the next month. My last though before I doze off is that I haven't thought of Will all evening. Perhaps this is the beginning of my road to recovery.

The next morning I waken, bright and early, with not the slightest sign of a hangover. I can tell my Grandfather is itching to hear about my night out, he looks at me curiously with a hint of a smile.
'It was wonderful. He was the perfect gent and totally respected the fact that I'm not looking for a boyfriend.'
'You see? I told you there are some decent ones around. So

what is the plan for today, then?' Granddad enquires.
'Well I'm going to head into London for a wander around Covent Garden, go for some lunch and maybe do something with this mop of hair. I was waiting until nearer the wedding, but...' I trail of as Granddad gives me a look of sympathy. We haven't mentioned it yet and it's been somewhat an elephant in the room at times. Granddad gives a chuckle,
'Remember your Nan used to call it having a wash and blow job until that nice Mrs. Stevens in number ten told her what that meant?' I splutter orange juice across the table cloth and down my nose, hic-coughing and laughing through watering eyes as I recall Nanny's shocked face underneath a newly coiffed do. 'She had to change hairdressers after that, she was mortified that she'd been asking for it for years,' Granddad coughs loudly and bends over to hold on to the table. I wait a few seconds for it to stop before scraping back my chair and patting him firmly on the back.
'Granddad, please go to the doctor, that cough should not be going on still.'
'Hush now, Ivy love. I've had two courses of antibiotics, it's just old age. It doesn't come itself.'
'I worry about you, Granddad, out in all weathers in that garden and allotment. You should be taking it easy at your time of life,' seeing him like this has alarmed me but he's a stubborn old git when it comes to his health.
'Righty-ho then, you get off up town, I'm off to the lotty to see what damage that idiot Jim has done to it. I'm sure he's sabotaging my plot so he wins first prize with his pumpkins.'
I walk upstairs for my bag and phone, looking back to see Granddad pull his oversized hanky from his pocket and wipe his forehead with it. I hate leaving him but he really doesn't like a fuss. At the moment he is reasonably honest about how he feels, albeit a played down version. I can't risk it stopping completely.

I catch the train from Richmond Station and switch instinctively from the District to Piccadilly line, and on to Covent Garden. It's funny how it's all still second nature to me, despite not being in London for so long. I walk out into the busy throng and feel immediately at home with the market atmosphere. My grandparents loved this place too; I guess it took them back to the old days of the stall. They taught me how to banter and bargain my way with the stall holders. My Grandfather hasn't been back since Nanny died. Too many memories, I guess. I wander around the market, admiring the hand-made jewellery and paintings. I'd love so much to have a stall here, proudly displaying my work but I don't reckon I'm even halfway in their league. I treat myself to a brightly coloured scarf and for Granddad, a small painting of Covent Garden itself; with the huge, imposing archways at the entrance and busy people hurrying by. If he won't come to Covent Garden then I will take it to him. My Grandfather tends to hide from anything that reminds him of Nanny and their past; he doesn't go down to the riverside now either. I'd love to see him rediscover their old, favourite haunts. He got so much pleasure from them. I'm planning on at least getting him out for dinner on the river. Perhaps we could go to Conor's place; Granddad's nose will get the better of him. I'd put money on him going, just to check Conor out. I walk over to my favourite cafe for lunch and take a seat outside. It's strange how everything is so familiar, and yet, I feel so much like a tourist. I take my phone out of my bag; I have a message from Ginny.
'Met the woman of my dreams last night, she's not 'come out' yet so I'm taking it slow. In fact she's so far in the in the bloody closet that she's actually in the bloke's three doors along. Working on it! How's your trip? Bert looking after you? xx'
I smile as I type my reply,
'Bert good but still has his cough, made a new friend. Glad

you're not pining too much for me. You go girl! xx' The waitress brings my panini and orange juice and puts them on the table in front of me. I've decided I will go and get a haircut and try to persuade Granddad to come out for dinner with me this evening. My phone buzzes again, Conor this time.
'Whatcha up to, Efferson?' I put my phone down and take a bite of my panini. I can't reply straight away, it looks too keen. I had been hoping he would text as turning up with Granddad at his pub for tea looks a little bit try-hard. I take two more bites and text back.
'Just having lunch in Covent Garden, then off to get my hair cut. Going to try to persuade Granddad to go out for tea. What's the food like down your gaff?'
'Fantastic, of course! Want me to book you a table? No going down to those sex shops in Soho now, young lady.'
'Ha! As if! I'm not sure if he will want to. Let me text you later.'
'Ok, no probs. Will put a provisional booking on my best table for now. x'
I feel a little buzz as I notice the kiss at the end, and tell myself off. I really need to be careful that I don't give Conor the wrong idea. It's not even passed my should-have-been wedding day yet. Yes, the attention is fun but jumping straight into a new relationship would only hurt Conor in the long run. It's just rebound feelings that I have. And besides, I'm planning on going it alone with my baby plans. What's to stop him, or the next man I meet, stringing me along for a few years then dumping me? If it can happen after eight years then anything can happen. I only mentioned going to The Inebriated Leprechaun as it's the best way to get Granddad down the river, and nothing more. I pay my bill and walk back up to the tube station. Now for my makeover.

I head home to Granddad's house with my new look. I've

been extremely brave, for me, and had three inches taken off the length, razored edges and a long sweeping side fridge. On a whim, I pop into a Richmond Hill boutique and buy a dark blue, floral prom style dress on my credit card. As I pass the shop windows I notice my reflection; who is this smiley, bouncy girl I don't recognise? Not even just from the past two weeks, I haven't felt this good for a long time. The summer sun has warmed my skin to a nice shade of light brown and I have a glow about me that had been lacking for a long time. Granddad isn't home from the lotty yet so I run myself a bath and carefully pile up my new hairdo in one of Nanny's long hair clips, shaped like a butterfly. By the time I hear the door open and Granddad greeting Archie and Dave, I am all dressed up and ready to go. I bound downstairs to the kitchen and see my Grandfather filling up the kettle.
'Hey, old yin, don't get too comfy. I'm taking you out tonight and you can't refuse because I got my hair done and bought a new dress especially.' Granddad turns to look at me and gives a low whistle.
'Well, well! Look at this beautiful girl I've found in my kitchen. You scrub up not too bad little Miss Efferson. So to what do I owe this pleasure?'
'Just as a thank you to my favourite Grandfather. For putting up with my miserable, Emo face this month.'
'You don't look like an emu, silly girl, and I'm your only Grandfather anyway. The local does a great pie and chips until 6, if we hurry we will make it, just.'
'Well, I thought we could go to the river, actually,' Granddad's face clouds over. His glance moves out towards the garden and settles on Nanny's fountain.
'I know I'm not your best girl, Granddad, but I'm hoping you will accompany your second best girl?'
'Of course you're my best girl, Ivy,' Granddad smiles wistfully. 'She was my best woman.'
'Conor is quite keen to meet you. He's put aside his best table

for us...'
Granddad gives the smile of a man who knows he is beaten and shakes his head with a resigned sigh.
'Give me ten minutes, Missy. I need to have a shave and get changed,' he strokes his stubbly chin thoughtfully.' You're a bad girl, Ivy Efferson, leading an old man astray on a week night.' Granddad wanders off, with a tut, and I hear him close the bathroom door.
'Affirmative, 7pm.' I text to Conor.
'Excellent, looking forward to seeing you and meeting Granddad,' he types back immediately.

We walk up the steps to the pub, Granddad holds the door open for me and I scan the area for Conor. We take our places at the bar and I order Granddad a pint of real ale and myself a white wine. I watch as the swing doors to the kitchen open and Conor appears. He stops abruptly on seeing me and seems a little taken aback. A smile spreads over his face and he holds up the two plates he is carrying before rushing over to a nearby table.
'That your friend?' Granddad enquires.
'Um, yes. That's Conor.'
'That's quite a look he gave you. You sure he's just after a friendship?' Granddad chuckles. I don't have time to reply as Conor is right beside us.
'Wow, Ivy, you look fantastic,' he gives me an approving once over. 'And you must be Ivy's Granddad?' Conor extends his hand amicably.
'George Efferson,' Granddad smiles, 'or Bert, if you prefer. That's mostly what the young 'uns call me.'
Conor smiles and picks up two menus, we follow him over to a table by the window. The river shimmers in the fading sun; I can see why this is the best table. A few people are sat on the water's edge and a few Canadian geese approach the tables for scraps of food. Conor whips away the reserved sign and

places our menus in front of us, with a flourish.
'I shall leave you to peruse your menu and be back presently. Our list of specials are on the board in front of the bar.'
'Very polite young lad,' Granddad says after Conor's retreating back. 'I don't remember Will being so attentive, Ivy.'
'Well, don't be digging out your best suit Granddad. I'm on my own from now on.' I study my menu, aware of Granddad's serious stare.
'Oh don't talk silly, darlin', there are plenty of good men out there, you were just unlucky with that last one.'
'There's no reason I can't go and get myself a job, flat and even have a baby on my own,' I glance up cautiously at my Grandfather. He nods slowly,
'Well that's true, Ivy, but being a single parent? That's not going to be easy. Some people find themselves in that situation and fair play to them for getting on with it, but by choice? It's good for children to have a father in their lives. You need to really think about that.' Conor arrives back at the table to take our orders and asks what plans we have for later.
'Well, I plan on catching last orders down the Nag's Head but I think Ivy is free,' Granddad gives me a knowing smile.
'Er, yes, I haven't got any exact plans for after dinner but I should really get an early night. I want to get some more drawing done tomorrow and...' I feel a kick from under the table, 'I guess I'm free,' I finish lamely, rubbing my shins. Conor gives Granddad a wide smile and heads off back to the kitchen.
'Oweee, that hurt you ol' bugger,' I shoot Granddad a dirty look.
'Just giving love a little helping hand, sometimes it does hurt.' I poke my tongue out and wander off to fetch him another pint. Conor pops over to see us after we finish our dinner.
'That was a good steak and ale pie, son. Great place you have here,' Granddad burps discreetly into his hand. 'That's a

compliment to the chef, in some countries.' I roll my eyes and give my Grandfather an indulgent look. Half an hour later and I'm feeling somewhat of a gooseberry. Granddad and Conor chat animatedly for the next hour about Conor's books, Granddad's allotment and where to get the best pint in Richmond. Eventually Granddad stands and says he will be making tracks. He puts two twenty pound notes on the table which Conor promptly hands back to him.
'On me, sir, I'll be offended if you don't accept.'
'No, neither of you are covering this, it's on me tonight. I said I was taking you out, Granddad. '
I rummage in my bag for my purse but Conor reaches out to stop me. I move my hand quickly away from his touch.
'Sorry. Thank you,' I bluster, 'you really didn't have to do that.'
'We must have the lad round for dinner to say thank you, Ivy.' Granddad smiles, 'When's your next night off, Conor?'
'Thursday and Sunday this week,' Conor shoots me a triumphant smile, 'I'd love to try Ivy's culinary skills.'
'Thursday's fine, Granddad nods his approval, 'I shall see you two later, no don't get up, I know the way well enough.' I watch anxiously as my Grandfather leaves the pub, I know he won't take the bus; he will want to reminisce on his walk home. It's getting dark now and the air is damp today.
'What a great guy,' Conor beams, 'I really like him, Ivy. So how about we go upstairs and watch a movie?' I drain my wine and wish I could think of something to say that would get me out of this. I'd much rather run to catch Granddad up and sit at the bar with him as he chats to his friends, down his local. But I can think of nothing, so I follow Conor up the winding staircase to his flat. He informs me I am all his until cashing up time. I take in the view of his studio flat; clean-ish, for a guy living alone, minimal but with a lot of gadgets, which I had expected. A few homely touches; a couple of lamps and an Aztec patterned black and grey rug, a small,

round dining table with a hopeful extra chair. Conor clears a pile of papers from the sofa and indicates me to sit.
'Here are a couple of new DVDs I picked up today, would you like to choose?'
'Please, you go ahead,' I have a sudden attack of shyness. Conor pops a disc into the player and fetches us a couple of cokes from the kitchen. He kicks his shoes off and pulls a footstool between us.
'Make yourself at home, Ivy.'
'Ha! I wouldn't say that or I shall fetch my jammies and raid your cupboards for chocolate,' I laugh. I take my shoes off and put my feet on the stool next to Conor's. I don't pay too much attention to the movie; I'm not really into action films anyway, but my mind keeps wandering back to the events of the past week. I relax into the comfortable cushions and enjoy the amicable silence. It's nice to share the experience of watching a movie with someone; Will on his games console, me alone in the bedroom watching my soaps, that's what has been the norm to me. I can feel the warmth of Conor's arm resting against mine and my eyes begin to close. I awaken as the end credits start to roll and see Conor looking down at me with an amused expression. I appear to have fallen asleep on his arm and I jump up with embarrassed horror.
'Gosh, is that the time? I'd best be heading for home,' I glance at an invisible watch on my wrist. Conor laughs and pulls on his trainers.
'Come on then, I'll walk you to the bus stop before I go and cash up.' We walk up the incline, wordlessly. This time the silence crackles between us and feels a little uncomfortable. Being so close to him felt wrong; I don't want Conor to get the wrong idea about us. He may be thirty-four and a hell of a lot more emotionally mature than Will, but I'm still not going there. I barely know a thing about him. My bus comes into view around the corner and Conor urges me to run for it.
'Thank you so much for tonight. I'll see you soon,' I shout

behind me before dashing up the hill. I just make it and gasp to catch my breath. I take my phone from my bag, Ginny has text with the ominous message,
'we need to talk, call me if you get this before eleven, early start tomorrow.' I check the time, 11.30. What now? I can't take any more revelations this week. I text her back anyway to ask if she's still awake and my phone rings seconds later.
'Oh my God, Ivy, you're never going to believe what I saw tonight,' Ginny is breathless with gossip overload. 'We were sat in that restaurant off North Bridge, you know, the Tapas one where you had too many shots and threw up down yourself? Will had to put you in a shopping trolley to get you home as no taxi would take you?' I cringe at the memory.
'Erm, yes, thanks for reawakening that for me after I've spent years trying to forget it.' Just a whiff of tequila can still send me off in a sprint to the toilet, these days.
'Well anyway, the missus got up to go to the loo and came back moaning about a man and woman in the corner's unnecessary PDA. Their public display of affection,' she shouts at my ignorant silence.
'Ahh OK, thanks for clarifying. So? Stop being such a heterophobe. Straight people have rights and feelings too, you know.'
'Oh do shut up, dear. Anyway, as you know I'm a nosey cow, so I walk past them just to see just how pathetic they really are and...'
'Oh for fuck's sake, Virginia! Drop the dramatics and tell me.'
'Do not *call* me that!' Ginny fumes at my laughter. 'Anyway,' she continues a little frostily, 'the canoodling couple in the corner were still at it and I suddenly realise I know the man.'
'Oh great! So you thought this would be helpful to my recovery, did you? That you saw Will out with his foetus?'
'No, no, nooooo! It was My Gerald! You know, your sister's husband?'
'Bloody Nora! Did he see you?' I demand.

'No, of course not, his tongue was firmly wedged down some blonde woman's throat at the time. I walked the other way back to the table and we bailed out pretty quickly after.'
'I'm going to have to tell her, aren't I?' I almost whisper.
'Well here's what I thought,' I can tell my friend is enjoying this, 'it would actually give me huge pleasure to be the one to tell her, and let's face it, she hates me anyway. All these years she's been scathing of my lifestyle and been smug about how perfect hers is, I have to be the one to do it.'
Wow, I can't believe I actually feel sorry for my sister. Yes, she has always looked down on us but to have Gin tell her out of spite is not going to happen. It's just too cruel.
'Look, Gin, can you leave this with me, please. I'm not sure I can actually take any more shocks in this week. I'll give you a call in the morning, but if we decide that you are telling her, it has to be nicely. It'll be enough that you are the one to do it, in her eyes.'
'Ha! I'm only pulling your pisser about me telling her, Ivy, I'm not a complete bitch. But I do think she needs to know, preferably from him. We run the risk that she may not believe it otherwise and will resent us instead.'
I go to bed numb. Well this just confirms my belief that I'm much better off on my own. The perfect marriage is a sham. It's what I have long suspected, to be honest, but I can't help feeling sorry for Evelyn. What an absolute shit. I don't even know where to begin on how to process this information. Bed, that's what I need. I shall sleep on it and work out a plan tomorrow. Luckily, I'm far enough away not to have to deal with the fallout of this. My life has become a soap opera, and to think, just last week I had been moaning about how boring it was.

Chapter Five

I waken the next morning disorientated. It takes me a few seconds to register where I am. I pick up my phone and check the time, 7.15am, Evelyn will be screaming at her kids to get up, doing breakfast and the school run. I can't phone until later. I roll onto my side and notice the sick feeling, my mouth waters and I sit up quickly. My first thought turns to food poisoning; Conor's place? No, don't be ridiculous, he told me he'd cooked it himself yesterday and he's banged on enough about how meticulous he is with regards to food hygiene. I swing my legs slowly out of bed before realising there's a little more haste required here and practically sprint to the bathroom to throw up. I lay my head on the cool cistern of the toilet and catch my breath. A bug, I've caught a bug. Didn't I overhear a parent at a bus stop mentioning one going around to a friend? It had spread like wildfire through their home. With relief I realise there will be no need for an awkward conversation with Conor over the state of his kitchen, and pad down to the kitchen for a glass of water. Granddad has thoughtfully laid the table for my breakfast. He leaves for the allotment at 7am most mornings. I bend to pat Archie on the head and open the door to let him out, he's too chunky for the cat flap these days but hates using a litter tray. I open the fridge to take out the milk and catch sight of a joint of meat defrosting for dinner. I quickly close the door and make my way to the downstairs bathroom. Hmmm, perhaps I should stick to a glass of water until my stomach settles. It's always best to starve this type of bug anyway, give them nothing to feed from but keep hydrated. Little germ fests, children; I'd best get used to this if I'm going to prepare for my own little rugrat. I carry my glass upstairs and run a bath, as I bend to pick my slippers up from the floor, my head spins. I clutch on to the side of the bed gratefully. Wow, this virus is sure knocking me for six. I haven't felt this shit since I caught the

Noro Virus three years ago, when it was doing the rounds at work. I turn the taps off and sink into the warm bubbles, searching Google for sickness viruses. I know I shouldn't, there will of course be a random story of someone who has died from one. Dr. Google has not been kind to me. The last one I read about was when I had a large lump on my arm, like a bite but not red. It turned out to be nothing but my search had informed me of a similar case that turned out to be a nest of baby spiders that erupted from under a man's skin. With alarm I scan all possible causes and the general advice is to take plenty fluids, let it run its course and stay away from others. I'm feeling a little better with the warmth of the bath and my little sips of water. No cramps or any other issues, therefore it's not the dreaded Noro come early this year. Clearly just your regular common or garden sickness virus.
An hour or so later I hear my Grandfather's return. He coos gently at his cats before shouting up to me,
'Weren't you hungry, Ivy, love?'
'No, Granddad, I have an upset stomach, I think I've caught a bug off of some kid at the bus stop the other day. Thank you for putting the stuff out for me, though.
'No problem, let me know if you feel up to lunch in a bit. I'm making some homemade, lentil soup.'
What a good man my Grandfather is, I smile to myself as I notice Nanny's shower cap hanging from a hook on the bathroom door. He's still not ready to let her go, I guess. Oh to have that lifetime love that they've had. From giggling teenagers stealing kisses in the back of the picture house, the thrill of their wedding; two wide-eyed smiling twenty-year-olds starting out on the adventure of life together. Their honeymoon to Cornwall, where they ate ice cream and walked hand in hand along the beach together. The birth of their two sons and one daughter; learning to be parents and laughing at how precious they were over their first and how blasé they were after the third. Seeing their kids have families of their

own, trying to let them learn their own mistakes and not butt in with advice. To an elderly couple, with different dreams; time to relax, time to reflect and most importantly time to reap what they'd sown. Except they couldn't, Nanny was cruelly snatched away from her adoring husband who is now still the same warm and loving person he has always been but like a shadow, an echo of himself. I think of Will and the infant he is now dating. How could he throw it all away for someone he barely knew? Well, there's absolutely no point in dwelling on the past, it won't change anything now. I sink beneath the bubbles and listen to the echoed sounds from around the house. It feels comforting to be cocooned in the water, safe and warm. When I can no longer hold my breath I rise up, disappointed to find that my problems hadn't washed away with the bath water. With a momentary panic I think of my dwindling bank account. I have no choice but to go back soon. Last I checked I had just over five hundred pounds. I really should be using that for travel expenses to interviews and giving Ginny some digs money, not to mention food. I pull out the bath plug and reach for my towel, feeling suddenly ravenous. Homemade soup sounds amazing. I can smell the bread that Granddad is baking; he hadn't been too proactive in cooking when Nanny was alive. It was her kitchen, she had informed him. She had been an amazing cook. Her Sunday roasts rivalled many a London Gastro Pub and her baking was talked about all over Richmond's fetes. I pull on a pair of jeans and a tee-shirt and head down to the welcoming kitchen. Granddad looks up with a smile, his sleeves rolled up to his elbows and flour on his rough old cheek. I laugh and brush it off before enveloping him in a huge hug, noticing for the first time how frail he feels for such a big man.
'Hey, what's this for?' he squeezes me tight.
'Just 'cos,' I reply into his cardigan, 'you've been so good to me. I feel lots better about things now. But, Granddad,' I hold him out at arm's length, 'I really am going to have to go back

soon and look for a job. I know I said I'd stay a month, but I'm running low on funds; much more so than I though.' He nods solemnly and places the bread basket on the table.
'Right, so, Ivy. If that's what you feel you need to do. As long as you know you can stay as long as you want. Hey, maybe you could get a job in the city?' he doffs an imaginary cap at the thought of me being an oh-so-important business woman.
'Oh yes, I can just see me shouting orders into my blackberry whist trying to juggle my Metro and briefcase. No, I best go back and face the music. I have a plan I need to put into action.' I tap my nose enigmatically. Granddad gives a chuckle,
'I don't suppose you'll tell an old man so I shall respect your privacy, even though I'm dying to know.' He dishes up a bowl of soup and holds it out to me.
'You will know soon enough, Granddad, I need to get things straight in my own head first,' I smile.

I put off my call to my sister and enjoy a quiet day of sketching in the garden; a gorgeous drawing of Dave and Archie for Granddad, and one of Nanny's fountain, framed by the fragrant jasmine that drapes down the wall. The sun beats down on my back and I feel so contented. I sip at the lemonade that my Grandfather has brought out to me and wish I could stay here forever. Could I really see myself in a city job? Would I fit in to London life? The thought warms me almost as much as the sun does. I fantasise about changing my phone number and only giving it to a select few people, reinventing myself as a confident woman of the world, bustling through tube stations and making new friends; ones who know nothing of my runaway groom. I could be whoever I want to be, in my new life. Be a little mysterious to keep people guessing or the life and soul of the office. I visualise after works drinks with young Hipsters in sunny beer gardens, weekends of seeing the latest shows and

hanging around Covent Garden. Maybe even the occasional dark, trendy club with its thumping bass. Although, of course once I put my plan into action and have my baby, things will change. London is a fantastic place for children. I can imagine wandering around the National History Museum teaching him or her all the names of the stuffed animals, watching the Christmas lights shine from my child's eyes with awe, in Hamley's toy store. Long walks by the river watching the boats chug back and forth. Both scenarios are too wonderful to contemplate. I wouldn't have to worry about bumping into Will and his pre-schooler either. Mum and Evelyn would be a safe enough distance away to merit just the occasional phone call. Glamorous career girl to yummy mummy, London would suit me nicely. The thought makes me smile. What do I really need to go back for? Gin and Dad can visit. They're the only ones I really would miss terribly. Ginny has her new woman; she may want her to move in soon if her past record is anything to go by. I'd put pressure on myself to leave as soon as possible and I may not realistically be able to afford that for months. A chill grips my heart as I think of having to live with Mum again. Her constant fussing and insistence on treating me like a five year old. So it's decided. I shall give it a go and job hunt in London. I'll keep it to myself, at least until I see what's out there. I don't want to get Granddad's hopes up if I can't find a job, but it's unlikely; this is London. A new home, a new life, a new me!
I finish off my sketch of Nanny's fountain with a flourish of signature. I take them in to show Granddad, but he's snoring in his armchair. I listen with concern at his wheezing exhalations. At least by staying here permanently I can keep an eye on him. I lay the sketches on the coffee table in front of him and tiptoe past to the stairs. Carpe Diem and all that; what better time to start my job search than now. I start with a critical overview of my CV, tweaking words here and there to make myself seem a little more special. I may not be great

at Sales but I am good at prioritising, office management, multi-tasking, er... fetching coffees and dry cleaning. Well, at least I'm versatile; I've had so many different jobs that I could pretty much do anything. I hit save and log on for a job search of the local area. Yes, plenty of office positions but mainly through agencies. All guaranteeing results; smiling people ooze enthusiasm and great claims of humble beginnings as an assistant and now, lo and behold, they are Managing Director! I'm not naive enough to believe this, of course, but I can't help imagine. I fill in a few agency forms and attach my CV before sending. My laptop lid shuts with a satisfied click; let's see what these three applications throw at me. I head downstairs again to watch TV with my Grandfather and hug my knees, enjoying the excitement of my little secret and the arrival of a glimmer of light at what seemed like a never-ending tunnel.

I awaken early again the following morning and check my email from my phone. There's a reply from one of the agencies that I submitted an application to. They don't waste any time. They've asked me to pop into the office at my earliest convenience. Well, today suits me. I still feel a little delicate from my stomach bug but I haven't thrown up again, just a fair bit of nausea and dizziness. I can handle that; it's more important that I find a job as soon as possible. I pop downstairs to make some tea and toast, Granddad has left a note to say he's playing bowls after the lotty so not to expect him back until late afternoon. Fantastic! Now I don't have to lie about what I'm up to today, I go through my wardrobe looking for a passable interview outfit. There are a couple of reasonably smart tops and skirts. I pull out a pale blue, frilled shirt and an A-line navy skirt. That will have to do, along with my beige, wedge sandals. It's the best that I have with me. I shower and dress quickly before heading out into the sunny Richmond day. As I pass the Doctor's surgery on the

corner, I pop in on a whim to see about registering. My heart thumps loudly in my chest. I'm doing this, I really am moving permanently to London. This may not be a big deal for many but I'm undoubtedly a play-it-safe kind of girl. I like the new me. New hair, new job and new location, it's a bold move. I wait patiently in the long queue as the medical secretary ploughs her way through the appointments and enquiries. A poster for antenatal care on the wall catches my eye. I wonder how long I can reasonably leave it until I go for IVF. I guess need at least a few months in a permanent job before I can even think about it. I watch on wistfully, as a young mum reads a story in hushed tones to the two year old boy on her lap. She catches me looking and we exchange a smile. Eventually I reach the front of the line and ask for an appointment to enrol as a patient. The secretary glances over her thick-rimmed spectacles as she scrolls the mouse down.
'Tomorrow at 9.15 OK?' she enquires. I nod appreciatively, so soon. On noticing my surprised expression she explains, 'we've just had a cancellation, luckily for you. We've been packed out with this sickness bug but it's calming down a bit now. Most people actually do more harm coming in here with it, we can't prescribe anything anyway. Now here is your specimen bottle. Please bring in a sample of urine with you.' I pop the sample bottle in my bag. The two year old waves at me as his mother watches on proudly. I wave back and whisper 'bye bye.' It will happen for me, I just have to be patient and reassess my situation over. My mind casts back to my conversation about Evelyn with Ginny, a couple of days ago. I've done absolutely nothing as I don't know what to do for the best. I need to give this more thought. Right now though, I have an interview to get through. I push my concerns to the back of my mind and head to the bus stop.

'Ivy Efferson? Amelia will see you now, please go through.' I've been offered an immediate interview at the

agency. I walk smartly through the door and greet the young woman behind the desk. Wow, she must be all of nineteen and she's the Recruitment Manager. There's hope for me yet.
'Hi, Ivy, take a seat. Do you have a CV for me look at? Our system has crashed and I can't access yours online.' I reach in to my bag, 'ahhh, just what I like in this office, an efficient person,' she smiles. I pull out my folder and the urine sample bottle with it. It lands with an unnecessary clunk on the tiled floor. Amelia bursts out laughing as I blush a deep red.
'My, you are organised but we ain't that thorough here. A couple of refs will do.'
'God, I'm so sorry,' I give a nervous giggle, 'I'm registering with a new GP too. Could have been worse, I could have filled it already.' Amelia laughs prettily.
'A good sense of humour, I can tick that box already. So, tell me, what kind of work are you interested in doing?' she casts an approving eye over my work history.
'I'm happy to do pretty much anything office related, really. Sales work isn't a particular strength of mine so we may want to avoid that.' Amelia flicks through some job vacancies on her screen.
'There are loads at the moment, mostly up in the city though. Oh, we actually have a post coming up here. A permanent role in this office dealing with recruitment, obvs,' she giggles, 'is it temping you particularly want to do, Ivy?'
'No,' I enthuse, 'I ideally want a full-time role and I'd be really interested in the position here.'
'Great!' Amelia smiles widely, 'You must be willing to go for drinks on a Friday night and take a Starbucks run twice a week. We have a rota and even Joe, the boss, takes a turn.'
'Sounds fine to me,' I smile, 'so when can I interview?' Amelia checks her diary.
'Joe can see you Wednesday afternoon at 4pm, any good?'
'Perfect!' I reply.
'I have a good feeling about you, Ivy. I think you'd fit right in

here at Essential Recruitment. I will put in a good word for you with the boss man. Should you not be successful we can look at other posts that may suit you better then.' I walk out into the street with a wide smile and a bounce in my step. Everything finally seems to be going in my favour. About bloody time too. Now all I need to do is make sure I get this job and persuade Granddad to go back to see the doctor and I'll be a very happy girl. I come around from my trance to discover that my feet appear to be taking me down to the river. I need to share my news and excitement with someone. I need to see Conor. I quicken my pace along the Quadrant and turn right into Water Lane. I feel like my chest may burst with excitement. As I walk into the bar I see Conor wrestling with a crate of Becks. He gives me a one hundred watt smile and heads around the bar.
'Ivy! What a lovely surprise. I was just about to head out for the afternoon at shift change. Fancy some lunch?'

We walk up to Tesco to buy some sandwiches and juice and lie on the grass in Richmond Green.
'I've got some news,' I break the amicable silence
'You have? You've decided not to go home to Edinburgh because you can't live without me.' Conor states.
'Half right, I raise my eyebrows and give him a gentle shove.
'The 'you can't live without me' half, or the 'not going back to Edinburgh' one?'
'The latter,' I smile and take a huge bite of my tuna mayo sandwich. God, I have got to stop eating so much. My skinny jeans were cutting me in half yesterday. Conor sits up sharply, 'Ivy that's fantastic news! Do you need a job? A place to stay? I have a mate who's looking for a housemate up on the hill in a gorgeous town house.'
'I may have a job already, actually. It's looking promising anyway, and I thought I'd stay with my Grandfather for a bit. He's not been well, but thanks anyway.'

'I can't believe it,' Conor shakes his head with a grin. 'I kind of hoped you would but I thought it was a long shot. What a shame I'm working tonight or I could have taken you out to dinner to celebrate.'
'Well, I have to register with a GP in the morning so I'd better not hand in a urine sample that's pure alcohol. How about tomorrow night?'
'It's a date!' announces Conor. I shoot him a warning look, 'or not...' he adds shamefacedly.

We take a walk around House of Fraser to shop for an interview outfit. It's not your usual type of office; trendy rather than formal. I find a few bright shirts, a plain black skirt and a pinafore dress. With embarrassment I buzz for the assistant.
'I appear to have grown from a ten to a twelve, I'm afraid. My Grandfather's home cooking,' I offer as way of an explanation.
'No problem,' she whispers and pops out to find my new size. I twist and turn in my underwear in the brightly lit mirror. Whoopsy, a few pounds gained here and there. It looks good actually; I have cleavage for the first time ever.
'Hoochy Mama,' I state to myself and unfortunately to the newly returned assistant.
'You're rocking it, babe,' she laughs, 'impressive rack. Best you head to lingerie next and accommodate that overspill. The double boob look ain't such a good look.' I make the mistake of telling Conor the saleswoman's suggestion and unfortunately he thinks it's a great idea.
'Conor. I am not lingerie shopping with you looking at me like a total perv.'
'Ahh c'mon, Ivy. You'd make my day, sure.' Five minutes of nagging goes by until I finally relent.
'Well hurry up then, and keep quiet in there. I'm not having you embarrass me any more than the situation is already.' Of course, this was the worst thing I could have said. Conor

makes me crease up with laughter as he minces around the lingerie department, loudly proclaiming to be my personal shopper. People stop and stare as he picks up bras announcing that bolds are *so* last season and the craftsmanship of a popular designer one is shoddy. Eventually, I stumble with an armful of underwear into a cubicle as I hear Conor announce to the sales girl that if she's a friend of Dorothy's she's a friend of his. He does 'do camp' frighteningly well. Maybe he should be acting instead of bar work and writing. I settle on some modest pastels and a cheeky, bold turquoise set, and leave the store with relief.
'Right you. Now back to work and keep out of trouble. I'm off to get a takeaway with Granddad to celebrate my groundbreaking decision. I shall see you tomorrow night at seven, prompt.' Conor ruffles my hair and makes me promise to wear the turquoise set for our night out. I inform him he will not be seeing it anyway so it doesn't matter what I wear. I head off to the bus stop swinging my bags with satisfaction, feeling like a new person. I can't keep it a secret; I can't keep anything from Granddad. I'm going to tell him what I've decided to do.

As I'd imagined, my Grandfather is thrilled to bits. I tell him it all hangs on actually getting a job and not to get too excited yet.
'They'd be stupid not to employ you, Ivy Efferson. You'll make MD within the week, I'm tellin' ya.' We order out a curry from Tiffinbox and settle down to watch a movie. Dave purrs contentedly on Granddad's lap and Archie lies on my tummy as I sprawl along the sofa. He has followed me everywhere since I got here. I have felt so at home and welcomed. By the ten o'clock news, I'm yawning loudly and decide I should have an early night. Yet again I have failed to call my sister; I'm making excuses, I know I am. I'm pretty sure she won't believe me and will say Ginny is making it up

because she hates her. I just can't think how to word it. I hug Granddad goodnight and head upstairs with a hot chocolate. I snuggle down into the duvet and check my email on my phone. Another agency is requesting me to come in to see them at 2pm on Friday. The Universe is turning and it's finally in my favour. My eyelids start to flutter; I'm so sleepy these days, since Will called it off I really haven't slept well. I'm so relaxed down here, in my spiritual home. The fresh air and hot chocolate make me feel punch drunk. With great effort I set my alarm before falling into a deep, dream-filled sleep.

Chapter Six

My alarm buzzes shrilly at 8am, I fumble blindly for my phone to check the time and roll over, groaning into my pillow. I really should have waited until I felt a hundred percent before going into the surgery. Who knows what joys I could pick up while I'm already ill? I sluggishly drag my legs out of bed and sit up. I still feel dizzy; bloody kids and their lurgy, but I probably should get the boring stuff out of the way now. I may be working this time next week. I take a sip of the water of my bedside table. I feel a little queasy still, but infinitely better than the other day. I wobble on Bambi legs to the shower and gratefully allow the warm water to wash over me. I press a hot flannel to my tummy. Cramps! Yes, just to add to the fun, my time of the month is looming. That may be contributing to my dizziness too actually; I haven't suffered like that since my early teens when I had blackouts every month, for around a year. It's not surprising, really. I may be feeling much more relaxed but losing my future husband, home and job in the space of a few days has got to take its toll somehow. I dress quickly and head downstairs. I only really have time for a quick coffee; I can eat when I return from the GP.

I walk into the surgery and take in the rows of patients. Three doctors and what looks like around twenty-five people. Fantastic, I'm going to be here for a while it seems. I take the only seat available is next to a teen; chewing gum loudly whilst rocking a buggy containing a screaming baby, with her foot. On my right sits a middle aged man who is sweating profusely, whilst coughing and spitting into a hanky. Why did I choose today; probably the hottest one yet, this year, to sit in a packed, germ filled surgery? It must be forty degrees in here. With great relief to everyone, the baby's name is called next. All around I hear grateful sighs and even the odd smile exchanged. I walk to a leaflet table opposite and absent-mindedly pick up a few to peruse. It's really an excuse to move along one seat to put some space between myself and the hanky spitter. My stomach heaved with each hacking cough and thorough examination of his tissue. Sure, he can't help being ill, but really? No need for the post-mortem of the contents of his lungs. A young woman opposite looks at me with curious horror. I smile nervously and look around. What's her problem? She's surely not looking at me; I'm clearly in the top ten percent of most normal and least ill in the room, for goodness sake. Perhaps she's in for an anxiety disorder. I allow her a little grace before launching on a game of guess the illness with the other patients. Two young babies, either in for their jabs or Mum in to sort out her contraception again. Teenager, nervous looking female; I'm betting on the morning after pill. Twenty-something, good looking bloke; tricky one, I shall come back to him. The receptionist interrupts my game, by calling the girl opposite to go through, as she passes, I note that she couldn't have given me a wider berth if she'd tried. Was she that weird before I picked up my leaflets from next to her seat? Do I smell? I raise a discreet arm; of course not; I'm literally just out of the shower. Bloody hell it's hot in here. I fan my face with my clutch of leaflets and lift my hair to fan my neck. I glance at the writing on my fliers. Fuck sake! I throw them down in horror. 'So you think you have herpes?' 'Chlamydia and infertility.' 'Genital warts, what you need to know.' Cough spitter shuffles along into a newly vacant seat in the opposite direction and one of the young mothers squashes her child to her bosom in disgust. I hastily pick up my leaflets and shove them into a nearby bin. 'Ivy Efferson, you can go to room three.' I smile my gratitude to the medical secretary and scuttle down the hallway to the room.

'So, how is your general health, Ivy?' Dr. Cameron smiles

kindly at me and leans back into her chair. She can't possibly be a doctor; she looks fifteen if she's a day!
'Very good, thanks. Although I have had that nasty sickness bug that's doing the rounds, I'm on the mend now.'
'Yes, most uncommon for this time of year. We've seen a lot of it in here, this past fortnight.'
'Let's start with taking your height and weight. When was your last smear?'
'Well, I'm actually due one, but cycle-wise, it isn't good for me today.' She looks at me suspiciously and even though I am telling the truth, my face defies me with a blush. Dammit!
'Well, I'd like you to book an appointment for two weeks' time,' she informs me sternly. I feel like I'm being told off by a High School student.
'Yes, of course,' I smile graciously as I step on the scale. She pulls down the height measure and then consults a colour coded chart.
'Well your BMI is a little on the high side but nothing too worrying. Let's check your blood pressure and then I will let you go for today.' Great! So I'm fat *and* a liar. The cuff tightens around my arm and the room spins a little. I hold on to the edge of the table with my free arm to steady myself. Dr. Cameron gives me a concerned look.
'Are you alright, Ivy?'
'Yes, I've had these dizzy spells on and off but I think it's just this sickness virus.'
'Have you had a recent ear infection?'
'No, I've been pretty healthy lately, just this sickness and nausea the last couple of days.'
'And you probably skipped breakfast this morning?' she raises a judgemental eyebrow.
'Well, yes, but I wouldn't normally,' I sound so defensive. 'I was running a bit late so I shall have some when I get home.' She nods her approval.
'Any chance you may be pregnant?'

'Well, I haven't had a recent visit from the Angel of the Lord, so at a guess, no.' She looks confused, 'I'm single, I offer as way of an explanation. Jilted, more or less, three weeks ago. Trust me, I'm not pregnant,' I finish with an embarrassed laugh. She whips out a little device with a torch on it and checks my ears, just in case I have an underlying infection which could be causing the vertigo.
'OK, they're clear, well that's us done. If the dizziness carries on then do come back in to see me, otherwise I will see you in two weeks for your smear. Oh, I'll take your urine sample off you before you go.' I hurry quickly out of the surgery, trying not to notice the receptionist spraying my chair with an anti-bacterial solution as hanky spitter looks at me with superiority. He told on me for my imaginary STDs? How very rude.

I sit in the Indian restaurant on Ham Parade, impatiently tapping my fingers on the table. A major funk of a mood descended on me this afternoon and it just won't shift. Conor is running late. I've ordered some popadoms and wine and now could quote the menu in reserve, I've read it so many times. That pre-pubescent doctor has pissed me off; nothing makes you realise how you've failed in life like someone clearly much younger than you in a good job. Saying that, I wouldn't actually want to lance boils and investigate ingrown toenails for a living. You only have to watch embarrassing bodies to see how glam being a doctor really is. I glance out at the darkening sky, even the clouds seem to be echoing my mood; dark, thunderous and heavy. Eventually, I see a flash of blue dash past the window and Conor bursts into the restaurant, jingling the bell over the door noisily.
'I'm so sorry, Ivy, two staff members called in sick with that lurgy. I hope you're not too mad at me.'
'Not at all,' I smile frostily. 'I've only been here forty minutes. No biggie,' I shrug. God, I'm a pre-menstrual grump. Pre-

minstrel Ginny calls it, due to her monthly, mad craving for chocolate. Conor's face falls and I rally some positivity from the core of my being.
'Of course it's OK, Conor. You're here now.' Luckily I start to feel a bit more positive as the evening progresses and I finally let Conor know about my should-have-been impending nuptials. Maybe it was the wine, maybe my mood, but it felt better to let him know. Now he will back off to a safe distance and drop the hurt bunny eyes when I say how much I want to stay single. He listens intently, nodding seriously in agreement at my occasional burst of anger. Finally I exhaust my story as we finish our curries.
'Shit, Ivy, I had no idea. I'm in awe at your ability to see this as an opportunity for a fresh start. That's a really good quality you have. I'd still be in bed surrounded by beer cans and pizza boxes if that were me.' I push my naan bread around my plate to gather up the last of the curry sauce.
'Well, I'm a Scot. It's rather self-indulgent to go on about things like that back home. The English have their stiff upper lip but us Celts get told to stop whinging ten minutes after the ordeal. Of course, then an automatic free license is given, to anyone who knows you, to take the piss out of you about it for the rest of your life. No, pick up, dust off and move on is my motto. But I won't get burned again, that's the reason I'm staying single and that's why I'm glad you realise we can only be friends,' I finish with defiance.
'Er, yeah, sure,' stammers Conor. 'I'm not surprised that's how you feel and I'm happy you are at least allowing a friendship and not wanting to cut my balls off, just for being a man.' Conor removes my dinner knife from my plate with a mischievous smile.
'Idiot,' I laugh, 'I'm not planning on punishing you for the sins of the brothers. Now Will's balls on the other hand...' I make a slicing motion in the air and Conor recoils a little.

We settle up the bill and head over to the pub along the road. Sitting in the peaceful beer garden, we chat until midnight. All too late I remember my interview tomorrow. I hastily gather up my things and walk Conor to the bus stop.
'Lucky it sounds like the job is already in the bag, Ivy. Talking of bags, I reckon you're gonna look pretty rough in the morning.' I give him a gentle punch to the side. 'Good luck, shall I see you on Thursday night then?'
'Yes, of course, seven alright?'
'Perfect.' Conor gives me a quick peck on the cheek as his bus rumbles around the corner. 'Text me to say how it goes,' he jumps on the bus and waves from the window. Right: a pint of water, two paracetamol and bed. I have got to get this job tomorrow. Everything is falling into place now; a job is the one final hurdle. But when I finally slide under the covers, sleep eludes me. I lie in bed, tossing and turning. Every position feels uncomfortable and my conscience is bothering me about Evelyn. Why should I be the one to tell her? Gerald should own up; it's the only way she will believe what has been going on. I sit back up in bed and type out a quick email to his work address. The personal one is one of those annoying family email addresses. He tends to not read those and leaves Evelyn to check. It's a basic one line affair, pardon the pun. I simply put that I knew what he was doing and he had been seen by a friend. He has one week to fess up to Evelyn or I will be taking action. No niceties spared. My guilt slides away as I hit send and I fall asleep almost instantly. Now it's in his hands, and I can copy any responses to Evelyn to prove the point.

My interview the next day goes fantastically, Amelia has clearly put in a good word for me and I walk in to the office to be greeted like an old friend. This job would be ideal; a ten minute bus ride or a thirty minute walk, which I will do on nice days since my BMI is higher than it should be. I'm still annoyed about this; she wasn't exactly Kate Moss herself. The friendly staff, M&S food hall and Starbucks just across the road, Conor, my new friend, just a stone's throw away to meet for lunch; it's too good to be true. I have to wait to hear at the end of the interviews, which is on Monday. I'm quietly confident; even the boss was informal and chummy. On a whim, I pop into M&S to pick up things for tomorrow night's tea with Conor and Granddad. It'll save me rushing around tomorrow when I will be short of time. I'm on the bus home when my phone rings from the bottom of my bag. I fumble around for several rings only to wish I hadn't bothered. It's Mum, oh give me strength; please don't let this be any kind of backlash from my email. I contemplate ignoring the call but she will only keep trying at ten minute intervals.

'Hi, Mum,' God I should like a sulky teen.

'Ivy! Where are you?'

'I'm in Richmond, Mum. I told you I was visiting Granddad for a few weeks.'

'Yes, yes, well I think it's high time you came home now lady. You should be looking for a new job and standing by in case Will decides he wants you back.' I smart indignantly. Should I indeed?

'Mum, I will not be *standing by* and waiting for anyone, and besides, I think I have a job. I'm just awaiting confirmation.'

'You mean you came back for interviews and never told us?' she huffs.

'Of course not, I mean in Richmond, with a recruitment company. I'm staying here, Mum.'

'Oh are you indeed? Your sister was just saying yesterday when I went round to see Matilda's star of the week certificate, that's twice this term now,' she adds smugly. 'She said you have no consideration for anyone but yourself at the moment. It's hard for all of us, Ivy. We could use some support too, you know.'

'What the actual fuck does any of this have to do with

Evelyn?' I bluster, 'Little Miss Perfect with her Boden catalogue family and pathetic husband. She wouldn't know hardship if it smacked her on the back of her perfectly lacquered head! Well, I *will* be speaking to her, Mother dearest, I have a few things I need to say to her that may make her realise that *her* life isn't a fucking bed of roses.' I hear Mum suck in air and choke a little. Her tone is low and angry, 'I always did suspect you were jealous of your sister, and now I have it confirmed. She is worried about you, Ivy, *worried!* ' She hisses the last word.

'Oh please, all either of you are worried about is saving face with Edinburgh's high society. She looks at me constantly like I just gobbed in her Chablis and crapped in her Fois Gras.' I'm suddenly aware that I'm getting rather a lot of attention from my fellow passengers. 'And another thing Mother, last time I checked, I was an adult and if I want to stay down here a make a life for myself, then I shall do so. I have nothing more to say to you but please do call again when you can show me the respect I deserve. Do give my love to Dad. Good day.' I click the end call button, dearly missing the days of a satisfying slam from one of the old style telephones, and to my surprise a small ripple of applause begins behind me. A few more people join in, culminating in a small cheer.

'Well done, dear,' a middle aged woman behind me pats my back, her face glowing red with pride at this gobshite of a stranger. 'I wish I'd had the guts to speak like that to my Mother, that woman controlled my life like you would not believe.' I give an embarrassed smile to all around me, thankfully, my stop looms in the distance and I gather my bags. I look back at the bus, giving a friendly wave to my new-found friends. Wow! That felt liberating, I really am a different person these days.

I potter around in Granddad's kitchen, putting away my groceries and humming contentedly to myself. Tomorrow I shall be chef extraordinaire; I do love to show off in the kitchen. On a whim I decide to bake a batch of muffins. I really shouldn't blow my own trumpet but my baking skills have always been a bug-bear to my sister. To the point that she actually banned me from supplying them to both the school and church fetes. My chocolate orange cookies and brandy truffles went in under an hour. Her crispie cakes and shop bought (and deliberately bashed up a bit) French fancies took an hour and a half. Did I really have such a dull life that this was once important to me? I think back to all the lonely evenings lying in the half light of the TV, watching endless depressing soaps and listening to the guffaws of Will as he 'nailed' another level on whatever godforsaken war game he was playing at the time. The click of yet another ring pull on a can of beer and his satisfied 'aaaah,' at the first noisy gulp. I shudder and open the cupboard door to find Nanny's slightly chipped baking bowl. I was with her when she bought it in Shepherd's Bush market that day. I remember staring in wonder at the strange looking Caribbean fruits on the stalls and the very smiley lady who patiently named them all for me. I remember Nanny buying me some plantain that I wanted to try, because it looked like a green banana; it tasted amazing. The brightly coloured sari materials in the Indian shops and stalls, the smell of the spices and the mixture of languages and accents I heard as I walked around; I was in awe. London seemed vibrant, colourful and full of interesting, warm faces. I've never understood why people find London unfriendly; sure, up in the business district it's ridiculously busy. You get the odd grumpy bus driver but so would I be, with all that heavy London traffic. People go to Oxford Street on a weekend away and think they know London; the real heart of the City is in the suburbs, in my opinion. I zone out in my thoughts, hypnotised with the soothing sounds of the whisk. Archie stretches up a curious paw at the smell of melting butter, breaking my reverie, I scoop a dollop onto my finger and he eagerly licks it off. In a strange way I'm almost relieved now that Will has cancelled the wedding. I was in a complete rut and I doubt we would have made each other happy in the long run. I know he will be straight out there looking for no-strings fun, if he tires of the one that he's with. I have my own aims now; my child doesn't need a dick-led jakey for a father. I tip the muffin mix into the cases, pop them into the oven and head outside to enjoy the sun.

The next day passes in a blur. I have another interview, in town this time and really not what I imagine myself doing. It had too much of a corporate feel to it and no eye contact in the corridors between staff. It felt tense and unnatural to me. In the afternoon I spent two hours prepping tonight's dinner with Conor. I've gone all out to impress with my culinary skills; garlic butter tiger prawns with bread rolls to start, with gastro pub style chicken breast stuffed with blue cheese and wrapped in Parma ham, with seasonal vegetables for main. For dessert I'm doing Granddad's favourite; tipsy crumble, with summer fruits that I soaked in Pimms overnight. It's a gorgeous afternoon so, on a whim, I decide to use the garden to host my dinner. I put on Granddad's radio, which remains permanently on classic FM. The soothing sounds of Vivaldi float out to the back garden as I lay the table. Right, I have one hour to freshen up before Conor arrives. My Grandfather will be home from the Farmer's market any minute. I dash upstairs for a quick shower and change. At ten to seven the doorbell goes and I skip downstairs to become the perfect hostess.

Conor looks a little anxious as I lead him out to the garden and pour him a Prosecco from the ice bucket.
'Hey, my cooking isn't that bad,' I laugh.
'No, it's not you,' he gives me a troubled glance, 'the brewery

has asked me if I'll run a pub back in Dublin for a few months, their Manager has just walked out.'
'Oh!' I gasp, why does this bother me so much. 'And, what have you decided?'
'I don't know, I'm supposed to be flexible so I really feel I have to say yes. It's only a few months.' I have the perfect opportunity to drive home my message, I decide. I feel rather cruel to say it but Conor is increasingly acting like we are an item.
'I think you should take it,' I announce over my glass of water.
'You wouldn't miss me?' Conor looks wounded.
'How can I miss you if you won't go away?' I laugh, unconvincingly. This sudden announcement has taken the wind out of my sails a little. He is my only friend in Richmond, after all. But it's not like he won't be back, I'll cope. Plus, I will hopefully have a few more friends when I start in the office.
The evening goes just as I planned. Granddad and Conor chat like old friends as I clear away the last of the debris. Once the last glass of wine is gone, I put on some coffee. The air is fragrant from my Grandfather's well-tended garden; I sip on my coffee and inhale the mix of lavender, roses and jasmine, my favourite smell ever. It takes me back to balmy, childhood summers spent here and makes me think of paddling pools and sandpits, both of which Nanny and Granddad bought for us and kept until we were young teens. We hadn't used them since around eight years of age but they were rather nostalgic about things like that. I'd spend hours sat cross-legged on the grass drawing an individual flower or a lazy, garden snail and felt like I wanted to stay forever. Edinburgh always seemed boring compared to Richmond. Edinburgh meant school and ballet class, learning violin and piano, which I had no interest in. Edinburgh felt grey; Richmond was where colours came alive. Mum never had home-baked cookies and a jar of sweets that were there to help yourself to, whenever we felt

like it. Dad was busy working all the time and Mum lived for her bridge club meet-ups and for 8pm, gin o'clock, when we went to bed. My Grandparents had infinite patience and all the time in the world. We chat until the sun goes down and Conor decides to make tracks. I fall asleep on the sofa until 2am, awakening to find a blanket over me and the house in darkness. I pick Archie up off my lap and carry him up to bed. With Conor's imminent departure looming in my head, it takes me the longest time to drift off. It's only for a few months; it's not like I'll never see him again. But still, I like having him around to hang out with. Maybe I can pop over to Dublin for a weekend; I've not been since childhood and don't remember too much about it. Yes, I'll do that with my first pay check. With that in my mind and something to look forward to, I roll on to my side and finally manage to doze off.

Chapter Seven

The days drag by as I wait to hear if I have the job. I'm tempted to pop into the office but don't want to appear desperate. Conor now has a date for leaving but not for a few weeks yet. They've put in a relief for now and he can cover until he takes up his permanent post. Hopefully, that will see me through settling into work and at least making a couple of friends to see outside of work. It's quite a young crowd; I'm probably the eldest apart from Joe, the boss. Mind you, it's about time I had some fun, for a little while at least before my plan begins. I fantasise about what kind of father I could choose, you wouldn't get this kind of choice with a partner. Clever, obviously and good looking; shallow, yes, but who cares. I'm not going to deliberately choose to have an ugly baby, am I? I could even have a mixed race child if I choose. My skin tone can be quite olive anyway. Mixed race babies are always gorgeous. I remember seeing a beautiful brown skinned child with ringlet blonde curls and the bluest eyes imaginable. I smile to myself at this thought, as I tidy my room. I'm just about to take my pile of laundry downstairs when my mobile rings.

'Hi, Ivy, it's the Jones, Cameron and Smith surgery here. Dr. Cameron asked me to call and see if you can pop in.

'Yes, of course, I will be in as soon as possible. Have I missed an appointment? I was sure my smear wasn't until next week.'

'She didn't say, sorry, she just asked me to call you.'

'OK. Give me, say, an hour? I'm not long out of bed.'

'No problem, Ivy, see you soon. How odd. I have a quick shower, throw on some clothes and head out to the garden.

'Granddad, I'm going out for a bit.'

'But your breakfast? Where are you off to so early?'

'Nosey, mind your own,' I laugh as I walk down the path. I hear him still chuckling as I round the corner.

I sit in the waiting area scrolling absent-mindedly through my emails on my phone. No reply from Gerald yet, I know he will have it, he's never off his phone whenever I've been round at theirs. There are a few funnies from Ginny and one from Evelyn, I groan as I open it. Does she know about Gerald? Or is this just a general rant about how much of a brat I am. It is, of course, the latter.

Ivy,
Mum and Dad are really worried about you. You need to come home ASAP! You can't just take off and leave everyone to deal with the aftermath of your bombshell. You should be fighting for your relationship and looking for work, not swanning around, drawing by the river. You will never pay the rent on a few sketches. Call me as soon as you read this so we can have a proper talk.
Evelyn.

No warmth, no kisses, I delete the message and click on one about changes to my internet banking.
'Ivy Efferson?' I raise my head. 'Dr. Cameron will see you now.' I storm down the corridor in a sudden foul mood. See, this is why I'm better off away from my family, they drive me insane, well Dad doesn't, to be fair, but the rest of them do, all the bloody time. Dr. Cameron looks at me with an expression of calm seriousness as I enter the room. She indicates to the empty chair and I sit obediently.
'Ivy, I'm sure quite how you're going to feel about this, given your current circumstances, but it turns out as I suspected. You're pregnant.'
'I...I'm...what?'
'Pregnant, Ivy.' The room spins around me.
'No, I can't be, I've had cramps for days now. My monthly will be here any minute...any minute now.' Dr. Cameron interrupts my rant.
'When was your last period, Ivy? I snap my head up.
'Well...around seven weeks ago but with the wedding and my

job loss...and the breakup,' I trail off. 'Look it's just stress, I've had cramps and I've been partying loads. Oh my God I've been drinking so much!' I shout in alarm.
'That's very common with a lot of women, before they know. I was smoking and drinking on a Hen weekend before I found out with my son, and he's fine,' she smiles sympathetically. I look at her in amazement, a doctor? Smoking? 'The embryo feeds from the yolk sac in the early weeks and isn't connected to your blood supply in this time. You will be fine if you stop now and start taking folic acid. The cramps you are describing are just the uterus stretching to accommodate your growing baby.' A baby? Will's baby! I put my head on the desk and thud it several times before the doctor asks me gently to stop. I want to be delighted, this is *all* I have ever wanted, and I even intended to do it on my own. On my own would be preferable, actually.
'But I've just been dumped, very publicly, very humiliatingly and he has a new girlfriend,' I wail. The doctor gives me a sympathetic smile and nods her understanding.
'Well, first of all we'll concentrate on you and baby, let me do an ultrasound and see what's going on in there,' her tone is calm and soothing, but I feel anything but calm and soothed. I lay on the bed as she switches on the ultrasound machine. She smears some cold gel on my belly and rolls the hand held device over. After a few seconds she points to a tiny blob. 'There's your baby. You see that tiny flicker?' I nod dumbly, 'that's baby's heartbeat.' I stare in awe at the tiny life growing in me. I can't take this in.
'What should I do?' I ask with desperation in my voice.
'Well, you need to decide if being pregnant is the right thing for you given your situation.' I stare at the doctor in horror at the thought that I could even contemplate an alternative to having this child, 'and even though the father hasn't been the greatest of supports at the moment, he does have a right to know, if you decide to keep it.' I shake my head in confusion;

every plan I have made this month has been turned on its head; a sea change. Just when I stop reeling from being dumped and losing my job and I've made up my mind to start over in Surrey, *this* happens. I'll have to go home and tell everyone. Much as they piss me off they deserve it face to face. I wipe the gel from my stomach, climb down from the bed and sit back on the chair.
'Would you like a prescription for folic acid or shall you just get it over the counter? The multi-vitamins in the shop bought ones are helpful too, for a mummy-to-be.'
'I will get it over the counter,' I gaze into space, 'and I will be going home to Edinburgh for a while, I don't know where I will be living from now on. I won't get my job, now that I'm pregnant.'
'Well, you are not under any legal obligation to tell an employer at this stage, morally may be a different matter. It may be tricky to admit later on that you knew. Another few weeks and you may start to show. I'll put a hold on getting your notes for now, but let me know what you decide, you will need an appointment to see the midwife and pre-natal care, which I can arrange if you decide to stay here.'

I dash from the surgery and almost run into my Grandfather walking to his car. He takes one look at my face and ushers me up the path and into the kitchen. He puts the kettle on and I shake violently as I sit at the table, grateful for the silence for a few minutes to gather my thoughts. Finally, he pours up two cups of tea and places one in front of me.
'Biscuit?' he enquires.
'No thank you,' I reply, taking one from the plate he has held out.
'Want to talk about it?' his voice is gentle. I snap from my thoughts and nod slowly.
'Well, you know how Will...I mean we should have been married...and we were living together,' he nods patiently.

'Well, somehow and I really don't know how...or when,' I sigh and shake my head, trying to remember, 'It seems that I'm having a baby.' Granddad stands and moves quickly around the table, holding me in his huge arms.
'Are we happy?' he half smiles.
'No! I mean, I don't know. Will's not exactly father of the year material, is he? I have to go back, Granddad,' I plead with my eyes to make him understand why I have to leave; God knows I don't want to. '
'But of course you do. He has to support his child, even if you're not together. You never know, he may want to be together again after all with this news.' I wouldn't count on it, I think to myself. I certainly won't be trying to force him. Where the fuck am I going to live? Not with Mum, I shudder. I cannot put a child through the years I had being a constant disappointment. I sit back down and finish my tea, searching for the train times on my phone. I glance at the clock; I can make the next one in an hour and forty-five minutes if I rush.

Granddad drives me to Kings Cross station and waves me off with a slightly concerned expression. I pull down the window.
'The irony of all this is that I think I was about to be offered the job in Richmond. I was going to take you out for tea and surprise you with my news.' I look sadly down at Granddad. He reaches up and squeezes my hand.
'You come back any time you want, and if they're keen to take you on then you can still take the job. I'm retired; me and junior will be just fine down the lotty.' I smile my gratitude,
'That's good to know, thank you.' The guard blows the whistle and the train jerks into action. I look at my Grandfather in panic.
'You'll be fine, Ivy, love. I'm always here, you know, come down any time.' I lean out the window and wave for as long as I can, until the train goes round a bend and I can no longer

see him. I wave for a few more seconds, just in case he can still see me, then head to my seat. I text Dad to tell him I'm on my way. He messages back to say he will pick me up at Waverly Station. Mum obviously calls to tell Evelyn I'm coming home because half an hour later I receive a message from her saying that she's glad I'm doing what I'm told for once. I silently fume, how bloody dare she think any of this is her doing, I couldn't give a rat's arse what she thinks.
'Fuck. Off.' I mutter as I delete her message.
'London tickets please? Although I'm almost scared to ask,' laughs the guard.
'Well, lucky for you that you are not my sister,' I smile back; just to show I'm not going to require the men in white coats to collect me from the next stop. I text Will and tell him I must see him, alone, this evening. There can be no excuses; this is of the utmost importance. To give him his due, he actually does text back within five minutes, but only to say,
'OMG why? Have you got an STD?!!!' Prick! I ignore the comment and message back,
'the cafe on the corner at 7pm, don't be late.' Let him worry, it'll make sure he turns up. He may be wishing it's an STD by the end of the conversation, it's certainly *something* sexually transmitted anyway. I cast my mind back to when this could have happened. It must have been that one off occasion we went out with friends and I got a little drunk. It was the only time I can remember anyway; being manhandled at 2am after he'd finished all his cans and switched off his games console was not my idea of romance. I turned him down on all those occasions but we did have that one barely memorable moment. I can't believe this idiot is going to have to be part of my life forever now. Why did I come off the pill on the run-up to our wedding? In just over two weeks' time it should have been taking place; I would have been thrilled to find out today that I was pregnant in some parallel universe in which we were still together. My phone beeps and I pick it up from

the table.
'Hey Efferson, what you up to tonight? I've mucked up the rota and put on too many staff. So, guess who has the night off? x' I groan and put the phone face down on the table. How could I have forgotten about Conor? I can't even think of anything to reply to him with. I text Ginny to see if she can meet me after I've told Will, I will need the moral support. She replies that of course she will and she's really happy I'm coming home. Four hours to go and I suddenly feel completely exhausted, I decide to close my eyes and catch up on a bit of sleep, to pass the time and so I don't have to think. I scrunch up my hoodie, to use as a pillow, and sleep for practically all the journey.

Chapter Eight

Will stares across the table at me as I stir a hole in the bottom of my teacup.

'How can you be sure it's mine?' he accuses, God, I hate this man. What a pillock!

'Because Will, I haven't slept with anybody else for *eight years.* I'm seven weeks and three days pregnant, of course it's yours. What are you going to tell your girlfriend?' I smile with satisfaction.

'I doubt she will be bothered, she spends half the time at her boyfriend's anyway, these days.' I choke on my lukewarm, too milky tea, but I'm far from surprised. Will shrugs, 'well you always were such a frigid bitch I actually believe that it's mine.' I stare at him in disbelief.

'Just because I didn't give in to your amorous attempts at stupid-o'clock in the morning does not mean I'm frigid!' That was perhaps a little loud. Will rolls his eyes at a couple at the next table, now taking a greater interest in us.

'So what did you think of Sasha then? She's pretty, huh?' Unbelievable!

'If you're attracted to the sort of age group that can't remember watching the first series of *Friends*, then I suppose so.' I give a nonchalant shrug.

'Oh, I just remembered, you left some of those bunny poop things in the bathroom. Sasha was using them; I said you wouldn't mind.'

'I left what?' I frown in irritation at how easily he can switch the subject.

'Bunny poops. You know, in that wee round tub with a sponge in the top, they're even in different shades of poo brown,' he chuckles to himself.

'They're bronzing pearls, Will.' I shake my head at his stupidity.

'Anyhoo, I reckon since we're having a sprog and that, you'd

probably better move back in so I can see it. Sash and I can have the couch if she comes round. '
'Excuse me? You want me to move back in and still have your bit on the side around? You really are a strange one, I guess I just stopped noticing after a while.'
'Hey, she's bloody brilliant at *Call of Duty,* I think that was the problem with us, Ivy; we had nothing in common any more. You weren't Interested in anything I did, or liked.' Will looks sadly into his builder's tea. Stewed, milk and two sugars, just how he's always liked it. I feel a minor pang of guilt, I've blamed him for everything but the reality is I can only blame him for cancelling the wedding. Maybe I didn't make too much of an effort. He paid all the rent for months while I found my next job and waited to get paid. He never complained once about that, at the time. I hated all his philandering friends so he had mainly stayed home. I took myself off to the bedroom every night even though he had asked me to play a game with him, I'm not blameless. And now we're having a child together. My voice softens a little.
'I'm not sure where I will be staying yet, Will, would you like to see a scan picture of our baby?' His eyes meet mine and sparkle with anticipation. God, those eyes! Please let the baby have inherited those. He takes the picture from my hand and gives me a strange look.
'We're having a kidney bean?'
'It's only small yet,' I laugh. It'll have more features later.'
'I know, just pulling your pisser, Ivy. Looks like ya. That's exactly how you sleep, curled in a wee ball.' I give him a playful slap across the table.
'Look, I have to go and see a few other people, and you have had a lot to take in. I'll give you a call tomorrow and we can chat again.' We walk outside the cafe to go our separate ways and Will gives me a hug. I embrace him awkwardly and head for the bus stop. He took it better than I expected to be honest. Now, number two on my list, Ginny.

'Oh my God, oh my God, you look amazing!' screams Ginny as she runs towards me. She holds my hands and takes a step back to examine me. London air suits you, and you're tanned, you lucky mare. It's pissed down here almost every day since you left.'

'Well, that's sitting by the river drawing, for you. Bert sends his love.'

'Awww Bert, my wee honey, if I was straight and forty years older he'd be my perfect man,' Gin scrunches up her features to make the kind of face you do when looking at kittens. 'A pint of Tennents and a white wine, please,' she instructs the barmaid before turning back to me.

'No! A soda and lime, please,' I hastily correct the barmaid. Ginny gives me a confused glance before shrugging at the barmaid, who looks at us in turn, like she's watching a tennis match. Ginny gives me a look up and down in contemplator as realisation slowly descends.

'Spill!' she demands, 'Coming home suddenly, meeting up with *Will!* Not drinking...you're not...you *are?* No waaaaay!' she screams and launches herself at me. This is the problem with Ginny, she knows me so well, I can hide nothing. She bustles me over to the table and pulls her seat in ready for the interrogation.

'So, was Will pleased?'

'Well...I had hoped for something more eloquent than "Yay, my baws work!" but you can't have everything.'

'Are you going to get back together? Where will you live? Of course, you can live with me and Tash, if you wish, we won't mind.' Ah, so Natasha has moved in, that's one less option for me.

'I could stay at Mum and Dad's, I suppose, although Will did say he'd like me to move back in. But how can I pay rent? Who's going to take me on for a job, *pregnant*?' Gin waves a dismissive hand.

'You'll get a job as a temp no bother. They won't care if they don't have to pay maternity leave. Hmm, your old flat is definitely a preferable option to your Mum's. So fuck if you can't pay rent for now; after all he's put you through, he deserves it. Yes, go with your old flat. Or ours.'
'Thanks, but I couldn't live with a couple. Much as I love you, I couldn't play gooseberry.' Ginny gives an irate tut.
'Hey, she's about to finish work, wanna meet her?'
'Of course, but I will need to go to see Mum and Dad in an hour. I've already had three voicemails asking if I'm dead.'

Just like three weeks ago, I'm sitting in the same spot in the good living room, except this time it's dark outside. The garden, mine and my father's distraction from Mum's steely gaze, has been removed.
'Oh how delightful,' Mum screeches, 'We can get the wedding back on and nobody will be any the wiser.'
'No, we can't, mother. Will cancelled everything; we've lost our deposit and they will more than likely have filled our space. Anyway, you don't have to be married these days. We can go back to living together for a trial period and if things go well when the baby is born, we can think about it then.' Mum looks crestfallen.
'Brian! Tell Ivy she must get married. You can't have a child out of wedlock,' she whispers the last word and shakily pours herself a generous gin. 'Whatever will your sister say?' she shakes her head solemnly.
'I couldn't give a flying fuck!' I announce indignantly. 'This is my life and my business, Evelyn can butt out.' Mum appears not to even hear my outburst, but paces along the rug in front of the fire. Dad gets up from his chair with difficulty and pats me on the head on the way past.
'Congratulations, lass. I know it's what you've dreamed of. I'll go and warm up some chicken pasta leftovers from tea for you.' I watch desperately as my father leaves the room. Mum

is now punching her way through the phone's call list.
'Evelyn? Yes, its Mummy, your sister would like a word.' But I've gone, slipped out behind my father who is gesturing wildly towards the pantry. I sit on the tiny Rupert the Bear footstool that belonged to me, as a child, and clamp my hands across my mouth to keep from laughing at the muffled conversation in the kitchen.
'Hang on Evelyn, your father doesn't know where she's at. I'll go and see if she's in her room.' I sneak out of the cupboard and Dad and I titter like school-kids as we listen to Mum clip-clop through the rooms upstairs. I sit down at the table and tuck into my pasta, served with a glass of milk, for baby's bones, Dad informs me.
'How did she...?' Mum gives us a puzzled look as she walks back into the kitchen.
'I've been here all along, Mum,' I frown.
'But Brian, you just said she wasn't...' Mum trails off.
'I haven't spoken to you, Barbara. Jeezo, you drink too much,' my father shakes his head in disgust. Mum clutches her hand to her bosom and rushes from the warmth of the kitchen. Dad and I exchange a knowing smirk. Oh, I could so happily live here if it weren't for Mum. The apple didn't fall far from the tree where Dad is concerned; he's just a younger model of Granddad. So, I've come almost full circle in three weeks, except instead of a wedding, I have a baby. Who'd have thought it? Tomorrow I have a lot of thinking to do but right now, all I want is a warm bubble bath and an early night.

I'm rudely awakened at 9.15, the next morning, by Evelyn, coming straight from the school run to give me grief; she must have thrown those kids out of the car without slowing down. She plonks herself on the end of my bed and runs a hand through her perfect, dark hair.
'Ivy, Mum asked me to come and talk some sense in to you. You really need to be with the father of your child. Mum and

Dad have a lot of friends in high places, think about what everyone will say.'
'Oh, good morning Evelyn, thank you so much for your congratulations and your concern about how I am keeping.' I sit up and give my dishevelled hair a shake. She throws me a sarcastic look.
'I already asked Mum.'
'Well thank you for your interest but I haven't yet decided what I'm doing. As soon as I do, I'll be sure to tell you first, 'I smirk. 'But, it will be *my* decision and nobody else's.' I say the last sentence defiantly to drive the message home.
'Actually, I've already called Will and he wants you back, so I'm here to help you take your stuff from here and Ginny's flat and to see you're settled back in.' I stare at my sister in disbelief. How can we be from the same stock and just so...different?
'You've had a wasted trip, Evelyn. When I have made up my mind I shall make my own plans. I don't need you, or Mum controlling my life. It's not just a case of Will wanting me back, I'm not used goods! Now, do be a dear and piss off.' I flop back down into bed and pull the duvet over my head.
'God! You are an infuriating little madam. My kids have more sense than you do. Fine! Be a single mother, I don't care.' My bedroom door slams shut and I exhale my relief, with a mental note to Google, 'how to divorce your family.' My phone beeps, it's Will.
'Good morning how is the mumma of my bubba? Made your decision yet?' I groan and roll away from my phone. What exactly are my options? Stay with Mum and Dad? No! Move in with Ginny and Natasha? A definite better option but it would be unfair to impose on a couple, especially with a baby in the mix. I haven't got the option of my own flat. With no income or savings, I couldn't even afford to furnish a council flat, should I manage to get one. Granddad's? I brighten at this; at the thought of long riverside walks, baby with a

childminder so I could still work part time. This is my favourite option so far. But Will, he is so excited at the prospect of us living together again and seeing his child; I really owe it to him, and our son or daughter, to try again. Granddad's words echo in my head about becoming a single Mum by choice. It really wouldn't be fair to take that away from my child. I try to visualise what my life would have been like without my Dad, it's not a nice thought. All those snuggles on his knee as I watched cartoons, teaching me how to shoot a hoop that led to my place on the netball team and all those sore knee kisses that instantly took the pain away. I probably wouldn't have been so close to Nanny and Granddad either. My life would have been even more music and ballet lessons, dumped with babysitters so Mum could play bridge. I may even have developed a dependency on gin myself by now. No, I owe it to my baby and Will to see if he can man up and be the parent that he should be. I guess I've made my decision then, I'm going back to my flat.

I walk reluctantly downstairs to tell my family my decision. Evelyn perches on a stool at the breakfast bar with a tiny cup of espresso in her hand.
'Has Gerald told you I emailed him, Evelyn?' I've heard nothing back and I need to know.
'No, what for? I didn't see an email from you and I've been checking twice a day. Seeing that I was waiting for a reply from you, for mine,' she huffs.
'Oh nothing, I'll text him later. Oh, and if that lift to Will's is still OK, then I'd like to take you up on the offer...thanks.' I say grudgingly. The thought of two heavy cases on the bus neither appeals nor is good for me in my condition.
'Oh, there's a good girl,' Mum beams. My sister shoots her a smug I-told-you-so look.
'Of course, Ivy, it would be a pleasure. I'm glad I've managed to talk some sense into you.' I turn about and leave the kitchen

before I say something I can't take back. God, my sister infuriates me. I walk upstairs to re-pack my case and shout for Dad to help me carry it downstairs. Evelyn and I walk out to the people carrier and she lifts my case into the back seat. I climb up to the passenger side and put on my seat belt. Evelyn reaches over and pulls the lower part of the belt over my tummy.
'You need to position it like that now you're pregnant.' I nod my understanding.
'How are things at home, Evelyn? Is Gerald working a lot of extra hours at the moment?' I enquire as we roll down the driveway. Evelyn indicates left and throws me a strange look.
'He's always busy. He never usually gets home before ten since the promotion. What's this sudden obsession with My Gerald?'
'Erm, nothing really, just that it's not like him not to reply to my email, is all. Although you do look a little stressed too.' My sister glances in the rear view mirror at her reflection and frowns. She looks immaculate as ever, of course. I stop talking, as I suspected he has told her nothing. I'll take it up with him; I don't want to have to be the one to ruin my sister's perfect life. We stop off at Ginny's to pick up the remainder of my things and finally pull up at my old flat. My stomach churns with anticipation and dread. Please let me be making the right decision. I really can't trust my own judgement any more.

Chapter Nine

Things go back to normal surprisingly quickly, once I move back in, almost like I had never been away. It's been a week now and although I have suddenly developed full on morning sickness, I still try to make an effort to interact more with Will. I'm really not interested in playing his X Box with him, I'm not very good, but I do try. Will puts on Eastenders in the living room for me but plays on his phone throughout. Still, we are both kind of making a half-arsed effort. He's been really understanding about me not working. That's the one complaint I never had of him, he is anything but tight with his cash. I have actually been for one job interview already and have two more lined up; it's important to me to still maintain some kind of independence. I never mentioned my pregnancy at the interview as it was for a temporary role anyway. I'd be leaving in three months' time so it's not relevant to them. The next two are permanent, so I really will feel obliged to say, I don't hold out much hope for getting those jobs. I can't get away with not saying I'm pregnant for very long anyway, they will see a bump in a few weeks and there is no way they will believe that I didn't already know.

I'm flicking through the Scotsman newspaper's job section and half watching Coronation Street, when the doorbell rings. I glance over at Will to see if he seems to be expecting anyone but he has already got up to answer it. I hear muffled whispers in the hallway and turn the sound on the TV down, peering curiously at the closed living room door. I hear Will inviting someone through and hastily arrange myself a bit more appropriately for guests. We haven't been expecting anyone tonight, or none that Will has told me about. My family and friends all know how much I hate unannounced visitors; a quick text half an hour before is the norm, to us. In a haze of cheap perfume and leopard print leggings, walks

Sasha. She scornfully gives the once over to my fleecy, teddy bear pyjamas, stained with Ben and Jerry's cookie dough ice cream. How typical that I'd just taken my makeup off. Cotton wool balls splodged with mascara and foundation line the arm of the couch; I really couldn't have looked less attractive if I'd tried.

'Oh so she's back then, is she?' Sasha raises her eyebrows and stares at me. 'Decided you wanted to pay your share of the bills after all, did you?' I can't believe the nerve of this...child!

'Actually, I thought it may be nice for our baby to have a father around. Sorry to ruin your plan of taking over my flat,' I retort.

'Funny, I could tell this place had been decorated with a much *older* woman's touch.' She shoots back.

'I'm just relieved you didn't Barbie it up in my absence, white trash pink is so not my colour,' I will not let her win. 'Anyway, what can we do for you this evening? We are about to watch a movie, you really should have called first.'

'I did, I called Will, it's his flat, I don't believe I need your permission,' she smirks. I glare at Will. How dare he not mention it? She picks up her iPod from the pile of letters, keys and pens in the fruit bowl and walks to the door with a smug look.

'Enjoy One Direction on the way home, dear.' I try to get the last shot in but she ignores me.

'Wi-iiiill, would you drive me, please. It's ever so chilly out.' Will reaches for his car keys on the table but the look on my face stops him in his tracks.

'Errr, sorry Sash, I forgot, I have a flat tyre. You need bus money?' I smile smugly at Sasha to let her know I've won.'

'Nah, s'ok, I'll call my Da.'

'Why not call your boyfriend?' I retort, 'or has he found out you had a bit on the side and ditched you.' The wounded look on her face tells me I've hit the nail on the head with my comment. I'd like to say I feel a little guilty, but I don't. Once

she leaves I have a proper go at Will for not telling me she was coming round. Hell hath no fury like a hormonal woman. He flits from feigning innocence, to outright lying before losing his temper and storming out. I head off to bed, where I silently fume. This is not an ideal situation; we've found ourselves thrown together due to circumstances, rather than choice. I miss Richmond, I miss Granddad and Conor and...oh bugger! I totally forgot to message him back when he text me on the train. How could I have forgotten about that? I've thought about him a lot, even considered messaging him; I just couldn't formulate in my head what I wanted to say. Nothing sounded right. I scroll through my messages. Where is it? Did I dream that text? I was in shock after all. I go to my contacts list but his name is not there. Will! I'm going to kill him, what a jealous, insecure prick. I hear the front door bang closed again, fifteen minutes later. Will has clearly only gone as far as the off-license. I've given him the perfect excuse to not sit there with a face on him all night, a cup of tea by his side. I told him the other day that he needs to cut down and he had grudgingly said he would although he didn't see why it mattered, since he's not the one who's pregnant. I round the corner to see his startled face. 'Where is Conor's number?' I begin calmly.
'Who the fuck is Conor?'
'Don't play dumb with me, where is it?' There's an edge to my voice that now that makes him take the defensive.
'Ivy, I don't know what you're on about, for God's sake.'
'You fucking do, you lying shit. He was a friend, that's all. I wasn't the one cheating in this relationship. I hate you for this, Will. Get *over* yourself; you are no bloody catch, these days.'
I storm back to the bedroom and call my Grandfather. Maybe he can pop into the pub and let him know I've come home. Of course, I could easily look up the Inebriated Leprechaun number and call myself, but I feel really bad about ignoring

his message all this time, I wouldn't be surprised if he slammed the phone down on me. What is my real motive for calling Granddad? Am I testing the water to see if I can move back? Maybe I just need to hear a friendly voice. I have no idea what to do, what to think. Just talking to Granddad can help sometimes. It rings on and on, he's never moved on with technology and doesn't have an answer phone service. I'm about to hang up when he finally answers.

'Hi Granddad...' I pause; I don't trust myself to speak any more. I feel overwhelmed with emotion just hearing his voice.

'Hello my little darlin', how's my favourite girl?'

Umm...OK, I suppose. Having a bit of a shit day; I've lost Conor's number and I wondered if you'd be up in Richmond tomorrow. I could call the pub myself if you're not, it just feels a bit weird doing that for some reason. '

'It's OK, love. I ran into him in the supermarket and told him you had to go home urgently. Don't worry, I didn't tell him of your delicate situation, that's not my place, but he did ask if you were back with your ex and I said you were giving it another go.' My heart fills with sadness.

'How did he seem?'

'He was ok; maybe a little shocked but said it explained why he hadn't heard back from you.' Oh poor Conor, I can see the exact expression he would have had at this news.

'Are you keeping OK, Granddad?'

'Yes, love, I'm fine. You just concentrate on baking that great grandchild of mine. I can't wait to meet him or her.' We chat for a few more minutes but Granddad can sense I need some time alone and makes an excuse to go. I hang up and pull the duvet over my head, what a bloody mess I've made of things; I can't even text Conor to say sorry now. Of course it was Will; he's the only one who knows my pass-code. He's clearly been looking through my messages and decided Conor was a threat. He never was, that's the thing that annoys me most. He was just a mate, like Ginny.

I don't remember falling asleep but I awaken the next morning, still clutching my phone, as it rings. It's an 0208 London number that's not logged in my phone. Conor? It has to be. Fantastic! He's decided to call from the pub landline and I can ask for his number again, to keep in touch as friends. I'm changing my pass code as soon as it's stored. I answer on the third ring.
'Conor?'
'Er, not last time I checked,' laughs a friendly female voice, 'It's Amelia.'
'Oh, hi,' I sit bolt upright in bed.
'Oh, hi to you too, new colleague. I'm so sorry it's taken an age to get back to you, but we finally finished all the interviews and you stood out by miles. We are hoping we aren't too late and you've snapped up another job already. Newbies get the first round in for Friday drinks and I'm making mine a double.' Amelia's laugh tinkles over the hundreds of miles, but it may as well be from another world.
'Ivy? Are you so shocked you can't speak?' It's a slightly nervous laugh this time.
'Oh, Amelia,' I can hear the pain in my voice, 'I came back to Edinburgh to try again with my ex-fiancé. I'm so sorry; I really wanted the job too. '
'Wow! That's fantastic; I'm so pleased for you, Ivy. I hope it works out well.' I can't bring myself to mention the baby, I'm telling nobody else until the end of the precarious first twelve weeks.
'Fingers crossed, Amelia. I'm so grateful for the job offer, and actually, I'm pretty gutted I can't take it. '
'No Worries, Ivy, I'll go call number two on the list. Good luck, I'm sorry you won't be working with us; I saw us becoming friends; you were such a laugh at the interview.'
'I know, I would have loved that Amelia. I'm so sorry. Please thank Joe for me won't you?'

'Of course I will, no worries, Ivy. Take care of yourself.'

I stomp angrily to the kitchen to make a cup of tea, ignoring a snoring Will on the sofa. In my other life, I would be celebrating right now, probably texting Conor to arrange an emergency, celebratory night out, before heading into Richmond to stock up of my new working wardrobe. Instead I have a pile of dishes from last night, a philandering drunk who will no doubt mooch around in a grump until he orders himself a takeaway and start drinking again to cure his hangover. I can't even say this is a new thing; I'd clearly become desensitised to it years ago. What was I thinking of, planning on marrying this idiot? And now I'm trapped, stuck with him in my life forever, just because he's the father of my child.

I head into town to meet Ginny for lunch on a spur of the moment. I make a mental note to apologise for the crack on the head she received when her phone rang whilst she was under a bath. I wait in the local pub closest to her work and absent-mindedly people watch. I spot two parents outside the window, the mother is chatting to a friend while the father chases his son around the buggy. The child squeals with delighted shock every time his dad catches him. I can't help but give a wistful smile at the child's laughter. Unfortunately, I can't see Will being that kind of parent. He's excited by the idea but the reality is that it will infringe upon his life too much. To him it will be a status symbol, a badge of honour of his virility. To me it is everything; my child will be my whole life, my reason for being. I can't quite believe how oblivious I have been to our differences, all this time. The family moves on and my attention turns to a couple at a table in the window. Their heads close, whispering and giggling at a private joke, over their glasses of wine. I can't even remember the last time I felt like that, we rarely went out together or

even ate together. With a sudden swing of the front door, Ginny arrives. She looks around for a few seconds before giving me a wave and making her way through the tables. She gives me a hug and a belly pat.
'How's mummy feeling?'
'Stressed,' I run a hand through my hair and shake my head. 'Why did I romanticise our relationship so much? Why couldn't I see that Will is a bloody idiot? That fling he had, well, she came round last night. He went out just after she left and I'm sure he went to catch her up.' Ginny gives me a sympathetic smile and reaches across the table to squeeze my hand. 'Oh, and he deleted Conor's number from my phone but hey! At least I got offered that dream job in Richmond, Oh wait, that's right, I can't take it because I'm up the duff and trapped in a relationship with a permanently pissed idiot, who shags around. God, I could even have the clap!' I mutter with disgust.
'You don't have the clap, Ivy. They'll have tested you for all that when you went for your bloods. I'm sure they'd have thought to mention it. Anyway, why can't you take the job? Go stay with Granddad Bert and have the life you wanted. Go on, call them back now and tell them you'll take the position.' Things are always so straight forward in Ginny's world. I'd love to have her philosophy on life; she's never unhappy because she refuses to remain in a situation that makes her feel that way.
'No, I can't, I know I don't have to tell them I'm pregnant but it just doesn't feel right to hide it.'
'Fair enough, well just because you're having a kid doesn't mean you're stuck with him. Stay with us, or your Mum,' Ginny sniggers at her last suggestion. 'He can see his kid on the weekends.' I don't know what I should be doing and I don't know what I want, except my baby, I definitely want my baby. But being with my friend does help, at least to temporarily forget my problems. I'm coming up for nine

weeks now, three more and I can see how much my baby has grown, at my twelve week scan. I'm really excited about that. Well, I guess I'd counted on being a single mum anyway; Will or no Will I can do it. We order our baguettes and chat about Ginny's new relationship; she has never been so happy. Natasha has decided to come out to some close friends and build up to telling her family. My friend glows with excitement when she talks about her girlfriend. It's good to see her so content; she's had a few runs of bad luck when it comes to women. Not just the cat thief, but one that refused to find a job and spent all Ginny's hard-earned cash and another who ran off back to her ex in Australia, after running up a phone bill of hundreds of pounds. All too soon, it's time for Ginny to go back to work and I have to face going home. I walk past the shops showing off their vibrant, autumn fashions and think how unfair it is that I don't even have the money to treat myself to lift my spirits.

I arrive home to an empty house. It's freezing and dark, but the relief I feel is palpable. A simple note declaring 'gone out,' sits on the table. No kisses, no mention of where; the pub, at a guess. I switch on the heating and rummage in the freezer for dinner. Pizza, nice one! I can have a whole evening of girly movies and a bubble bath without Will hammering on the door announcing he needs in. I'm sure he does it on purpose just to ruin my enjoyment and solitude. With my dinner in the oven, I decide to see if I can find Conor on Facebook. At least then I can keep in touch. A friend request seems a little less stalkerish than calling him at work. I'm sure he wouldn't mind but by not texting him back and not telling him where I was going, it may be an awkward conversation. He may not even want to talk to me at all. I wouldn't, if I were him. Why had I never added him as a friend when I was down in London? Probably because I'm rarely on there these days; there's only so much I can take of the fake, perfect lives that are created just to make you feel inadequate. 'Friends' who lurk without posting and pass you by on the street. I guess I never thought and Conor never mentioned having an account. But his name is far too common and half of Ireland seems to appear on my screen. After half an hour I throw my phone down in defeat. There's an awful smell wafting down the hallway, burning, that's what it is. Fucking great, now I have no dinner; because things clearly weren't shit enough. I tip the charred pizza into the bin and make some toast instead. This time last month, I didn't have the baby I so desperately wanted, well, I did but I didn't know it, and I was the happiest I have been in years. Now, I have the thing I want most in the world and I'm the most miserable I have been in a long time. Maybe I'm just hormonal, or a more likely explanation is that it's Will. I've tasted life without him, and I loved it. Maybe we could go to couples counselling, maybe he could go to rehab. I remember his cruel comment about 'AA being for quitters' and realise there is probably no point in even suggesting it. I decide to vent my fury by emailing Gerald again, this time with the simple message, 'You're out of time. I'm serious! Tell her tonight or I will.' This makes me feel marginally better; at least there is one situation I can control. My own one, well I shall just keep out of Will's way for now. As I see it, I have two options; see if I can get a temp job to save up for my own flat. Dad would loan me a deposit, I know he would. Or go back to London and explain my circumstances to Amelia get some temp work and do the same at Granddad's. Save for my own place; infinitely trickier in London due to the cost of rent being so high. Unless I move a little way out, that could work. I'd be happier, I know I would. I know my original thinking was for Will and the baby to have a close relationship but at this stage I'm beyond caring. If he can still mess around behind my back when I'm pregnant, he's not going to give a shit once the baby is here. Some people will never change. My phone alerts me to a new email. Gerald!

Dear Ivy,
Thank you for your concern and relationship advice but Evelyn is more than aware of the situation. We have an open marriage these days, after deciding this would be for the best a couple of years ago. It works well for the kids as we would have split up otherwise. I'm sure she is seeing someone herself but she isn't quite as open about it. I'd prefer it that you don't discuss this with Evelyn or anyone else. It's a private arrangement that she would be ashamed to discuss.
Good to have you home and congratulations on your pregnancy.
Regards, G.

I reread the email in puzzlement. Really? It would explain why she has a face like a smacked arse most of the time. So now what? If he's telling the truth then she will be mortified that I've mentioned it. If he's lying then she really needs to know. Oh he's good, I'll give him that. If it wasn't for Dad and Granddad to show me how men *should* be, I'd probably have given up years ago. I file my correspondence from Gerald into a file named 'Twat.' I need evidence to prove to Evelyn that I at least tried. With that little distraction out of the way, I reluctantly turn my attention back to my own situation. I really don't want to be financially dependent on Will; I don't actually want to be with him at all now. Therefore, my first port of call needs to be an employment agency. No more messing about with job applications, two weeks here and there will have to do for now. But what to do about maternity leave? How do I pay rent then? I thump my head onto the table. I feel trapped, completely trapped in this shit relationship. Of course, Will would support his child but I know the cost of Edinburgh rentals. At least my way I could have got some savings together before having to leave work. Fuck it! I'll send out applications anyway. At least I have some time to save something whilst I decide. I'm astounded

Will actually managed to make me pregnant in the first place; he drinks so much that I'd assumed they'd all be swimming sideways and backstroke, perishing before they'd even made it to the Fallopian tubes. Just goes to show, you can never take anything for granted. This thought is barely out of my head when the front door clatters against the wall, announcing Will's arrival home from work. We need a proper talk and I want to catch him before the Playstation goes on and the first can is opened.

'Hey babymomma, what's for tea? I'm starving.' Will, beer can in hand stands up from the fridge. I hate that even though we have argued he can act like nothing is wrong. Well I can play that game too.

'Sod all, you either go to the supermarket or call for a takeaway. Oh, and can we have a chat before you get settled for the night, please, Will?' He looks at me cautiously, like a child who knows he is about to get a telling off. 'And must you drink every night? It's not healthy. Do you ever wonder if you have a drink problem?' Will looks down at the can in his hand, as if he couldn't quite recall how it got there.'

'Of course I have a drink problem,' he looks at me seriously, 'I have two hands and only one mouth!' Will cackles at his own joke before cracking open the can and making that glug and ahhh sound that makes my entire body tense up in disgust.

'You crack yourself up, I'm sure. Look, I just want to talk about work and the baby; how I can best support myself while I'm pregnant.' Will squints as he points the remote at the TV, as if trying to block out the sound of my voice.

'It's cool, Ivy, pay me in sexual favours,' I roll my eyes. 'And by that I mean do me a favour and keep the fuck away from me.' Will throws himself on to the sofa and clutches his stomach through his mirth. What did I ever see in this idiot?

'Thanks for that, but I'd rather shit in my hands and clap than sleep with you again, Will.' He gives me a wounded look.

'Well lucky I got Sash for that then, isn't it.' He watches the

TV intently as his game loads.
'Do you find it easier having a brainless bimbo in your life then, Will? I mean, from what you've told me, that is. I mean, I'm not exactly a rocket scientist but you'd never catch me paying fifteen quid for an air guitar.' Will glances up with a frown.
'She was *pissed*, Ivy. It was at T in the Park, we were all hammered. It was a hilarious moment, seeing her walk away with nothing. Not that you'd know fun if it smacked you on your fat arse. At least Sasha is a good laugh, stop being so nasty about her.'
'Stop being so nasty? She messes around with my fiancé behind my back, slags me off in my own home and *I'm* the bitch?'
'Well, if the lead fits...' I storm out of the room and angrily pull on my boots and coat. I'm just about to slam out the front door when I notice Will leaning against the living room door frame with a sheepish look on his face.
'Ivy, I'm sorry, I didn't mean that. You don't need to worry about money, even if we don't end up together forever, I'll always make sure you and the sprog are OK. We nearly got married after all.' I give Will a sarcastic smile and push past him towards the front door. I know he means that but I'm still mad at him for messing around behind my back and then having the nerve to defend his bit on the side.
'You gonna bring back a chippy for me then, Ivy?'
Nope, I'm going to be out all evening, get it yourself.'

Now what? I look left and right along the darkening street. Now I have said I'll be out all evening, I actually have to do it. I know that Gin and Natasha were planning to go to the cinema. I curse myself for neglecting my friendships over the years; all those calls for nights out that I turned down in favour of staying home with Will. Well those friends eventually stopped asking, and I was relieved. I'd got my man; I didn't need nights out on the town anymore. What an idiot. Sod it, I'll go and pay my sister a visit and see what Gerald's reaction is to seeing me, I will know then if he is telling the truth. How sad my life has become when things like is how I get my kicks. Who cares, in the absence of being able to get ratarsed, I need a way to vent somehow. I take a right turn and walk purposefully towards the bus stop. I'm going to put this open relationship theory to bed, once and for all.

Chapter Ten

'Ivy! We weren't expecting you this evening.' My sister looks annoyed and dishevelled; I give her holey leggings and baggy sweatshirt an approving look.
'Oh I know, Sis, but I was just passing and thought I'd pop by,' I give Evelyn a broad smile and follow her down the hall. 'See, I know what an expert you are on raising children and, well, I'm so new to this. I wanted to pick your brain a bit.' I can feel the superiority emanate from my sister, even though she is facing the opposite way, as we make our way down the endless hall and into the obsessively clean, open plan kitchen/family room. My sister is fairly open about her OCD; she can even laugh about it, but only if it's an even number of times, so Dad says. My fifteen year old nephew, Christopher, sits at the dining table surrounded by text books. His hair sticks up at a jaunty angle where he has pulled his fingers through it. An old childhood habit of his that I remember fondly.
'Hey, Chris, how's it going?' He engages me in some complicated, 'rude boy' handshake ending in a gentle knuckle punch. He is going through a 'Jafaikan' phase' right now. It seems to be doing the rounds at his high school at the moment, since those two 'well cool' Jamaican brothers arrived and everyone tried to copy their accents and actions. Well cool, *they* may be, but copying them makes Chris sounds like a pillock. He formerly had a snooty, Corstorphine public school boy accent. Actually, Jafaikan' was a humorous change for a short while; mainly because it annoyed his parents, who now refuse to speak to him unless he talks in his normal voice. Evelyn dashes upstairs to 'freshen up,' or put on a bra Christopher informs me with a chortle.
'Thank fuck, man. Seein' those ankle swingers while I'm eatin' No need, like. Innit, blood?'
'Hmmm,' I nod my agreement, hoping that's the right thing to

do. I have no idea what any of that meant.

'Hi, Matilda.' I walk over to my niece, who is carefully tying off the friendship bracelet she has just completed. The tongue of concentration pokes out the side of her mouth before she looks up at me with a beaming smile.

'Tadaaaa! For you, Auntie Ivy. Well, actually it's for my cousin, in there,' she points at my stomach with a mischievous giggle. She's eight now and at that weird age where kids start finding out the facts of life and find it embarrassingly hilarious and horrific, all at the same time.

'Aww thank you, Matty, that is so sweet of you.' I'll keep it safe until your cousin is old enough not to eat it.' I wander over to James, my other nephew, at the awkward age of thirteen. He doesn't look up from his DS as I flop down beside him.

'Whatcha' playing, James?' I enquire.

'Oh, my God! Why won't everyone just *leave me alone*?' He storms of to his room and slams the door, Chris, Matilda and I guffaw loudly. My sister struts down the stairs like she's off to a dinner party. Why bother? It's only me here for goodness sake. I notice that she's put on a no make-up, made-up look. She walks over to the kettle and fills it in a sink not far off the size of my bath tub.

'Gerald not home yet? I ask, nonchalantly.

'No, he has late surgery tonight. Probably won't be home until ten-ish.'

'He's neva' home 'til ten, man. Youse is always on his case, innit?' Chris gives his tuppence-worth.

'Ginny saw him out for dinner last week, with a...colleague?' I get straight to the point. I see my sister stiffen slightly, before she moves to the cupboard to take out two cups.

'Right, Matilda, off for your bath, Christopher, finish off your homework in your room, please. Aunt Ivy and I are talking parenting.' With two dramatic sighs, my niece and nephew drag themselves off their chairs with huge effort.

'I'll come say goodnight before I leave,' I smile as they pass me by.
'Never good to let them have inside information; remember that, Ivy. When you talk parenting, check all areas in the vicinity for ear-wiggers. Raising children is not an easy job, no wonder Mum takes the gin-and-bear-it approach. ' I chuckle at this, even when we were young I can recall Mum declaring it almost gin-o'clock. Usually in the half hour before we went to bed. There was a time when she'd wait until we actually were in bed but this crept up. Now, of course, lunch time is acceptable in her eyes. I'm struggling to find a way to go back to my last comment, regarding Gerald. Evelyn has chosen to simply ignore it. I hadn't expected that, I decide to try another tactic.
'Evelyn, I do need some suggestions on how to parent but what I really want to talk to you about, is Will.' My sister gives me a curious glance over her mug of tea. 'He was messing about behind my back and he's still seeing her.' I don't really need advice on this; I've made up my mind to dump the philandering tosser at the earliest convenience. I won't put up with crap like that anymore; I just need an 'in' to talk about Gerald.
'How do you know? Has he said anything?'
'Well, he's pretty open about it, actually. He's out all the time, she was round the other night and he said if she wants to stay over then they can have the sofa. Handy for him, I guess, since he sleeps there just about every night anyway, because he's too pissed to make it to bed. He clearly thinks we are living together just because we are having a baby. It seems he thinks there is nothing wrong with having a girlfriend, right under my nose. '
'Ivy, you need to put your foot down! Tell him this is not acceptable and reschedule this wedding as soon as possible; he needs to take his commitments seriously. Who is this person he is messing around with?'

'Sasha somebody, she's a waitress in that new Greek place down past the Playhouse, apparently. She's early twenties at a guess. She had a boyfriend but he just ditched her.'
'Oh, I know that place. Eliza and John, two doors down, were there last weekend, fantastic souvlaki, they said.'
I gaze into the bottom of my cup, like it holds all the answers.
'You could always pay a visit to his parents, you know, he's always been slightly terrified of his ex-military father, hasn't he?'
'How do you keep Gerald faithful, Evelyn?' I watch her reaction closely but she looks off into the distance, making her expression impossible to read.
'You can't *keep* anyone faithful, Ivy, you just have to be the best partner you can and hope that they appreciate you. No relationship is perfect.' Jeez, she's so vague, that comment told me nothing. I wish she'd stop 'third personing' everything and then I'd find out if she knows or not.
'I guess what Will really wants is an open relationship. Do you think I should go along with that? Could you?' Another leading question, this one should tell me what she really thinks.
'I don't think that's what would make you happy, Ivy. This isn't about what I'd do; it's about whether or not you can put up with not being exclusive. I personally don't think you can.'
Feeling defeated, I make my excuses to leave. Much as I'd like to see Gerald's face when he walks in, I'm so tired that I'm not sure I can even make it to nine, let alone ten. I pop in to see Matilda, who gives me a big, sleepy hug, before rolling back onto her side and surreptitiously sucking her thumb under the covers. At eight, her mother tries to stop her by painting her thumb nail with that awful tasting stuff. Matty has got used to the taste now and short of amputating her thumb, there's not much more that Evelyn can do. I knock on James' door and shout goodbye, he doesn't reply, so I leave him to it. I think back to Evelyn's joke last week; how many teens does it

take to change a light bulb? None, they just hold it up there and expect the world to revolve around them. I'd laughed so much at this that my sister looked both surprised and proud at 'making a funny.' For a second I'd glimpsed the old, chilled out Evelyn. I knock on Chris's door and a grumpy sound implies that I may enter.

'So, get many tips from shit mother of the year, Ivy, man?'

'Hey, don't speak about your mum like that; she's very good to you all.'

Chris gives a snort, 'Yeah, right. For years I thought I was the son of God, you know.'

Really, why? Can you turn water into wine? If so you're definitely coming to my next dinner party. You'll save me a fortune.'

'No,' she shakes his head aggressively, 'because everything she's ever fucking said to me started with the words, "*Jesus Christ*!"' I laugh loudly and rumple his hair. He's always been so funny in his own right; I hate to see him compromise his identity by copying people he thinks are cooler than him. I'm quietly confident of seeing my nephew on the stage doing stand-up comedy one day. I head back downstairs and shout goodbye to my sister, just as I'm about to open the door, I hear a key in the lock.

'Ivy!' the colour drains quickly from Gerald's face. 'What...what are you doing here?'

'Just needed a bit of a chat with my big sis,' I smile ominously. He looks at me seriously over the top of his glasses. 'Hard day at the surgery?'

'Darling, you're home early.' Evelyn bustles past me and gives her husband a gentle hug. He gives me a look of relief from over her shoulder. She clearly hasn't had any bad news from me if she's giving him a hero's welcome like this. He's lying about this open relationship; I can see it now with my own eyes.

'I'll see you later, Evelyn.' I can't stand by and watch this charade, I click the door shut behind me and head toward the bus stop.

Two fairly uneventful days later and I sit sheepishly in the office of a recruitment agency on Queen Street. This is my third attempt at joining one; having had an attack of the guilts and been upfront about my condition, I'd been told there wasn't much around at the moment, I'm keeping my gob shut on this occasion. I have no bump yet; I can get away with it for at least another month.
'So you're available for an immediate start are you, Ivy?'
'Yes, the sooner the better,' I tell the teenager, whose name plate informs me that his name is Scott.' He hadn't even bothered to introduce himself and looks generally full of his own self-importance. After an agonising hour of hearing how great he is and how fast he has risen in his job, I leave with one interview for this afternoon and another for later in the week. They are both sales positions, it was pretty much all they had. I have doctored my CV to take out my last job and in its place I put that I'd taken voluntary leave to do a bit of 'travelling.' London loosely covers travel. I can't take any chances on getting a poor reference from my last job; I need out of my flat and away from Will too much. I kill some time by heading to Taff's Caff for some lunch, I'm due at my interview in an hour and a half, there's no point in going home. Taff isn't around, just one of the less friendly waitresses and a new girl. I'm relieved at the lack of inquisition and take a seat in the window. I absent-mindedly eat my chicken sandwich as I glance at the office workers buzzing by. Across the road I see a familiar face, Will, walking hand in hand with Sasha, who is wearing the shortest black dress imaginable as her waitress 'uniform.' One dropped fork and you'd see what she had for breakfast, I think to myself, calmly. I'm a little taken aback by the lack of emotion I feel at the sight of them; I really don't think

anything could surprise me anymore. I don't even have the energy to run after them to give him grief. I simply pick up the other half of my sandwich and turn my attention to the others passing by.

My new zen-like state seems to carry me well through the day as I'm offered the sales job after my interview. I clearly wasn't my usual, nervous, babbling self today. A kind of stillness has descended on me and I feel strangely more mature all of a sudden. I start on Monday, 9am, selling tickets for the festival in an office off the Royal Mile. I get ten percent off for myself too, like I have the money to go to shows. It sounds like a fun job for now, it's kind of a secondment position until after the festival when I will go to the usual office in Charlotte Square. It's a permanent position and I do feel rather guilty for not being upfront about my pregnancy; but needs must, I'll bluff my way out of it when the time comes to tell them. The location is great, I love the Royal Mile; it feels like stepping back in time with its low wynds leading into alleyways where people of a bygone time would string their washing across. It's steeped in history, ghost stories and tales of the horror of the plague. It gives me a lovely, creepy buzz being there after dark. I just wish I felt the excitement I had when I was certain I'd got my job in London. Without Conor and Granddad to celebrate with, I feel somewhat empty. Ginny, of course, will be thrilled to bits, but I know that she and Natasha are out at a gig after work tonight, I've barely seen my best friend since I got back. With a sudden rush of adrenaline, I remember the call log on my phone. I bet if I go back a couple of weeks I will find a now unnamed phone number that will be Conor's, I scroll excitedly through the past week's calls, only for it to stop at a week and a half ago. *Damn you, Will!* Not only has he deleted Conor's number but he has deleted my call history too. Determined to get one up on him, I search the internet for The Drunken Leprechaun. So what if he hangs up on me, I'll never know if I don't try. He's a decent bloke; I'm sure he will listen to my reason for leaving so abruptly. It pops up almost immediately with a call option and I listen to the ring for what feels like eternity,

'Drunken Leprechaun. Cal speaking, how can I help you?'

'Hi! Cal, is Conor there, please?'

'Conor? Just a moment.' A smile splits my face for the first time in two weeks. I wait patiently, listening to the familiar banter in the bustling pub. I imagine the sun filtering through the window, lighting the dust particles as they dance in the air. I close my eyes and I'm there; Richmond, my favourite place in the world. Sketch pad in hand, relaxed after a few hours' work and waiting on Conor to finish and take me out for dinner. I think of Granddad's garden, Archie and Dave taking shelter from the sun under the patio table and enjoying the sound of Nanny's fountain. Granddad whistling tunelessly along to Classic FM while he makes himself a cup of tea.

'Hi there.'

'Conor?'

'No, sorry love, I'm the new manager, just started last week. The guy you just spoke to is new too, didn't realise that Conor was the previous manager.'

'He's gone? Already?'

'Yeah, asked to go early, they were happy about that as the relief guy was shit,' he gives a hacking laugh.

'Do you know the name of the pub he's in?' I try and fail not to sound desperate.

'Nah, sorry. Dublin...somewhere. It's a big place, you know.'

'Thanks, never mind.' I hang up and clutch my phone to me, turning down into the Royal Mile and head for home, feeling utterly devastated. Well that's it, he's gone forever now, I couldn't find him if I wanted to. With a fresh surge of anger for Will, I quicken my pace. He can get to the far side of fuck if he thinks I'm putting up with any more shit. The second my first pay cheque is in the bank, I am gone. He can see his kid but I do not want to interact with him in any way after I leave. And this time, I'm taking my fucking table and chairs with me.

Chapter Eleven

It's seven in the morning that I first notice the pain. I wake up, instinctively protective, in the foetal position as the wave of cramps wash over me. My eyes spring open in horror as I become aware of the warm, wet sensation. I sit up as carefully as I can and pull back the covers. No, this can't be happening. How many times have I complained about being stuck with Will because of this baby? Right now I'd do anything for this not to be real. Guilt creeps its way into the mix of emotions I'm feeling. Blood seeps through my pale blue pyjama bottoms as I stumble to the bathroom, I clutch my stomach as I sit on the toilet, whimpering in fear. The two week silence between Will and I is broken, as I give out a loud wail, when another wave of pain washes over me. He rushes from his slumber on the sofa and hammers on the bathroom door.

'Ivy! Are you alright? What is it?'

'It's the baby! I think I'm losing it, Will. There's so much blood! I'm going to need you to take me to hospital.' I hear Will leave the door and clatter around the bedroom, getting dressed. I stand in the shower and look down in terror at the pool of blood that I stand in. The water washes over me and takes it down towards the plug hole. I steady myself against the tiled wall, feeling sick and faint. To give Will his due, I eventually exit the bathroom to find him fully clothed and pacing worriedly. I dress as quickly as the pain allows me and walk carefully down the path to the car. Will is silent and ashen on our short drive to the Accident and Emergency department and for once, the traffic lights are on our side, either remaining on green or changing as we drive up to them. Will stops and rushes round to my side, opening the door to help me out and up the ramp. He dashes ahead and grabs the receptionist, who is filling up some information leaflets. He babbles incoherently as she walks over to me with a smile.

'Take a seat, dear. Someone will be right with you.' Will looks from me to her, in confusion.
'Why aren't they fetching you a trolley? They should be taking you straight through as a priority.'
Will indicates to the waiting room where a young child has a small piece of Lego protruding from his nose and a middle aged lady in flip flops has her leg raised and what looks like an ingrown toenail. After around ten minutes or so, a kindly looking porter arrives with a wheelchair and informs me he will be taking me to the Early Pregnancy Clinic. He tries to make polite conversation as we turn into the never ending corridors, but other than Will politely giving one word answers, there is silence. We finally arrive and a bosomy midwife helps me onto a low bed.
'Is Dad coming in to join us?' she enquires with an encouraging smile.
'No, he can stay out there. I don't even want to see his face,' I hiss. The midwife looks concerned but wheels out the ultrasound.
'Let's see what's going on in there then, shall we?'
As expected, my womb is empty. I ask where the baby went and I'm told I probably just didn't notice passing it whilst sat on the loo, in my pain and shock. Miscarriage is very common in the first trimester, apparently. Fifteen percent, or some such statistic, that brought me absolutely no comfort, whatsoever.
'Is everything OK with you and your partner? You didn't seem very keen on having him in here,' the midwife asks with a concerned expression. My vitriol towards Will isn't probably the usual scenario in this situation, I shake my head and glance down at the bottom of the bed.
'Has he hurt you in any way, dear? If he has we can help, you know.' Her voice is kind and soothing.
'He hasn't hit me; he's just a dirty sha... I mean, he was unfaithful to me and we really were only together because I

found out I was pregnant. '
She shakes her head with disapproval as I tell her my tale of woe; including the cancelled wedding and him still being with his bit on the side.
'You deserve better than that, dear. I know you are devastated about the loss of your baby but there is someone out there who deserves to share this happy time with you.' I nod sadly. I know exactly what she means. In the kindest way possible, she is telling me I have choices now, I'm not tied to this idiot anymore. I have no intention of being, either. I n a rare moment of clarity, I now know exactly what I need to do. I leave with several leaflets on miscarriage and an assurance to call again should I need to. I don't need any medical management, thank God. I can go straight home.

Will and I sit wordlessly in the car. When we arrive home I strip the bedding and mattress protector and chuck it in a bin bag along with my pyjamas. I calmly pack my things and sit on the edge of the sofa, waiting for Ginny, who I text on the way home. She walks in without knocking, and pulls me into a hug, throwing Will a filthy look, as he loiters ashamedly in the hall. She then effortlessly picks up my table and puts it into the back of her van. When all my belongings are safely removed, she turns to Will and leans her face in close to his.
'I'm not blaming you for Ivy losing her baby but you have really not made her life very happy over the last few weeks. Stay the fuck away from her from now on; she doesn't need the likes of you in her life.' With that, she takes hold of my hand and slams the door behind us. I've never seen my friend so angry before; not even when that cow, Emma from a rival school deliberately tripped her up on the netball court, making us lose the championship cup after three successful wins. Once we get to the Bitchelor pad, she changes her sheets and insists I get into bed. She and Natasha will take the sofa bed for a few nights to let me have a proper rest. She

then calls my new employer and explains that I won't be in for a week or so due to a personal bereavement. I fall asleep almost immediately and waken to find she has slipped a hot water bottle under the covers to ease my cramps and has placed a glass of water on the bedside table.

I must have dozed off again, because when I awaken, it's dark. I wander down the hallway to find Natasha and Ginny watching TV. The clock on the wall tells me that it's six fifteen.
'Hey, gorgeous,' smiles Natasha as she gets up to give me a warm embrace, 'we were waiting a while longer before having tea to see if you were up to joining us.'
'Thanks, Tasha. I'm feeling slightly better, just in shock, I think.'
'I'm not surprised,' she soothes, 'what a devastating thing to happen to you, love.' My eyes well at her sympathy.
'The only upside to all this is that I never have to see that dickhead again. After all these years I'd been blind to the fact that he actually wouldn't have made a good father. He's an alcoholic, albeit a functioning one at the moment. Drinking every night until he passes out on the sofa; I would have been as much a single parent as I'd planned to be anyway.' Ginny and Natasha nod their solemn understanding. I'm absolutely gutted to have lost my baby, of course, but I'm relieved that Will is no longer part of my life. I'm annoyed with myself now that I didn't speak to Amelia about my pregnancy; had they been fine with it, my life in Richmond could have continued quite happily. Now I have a job it would be silly to go back to square one by moving away again.

Life goes back to predictable normality, I'm staying on with Tasha and Ginny for a couple of months until I can save up for a deposit and first month's rent on a flat. Surprisingly I don't feel at all uncomfortable; they're not one of those

coupley couples, snogging on the sofa and making me feel like a gooseberry. We take turns to make dinner, watch movies and drink wine. I've never seen my friend so happy; Natasha is good for her. Down to earth, hardworking and doesn't go in to jealous rages at the thought of previous girlfriends; just a few of the qualities lacking from previous women in Gin's life. My job is going well, the buzz of the festival is infectious and I've even lined up a few plays and comedy acts for us all to see. Today is Friday and I'm off for the weekend for once, in just under half an hour Tasha, Ginny and I are heading down to our favourite Italian restaurant, Ciao Roma, on the Bridges. The sun beats through the window of the office, lifting my spirits no end. I chat amiably to my customers about the shows, reviews and what else they may like to see. At five o'clock I skip out into the sunshine and make my way down the Mile, I find Ginny and Tasha in an excited huddle as I arrive at the restaurant.
'What are you two smiling like Cheshire cats for?' I view them with suspicion.
'Have a wine first, Ivy. I have a feeling you're going to need it,' beams Ginny.
'Oh my God, you're getting married,' I exhale.
'Er, no, but it's a commitment of some sort,' Tasha raises an enigmatic eyebrow at me. They keep exchanging smiles with each other and I drink my wine quickly, to be in on the secret. After an agonising ten minutes and a top up for my glass, Ginny finally asks if I'm ready to know.
'Yes!' I shout at her, 'it's killing me.'
'Well, as you know, I'm really not in to marriage, and Tash isn't too fussed either and most definitely doesn't want kids; every gay, lesbian person and their dog is having a civil partnership now and we aren't into getting hitched, just because some straight person has decided to treat us like human beings and allow us to.' I nod slowly, confused as to why they are telling me what I already know. 'But, I do love

the idea of a kid and I know you've set your mind on going down the IVF route. The only way I'm ever going to have a kid that doesn't involve a turkey baster is to have parental rights with a partner or go down the adoption route. '
'What? Start again, Ginny I'm totally confused,' I eye the volume percentage on our bottle of wine, to see how pissed she could possibly be, as Tasha takes up the story.
'What Ginny is saying Ivy is that she wants you to have her baby.' I look from one to the other, in shock, before the uncontrollable giggles begin. They smile patiently at me until I'm done.
'I'm serious, Ivy,' Ginny laughs, 'We get a donor, I'll adopt the child and take half of the parental rights, see our kid whenever I can, pay half of the school uniforms and stuff. This way I get to be a parent too, but with no pain or yucky bits for me. I don't mind being there for them but you know what I'm like with blood and needles,' she shudders.
'Really? You'd do that for me?' I give Ginny a puppy dog look, before thinking about how complicated that all sounds and giving myself a reality check. 'I don't know, it's not like we ever have been or ever will be partners. And Tasha, would you be OK with your lesbian lover having a child with her best friend? Or is that just too Jeremy Kyle for your liking?' Tasha shrugs,
'It's not like we haven't discussed it. Gin wants a kid and I don't, end of. I don't mind him or her staying over and stuff, that'd be quite fun. I just don't want that full-on commitment of having one myself.'
'Look, can we order some food now, I need to get my head around this,' I laugh.
'Sure,' Ginny picks up the menu and scans it even though she always has the same penne pasta dish. 'But seriously think about it, Ivy. At least this way the kid will always have two parents to love him or her, you get some valuable time off and financial input, and we both get what we want, a baby.'

When you think about it, it's a genius idea. I had noticed that Ginny had been in awe of my pregnancy and her glance lingered a little longer on babies in prams lately. Also, I don't have the scary concept of going it alone and Ginny can be an official parent without having to do the yukky bits, as she calls them, like giving birth or being inseminated. I laugh when she tells us how men have never really appealed to her.
'Hey, but what about Ronnie in high school?' I smirk, 'School disco? Second year? You snogged him to Careless Whisper right in the middle of the dance floor.'
Natasha snorts into her wine and looks at Ginny incredulously. 'You snogged a guy?' she laughs.
'Well, I was young and stupid, and everyone experiments in high school,' Ginny huffs.

The conversation moves on to other subjects but I keep going back to Ginny's suggestion in my head. Could it work? It's certainly one of her more bonkers ideas, but given how many she's had over the years, I can't say I'm surprised. We move on to a pub on the Mile and join the raucous post Festival crowd. What a difference in my enjoyment of my home city just by being with the right people. My parents and sister had been saddened by the loss of the baby but I could tell that they had thought the whole set-up was less than ideal and that I'd never truly be happy with Will. It took them long enough but after the fact sunk in that the wedding wouldn't go ahead regardless, they realised just how serious I was about it all. Evelyn had even made the odd nice comment to me; just a compliment about my new shoes or the brave - for me- new haircut, which I always seem to do after a breakup. I still miss Richmond, Granddad and Conor, but I'm happier than I have been in a long time, in Edinburgh at least. We have a few more drinks in a stop-off closer to home. It's a long walk back to Lothian Road, is the excuse, in reality we are just enjoying each other's company and none of us want the evening to end.

We finally arrive home just after midnight and my drink-addled mind plays over and over what we talked about, earlier in the evening. Maybe it's the alcohol, but it's increasing in its appeal to me. Why shouldn't we? We are both grown adults, entirely capable of making our own decisions. With this thought, I roll over and hug my duvet to me. IVF feels instantly less scary with the thought of my best friend by my side.

Ginny and I begin our research into the IVF process and donors. We have decided on a few things, such as we need an intelligent and dark haired, brown eyed donor. Looks-wise, because it matches both of our colouring, intelligent, because neither of us are particularly academic, or perhaps we were and just mucked around too much in school. Ginny doesn't even mind if our child grows up to be straight; very open minded of her, I thought. The child will stay predominantly with me but we will split the costs 50:50. Having read up on everything, I feel slightly sick at the thought of the egg collection bit; a needle will be inserted *via the vagina* to collect the eggs, thankfully, under sedation. I shudder and skip past this bit quickly to pictures of adorable little babies. The end result will be so worth it. Who needs a man? Well, other than to donate. Ginny and I book our consultation, the website features a lesbian couple, which I know we are not but it shows they are 'gay friendly,' and rather than have the drama of explaining and our decision being scrutinised, as far as the clinic is concerned, we are a couple. I feel rather uncomfortable about lying but Ginny thinks it's a hoot. The prices are eye watering, but it's the way it has to be, if Ginny is to share the parental rights. I don't need some male friend who initially agreed to a no responsibility donation turning up on my doorstep all doe-eyed and looking over my shoulder to try and catch a glimpse of his offspring. No, we will just have to suck it up and fork out. Gin is happy to pay it all up front, I can catch up later on once my flat is all set. I haven't told anyone in the family about this; they will only try to talk me out of it. I doubt my decision will surprise anyone, to be honest; the controversial does seem to follow me around. From arranging a wedding, to having a child with my lesbian friend, all in the space of a couple of months. I'd best stock up on the smelling salts for when I drop this bombshell.

Chapter Twelve

Armed with my Follicle Stimulating Hormone and an appointment for egg collection, I embark on a healthy eating, no alcohol and early night plan. Yes, it sounds boring but I fill my evenings watching movies or heading to the gym and taking long, leisurely swims. Gin says that she is happy to drink for two and has a last hurrah, party-wise. She and Natasha have lots of weekend date nights before their big stay-in to support me begins. Much as I love flat-sharing with them, it's nice to take stock and reflect on my hectic few months. They are out around three nights a week, sometimes not rolling home in the early hours, when I've long since gone to bed. I do have a momentary panic that maybe I'm overstaying my welcome a bit but when I voice my concerns, I'm assured that this is absolutely not the case. I've bought up just about every pregnancy magazine I can get my hands on and a couple of baby-care and weaning books. I feel confident in my abilities; like it will come naturally to me, an Earth Mother, almost. I visualise myself in long, flowing, muslin dresses, steaming organic fruit and vegetable purees for my baby, with soothing lullabies playing in the background that my little one dozes contentedly to. I imagine myself to be the calming, indulgent influence on my child. Gin will be the rough and tumble one, and will take no shit, she's big on manners and respect. It will be a good balance of parenting, I'm sure, if a little unorthodox in some opinions.

Our first appointment at the fertility clinic had gone well; although due to the fact Ginny and I always get the giggles in formal environments, over absolutely nothing more than looking at each other, it had been embarrassing being called for our appointment as both of us chortled in the waiting room. We'd followed the doctor down the endless, narrow, squeaky floored corridor giving ourselves a mental slap. We walked into the meeting composed but with aching sides. The last time we had lost it in such a manner had resulted in the Minister of our school's church not only putting us out during the Christmas service but giving us a stern talking to afterwards. It wasn't our fault that one of our male classmates had decided to do a pant ripper of a fart in the Lord's house, during a prayer for the poor and needy. I guess it did look rather insensitive at the time, but it was not done out of malice or lack of compassion, which is what Reverend Brown had assumed.

The fifty-something, grey haired, doctor had been most encouraging in our quest to have a baby. She coo'ed over our commitment to one and other and seemed delighted that we were only her third lesbian couple, the other two were now proud parents of two boys and one girl, respectively. At my age they only recommend the implantation of one embryo, there was no rush, she'd urged. Time we may have, but we aren't exactly rolling in cash. I was disappointed and had hoped for two embryos for our first try. The thought of an instant family and not going through this again had been ideal. She hedged a little around our questions of success rates, stating that it was based on age and lifestyle factors etc, but that our chances were good and that the majority of patients had successful pregnancies by their third attempt. I guess she didn't want to get our hopes up too much, and now I think of it, her hesitancy came after I mentioned my miscarriage. She did assure me that miscarriage was very common and often just Mother Nature knowing that something wasn't quite right and that most women will go on to have a normal, healthy pregnancy next time. There were a few awkward personal questions about our relationship; which seemed more out of friendly curiosity than necessity. Luckily we had worked out our story before going in there, keeping it as close to the truth as possible. We met at primary school, had been going out since around seventeen; by this we meant going out to pubs and the like. Not a lie, just a slightly misleading answer. I did feel guilty for fabricating the truth to this lovely lady; she was so genuinely pleased that we had made this decision to be parents together. Ginny shook her head firmly when asked if we had any plans for a civil ceremony, before quickly adding that she did believe in monogamy. The consultant had laughed and said that it wasn't in her interest to judge who was worthy of a child, based on whether or not they made our relationship official. We had a discussion about lifestyle factors such as how smoking and drinking can affect chances of getting pregnant and a baby itself, with a very generous gap on the stated and real amount of alcohol on my part, when not pregnant, obviously. We walk back down the echoing stairwell trying to suppress our excited giggles and head out into the sunshine towards Taff's Caff. Over lunch we chat excitedly about the future and what the kind of parents we will make. We agree to tell no one about this until after the first trimester; to get through the safe period but also to postpone the inevitable shit-storm that will ensue. From my family at least, Ginny's tend to be chilled out Bohemian types who rally around each other like a flash support mob. They will just be delighted that she has a chance to be a parent; it won't make the slightest bit of difference that the child isn't biologically hers. If it had been the other way around, I doubt that my mother would consider the baby her Grandchild. Wrong, of course, but that's just how she is.

The weeks pass by so quickly, as I work lots of overtime in preparation for renting and furnishing my own flat. The day of the egg collection is upon us and in spite of my nerves, it goes surprisingly well. It was completely manageable, pain wise; the thought of it was so much worse than the reality. I had assumed they had fudged the details on the website, about just how painful it would be, like they do when giving you an injection; a sharp scratch? My arse, it's a massive, fuck-off needle you've just shoved in me. I experienced a little cramping afterwards but nothing worse than the ovulation pain that I get. Ginny had calmed my nerves by being present the whole time and pacing impatiently in the corridor when the egg extraction was taking place. Because I've had a general anaesthetic, I have an overnight stay in the hospital. I doze on and off as Ginny reads a magazine by my bedside for a few hours. Eventually, one of the nursing staff tells her she may as well head home; I'll be ready to leave tomorrow around lunch time and I need my rest. In just a few days the transfer of the egg will take place and there's a real celebratory buzz in the flat. The donor we decided on was a twenty-five year old, dark haired, brown eyed, Caucasian, University graduate. At least our child has half a chance of being academic. Ginny has paid for the whole thing up front and I will set up a standing order to pay her back in monthly instalments. She can make in a day what I make in a week but I want this to be straight down the middle, it's the only fair way. Ginny is beyond excited and already talks about big happy, family holidays we will go on.

The day before the egg transfer and with Ginny out on a call, Tasha rushes me into the bedroom where she had been rummaging through Ginny's bedside table for some face wipes.
'Look!' she squeaks, and holds out a teeny, tiny pair of red fabric Converse trainers.
'Oh my God, look at those. Have you ever seen anything so cute?' We exchange a smile at Ginny's purchase. 'We decided we shouldn't buy anything in case we jinx the whole thing, but she obviously couldn't resist these,' I laugh. I cross my fingers that the implantation will be a success, at this rate I think Gin would be more gutted than I would if things didn't go to plan. I've really warmed to the idea of co-parenting

with my best friend. Men have come and gone but she has been the one stable in my life, other than my family. We will have a life-long bond anyway, regardless of the child. It makes perfect sense to have a child with Ginny, that and she will be a great parent and it would be tricky for her to do this any other way. Natasha pops the little shoes back in the bag and places them back in their hiding spot under a bag of cotton wool. We just make it back to the kitchen in the nick of time, before we hear Ginny's key in the lock.

With the egg transfer done, a few days later, we settle in to a nervous two week wait to see if the procedure has been a success. Ginny asks me at least five times a day how I'm feeling; any nausea, twinges, dizziness? I try to tell her I'm not the best authority on being pregnant since I didn't even realise last time but she asks me incessantly, regardless. I don't really know what to expect, sure, the baby books tell you, but it's impossible to know the very early signs by description only. A lot of it sounds like PMT symptoms to me, anyway. I've often read about, or seen TV shows where women didn't have a clue they were pregnant, and wondered how it could happen. Surely you'd just *know.* Well, I hadn't and I have a new sympathy for anyone else who says they had no idea. I feel no different whatsoever, other than slightly healthier due to eating well, not drinking alcohol and having endless early nights. I try to dissuade Ginny from dragging me around Mothercare to admire itty-bitty outfits and discussing the merits of each buggy with the sales assistant. I'm not overly keen on the term 'BabyMomma' that she now refers to me as. But she's ecstatic about the whole possibility and as ever, I indulge her.
Three days before my period should be due, I start to get an oh-so-familiar dull ache in my back. I'm wary of mentioning anything to Ginny as Dr. Google informs me that this can also mean a loosening up of the joints to prepare for a future birth.

Similarly, my pizza face could be down to hormones and my lower belly ache, which arrives the next day, due to implantation. I deliberately don't mention any of this as Gin will take these as sure signs of pregnancy, whereas the reality is they could also be down to being pre-menstrual. Never in my life has my body and cycle been subject to such scrutiny. Usually I'm such a private person about these sorts of things, unless it was an excuse to get out of gym class at school. Back then it was easy; our male gym teacher would wave away our notes whilst blushing a deep crimson colour. It got to the stage where we would live dangerously and actually turn up with a blank piece of folded paper instead of the usual forged parental signature one. This went well until the class bitch paled as we walked into our swim class and saw that Mr. McKay was off sick that day. A militant looking, female, supply teacher loomed over us all. Hilarious for the rest of the girls, however, considering she had just smacked a whole can of coke out of the hands of the most timid girl in our class. Her week of detention kept everyone safe for a few, blissful days.

On the morning of the day that I am due my period, Ginny bounds into my room and stares intently at me from the bottom of my bed. She holds out a two pack of pregnancy testing kits, and gives me the hugest of grins.

'Pee!' she squeaks. 'Morning pee is the best to use; I opened the packet and read the leaflet already. Now would you like this?' she holds out a shot glass towards me, 'or are you happy to go with the flow, pardon the pun.'

'I'll go with the flow,' I sigh and swing my legs out of bed. I'd be happier to hang on and see what happens instead of wasting the best part of a tenner but I know she is beyond excited. There is absolutely no point in arguing. She follows me to the bathroom door where I raise a questionable eyebrow at her.

'OK, I'll wait here, shall I? But can you come out so we can

see the results together, please?'
'Yes, but don't stand and listen, you'll give me stage fright. Go make some coffee and I'll be right through.'
'Fine, but it's decaf only, for you,' Ginny shouts as she wanders reluctantly down the hall. I'm just about to do the test when I hear my mobile ringing from my bedroom. It'll have to wait; Gin will have a coronary if I hold off any longer. I pee on the stick, not as easy as I had assumed it would be, and replace the cap on the test. Already the liquid has soaked up into the window. I squeeze my eyes shut and turn it over so I won't be tempted to look. I wander down the hall with my test stick, putting it behind my back as Ginny makes a grab for it.
'No, we are waiting a full three minutes and looking together. Haven't you heard that a watched pot never boils?' Ginny flops down at the table and occupies her fidgeting hands with grasping onto her cup. I pop the test on to the work top and sit opposite, throwing her an amused expression as she jiggles her leg under the table. In reality, I'm nervous. I really want this to work out for us; the procedure cost so much that we could really do with being lucky first time. The clock ticks ominously to fill our silence. This is excruciating, I can feel the tension in the room. Finally, I stand and walk over to the counter. Ginny's chair screeches across the floor as she tries to reach the test before I do.
'One, two, three, turn,' I announce. The test line is clear and strong but there is no second line. Not even a faint one.
'Oh, crap, Ginny. I'm sorry.'
'No, it's all right, the leaflet says it can take up to ten minutes, it could change yet.' I leave her angling the test in all directions and head off down the hall to fetch my phone. The missed call was from Evelyn. I hurry back to the kitchen to see a disappointed Ginny flinging the test in the bin.
'Maybe it's just taking a while for your HCG levels to build up,' she shrugs. I nod sympathetically but rather

unconvincingly.
'We can keep trying,' I give her arm a little rub, 'and at least we can go out and party for a couple of weeks. That will be fun.' Ginny brightens a little at this.
'Tasha will be pleased; she's missed our silly nights out. Let's plan one for Friday if your test is still negative, yeah?' She gives a half-hearted smile when I nod my agreement.
'For sure. Look, I'm sorry to abandon you but I've just got to go phone my sis back. You sure you're all right? It's just that call from my Evelyn at this time of the morning is most unusual; I just have to check nothing is up.' Ginny nods her understanding and heads off down the hall to the shower.

'Hi, Evelyn, how are you?' I settle back on my bed for what may be a long conversation.
'How am I? *How am I?* You can ask your little shit of a nephew how I am!'
Chris? Why what's he done?'
No, James. He's been excluded from school for drawing a picture of a dick on the white board and writing 'Mr. Thompson,' next to it.' I choke back a laugh but Evelyn hears it.
'I'm sorry,' I explain, 'that doesn't sound serious enough for exclusion.'
'No, not on its own, it's not, but they've been trying to get me all morning to collect him after he was caught smoking a joint in the boys toilets!'
'Oh...I'
'But I was in a W.I. meeting all morning, I missed the call and this afternoon I'm in another for the planning of the church fayre. I really don't want to have to explain my absence at the meeting to Rev Brown. Ivy, please will you go and collect him from school and stay with him until I can get back? I'm sorry to ask but I know you're off today and I'm desperate.'
'Er, yeah, sure I can.' I'll see if I can borrow Ginny's van and

go get him now.'
'You're a darling, thank you, Ivy. Punishment of the week is in the top drawer under the DVD player. Make sure he pays attention, I *will* be asking questions. I'll go call school, see you at five.'

I walk along the old familiar corridors that I haven't seen in twelve years. It still smells like a mixture of pickled onion crisps and well-worn boy's trainers, how strange. I knock on the Headmaster's door, in what I hope sounds a businesslike manner and the door swings open almost immediately. Mr. Millar gives me a wide, beaming smile.
'Well, I never. Ivy Efferson, what a pleasure to see you. How long has it been? Five years? ' He gives his familiar chuckle. He looks just the same although his face appears even redder than I remember and he has a new black toupee that's not in keeping with his ginger eyebrows.
'Haha, I wish it was only five years, Mr. Millar, try twelve.' I shoot my nephew stern look over his shoulder.
'And what are you doing with yourself? Married with a squad of rugrats, I'm guessing. You always were very maternal.'
'She got dumped, just before her wedding,' hisses James from the background. Mr. Millar gives an embarrassed cough.
'Actually I'm working in sales at the moment, for the Edinburgh Festival,' I smile through gritted teeth. I'm so going to kill that little shit. 'No marriage or kids as yet, but I'm only thirty. There's no rush'
'Goodness, not at all. You enjoy your youth, Ivy. You'll be my age before you know it. Oh don't look so worried, I'm just kidding, dear. Now I assume you are here for Mr. Funny over there?'
'Yes, his mother is in a meeting so I have the pleasure of his company this afternoon.'
'Good, good. Well I'm all for creativity in children but I'm

afraid his portrait of Mr Thompson was neither lifelike nor very tasteful. Young James here was in seclusion in that class over lunch. It was quite a shock to come in to that. Poor Mr. Thompson is not long back from an extended leave period. '
'I can assure you, Mr. Millar, James will be dealt with in an appropriate manner. I'm very sorry for the trouble he has caused. Has he apologised for his bad behaviour? *Have you apologised?'* I turn my attention to the one who deserves a bollocking. 'Well? I'm waiting.' James shrugs,
'I'll say sorry if he does, for throwing the best doobie I've ever made into the toilet,' he snarls sarcastically.
'Actually James, you're very fortunate, because if it had been me that had caught you with it, it would have been shoved in an entirely different and much less appealing place.' Mr. Millar raises his eyebrows and inhales deeply; I know I'm saying what he would dearly love to. 'You have precisely ten seconds to say sorry to Mr. Millar for your behaviour or any punishment that your mother has planned, I will be doubling.'

So, watching four hours of a documentary on the Socio-economic climate of Outer Mongolia was not how I had intended to spend my day off, but I had said I would double his punishment and I had to stand by my word. Once I had wrestled his iPhone from him and finally got him seated, I opened the top drawer to find the punishment. A DVD, with a post-it stating that dependent on the crime, that this may just be for starters. By the time Evelyn arrived back, soaked and windswept from a sudden late summer storm, I would have happily signed that brat up for National Service for my sufferance. I had to hand it to Evelyn, that was a bloody genius punishment for a kid. I certainly wasn't planning on crossing her any time soon. I hand over James' iPhone, which I had fiercely guarded since we had arrived home and fetched Evelyn an ice cold Chablis from the fridge. She needed it, if I hadn't have been driving I would have joined her for sure.

'I shall leave you to it, Evelyn. He refused to apologise to the Head or to the teacher so I doubled his punishment,' I indicate towards my now catatonic nephew huddled in the foetal position on the sofa.
'Here, Ivy,' she thrusts fifty quid into my hand, 'take Gin and yourself out for tea, and don't argue, you have more than deserved it.' I make a halfhearted attempt to hand the money back but she pushes my hand away.
'Now, go get home before that rain gets any worse. The traffic is horrendous tonight.' I smile my gratitude at my sister and with a backwards glance at James I head off into the early evening rush.

The storm has darkened the sky to the point that it feels like night-time. I hastily search for the van keys in my bag and pull the door open, against the wind. I rev up the engine and edge my way into the traffic. God knows what else Evelyn has lined up for him but with Matty and Chris shipped off to friend's houses for tea, I can only imagine it's not going to be pretty. Her previous punishments have included scrubbing the all-tiled bathroom with an old toothbrush and twenty hours of manual labour for the next door neighbour. The last one was for kicking a ball through the old guy's greenhouse. Granted, he had been in it and lost first prize for his tomatoes, which he had tipped over and landed on as he ducked for cover. This was much more serious this time. My sister and My Gerald have zero tolerance for drugs. I wouldn't be surprised if they sent his sorry ass off to borstal for this.
I sit in traffic in torrential rain for over an hour, impatiently tapping my fingers on the steering wheel and humming mindlessly along to an old eighties song on the radio. I wipe the condensation from the side window and watch the people scurrying by, inappropriately dressed for the summer weather; all city shorts and sandals and not an umbrella in

sight. Poor buggers, we get so complacent after a few weeks of nice weather, with our harsh winters a distant memory. I'm just thinking how grateful I am for Ginny's works van when out of the corner of my eye I see a familiar character. It's the skinny jeans and pointy toed boots that catch my attention first, before my eyes travel up past the battered leather jacket and too long, floppy hair which is quickly slicked out of his eyes. It can't be! Conor? He's in Edinburgh? I switch on my hazard lights and push the door open against the force of the wind. The rain drives sideways into the van and catches my breath. I hurriedly lock the door and take off at a sprint in the direction I saw him go. Behind me several car horns go off, such is their disbelief that someone could be as stupid as to abandon a car at a set of lights. I pick up my pace but he disappears from sight at the bus stop.

'Conor!' I shout as loudly as I can, but my words are whipped away and the driver pulls out of the stop. He's gone. I stare at the retreating bus with dismay as it rumbles towards the green light. I know the routes well enough to know that it's going to Morningside but I'm jammed between so many cars I will never get turned in time. I dash back to my vehicle and a white van driver shouts his disgust at me. First right, second left, could I make the short cut to Morningside before the bus? I reckon I could. With a loud beep of my horn I cut around the driver in front, squeezing through the gap between him and the car next to him with millimetres to spare. Thank goodness for those advanced driving lessons that Dad had insisted on when I passed my test. The light turns green and I'm off. The guy behind raises his hands in disbelief and angry blasts echo in my wake. I pray no one has read the signage on the van and will give Ginny a nasty call for this but I can't let Conor disappear from my life once again. Damn you Will, I fucking *hate* you for deleting his number. I grip the wheel with steely determination. Hate is not a word I use lightly but it's exactly how I feel about him right now. All that time he was messing around behind my back and he has the nerve to delete the number of a friend that I met when we weren't even bloody together. Having memorised the last bit of the buses registration, it's only ten minutes later that I see it pulling out of the junction that I've stopped by. We are heading into mainly residential areas now, but there are a few pubs scattered around that he could be running. I stop behind the bus at each stop, offering up a variety of prayers that Ginny will neither get in trouble for reckless driving or stopping dead in the bus zone. I'm insured for the van, of course, and I'll take what's coming to me in the form of fines and points.

'Hi, Conor Byrne, sorry for the nick of me, I'm soaked and was almost hit by a bus trying to get here on time.'
'Haha, no problem, Mr. Byrne, I'm Alan, the founding member of the agency. We were very impressed with your work. Tell me, have you been to Edinburgh before?'
'I have, actually. I used to run a pub here for a while, gorgeous city you have.'
'Are you staying with friends here or have you booked into a hotel?' Conor looks uncomfortably at his feet.
'No, I haven't any friends in Edinburgh, unless the very chatty barmaid at the Premier Inn counts.' Alan's assistant gives a flirty smile at Conor's trade mark hundred watt grin and twists the end of her pen in her mouth suggestively.
'Emma? A coffee for our guest, please?' Alan gives her a knowing smile. Emma jumps up from her seat and does a little shimmy out of the room.
'It seems some of us are more than just a fan of your work here, Conor.'
'So, what was the verdict on the full manuscript, Alan? Can I retire from the pub game yet?' Conor can contain himself no longer.
'Well, further to our phone conversation, I have read the full

MS and the sample chapters of the sequel,' Alan pauses dramatically. 'We loved it, Conor. We are looking to sign you for a three book deal with an advance of seventy-five thousand pounds.'
'You what? I...I don't know what to say. Yes! Yes, of course I'd love to sign with you,' he blusters.
'Fantastic news! Well how about we get the boring paperwork out the way and say sod the coffee, I'm taking our newest writer out for dinner and a pint.'

'I can't believe it, Ginny, he was *there*, right there in front of me and I lost him. I'm so sorry I got pulled over in your van. I knew you'd understand the situation, even if the police didn't,' I finish sheepishly.
'Don't worry, lovely,' Ginny rubs my shoulder soothingly. You had to go after him; I would have done the same in your situation. Well, not for a man, obvs. Are you sure you don't want to have another look on Facebook?'
'There's no point, I have actually gone through all five hundred or so and none of the pics are of him. About seventy are of inanimate objects but none of those even look like something he'd put as a profile picture. And Twitter is even worse for finding someone on. I tried the bar in London again and nobody knows where he's gone. I even tried the brewery but they wouldn't give out that information. I'm bordering on psycho territory now. There's nothing else I can do, I'll never find him, ever,' I shrug, defeated. Ginny sighs and gives my back a gentle rub.
'Don't worry, we'll think of something. Tasha has friends in IT; we'll see what they come up with.'
I wander down the hall and peel off my sodden clothes for a bath. I had almost come to terms with the fact that Conor had gone from my life forever but to get so close to him again has left me feeling deflated. With sad realisation I accept that I do have feelings for him. I probably knew way back in

Richmond but I was so bloody stubborn and single minded in my misery and shame at the time. I only have myself to blame for this mess.

'Cheers, to our newest, outstanding author. I wish us a long and happy career together,' Alan clinks his pint glass against Conor's and takes a noisy gulp.
'No, *thank you!* I'm chuffed to bits to be represented by your agency. I've heard so many good things about you. You have so many big names on your books.'
'This time, next year, Mr. Byrne, you will be one of those big names. You wait and see; I've not been in this business twenty-five years and been wrong yet. Now, this is the best restaurant in Lothian Road, let's eat.'

Less than twenty feet above, Ivy lowers herself into the warm water, washing the chill of the rain away. Conor was out there somewhere, but trying to find him in a large town like Edinburgh would be like looking for a needle in a haystack. There was nothing left to do but admit defeat.

Chapter Thirteen

The weeks pass by and Ginny's disappointment turns back into excitement, as our next fertility appointment date looms. The Edinburgh Festival is over and I'm now office based with the sister company in Charlotte Square, which means it is even quicker to get to work in the morning. I was ecstatic to be kept on in my sales role; given my history, and even though the role is permanent, I felt that after the three month probation period was over they'd find an excuse to get rid of me. It does wonders for my confidence to know that someone thinks I'm good at it. I've made a good few new friends and there are some rather cute men. I have been asked out on a few dates but my heart isn't in it. I've never quite recovered from seeing Conor that day; I keep hoping that he'll drop me a random text at some point, but in his mind I'm probably married by now and he won't want to interfere. I've already called around the Irish pubs in Edinburgh before realising I was teetering on the edge of stalker type behaviour. Of course, he may be in any pub, not necessarily the Irish ones, or have been covering only for a few weeks; he could have been and gone long ago. Ginny's hyperactivity is a good distraction, as is the fact that I've saved enough for a deposit on a flat plus the first month's rent. In another month I'll be ahead of myself with a fallback of an extra month in case I lose my job and with this month's overtime I have almost an extra grand to furnish my new accommodation. I do love living with my friends but I'm aware of the fact that they are a couple and need their own space. Having a flat for just myself and my baby does sound blissful too; I've never had my own place, going from Mum and Dad's to halls of residence, to a share flat with Ginny and then Will. Full control of decor and what I watch on TV sounds amazing.

Our next attempt at IVF is planned for a few days' time. We

know what to expect this time, of course and Ginny's enthusiasm is infectious. She has a good feeling about this attempt and I have to admit, so do I. That may be her influence rubbing off on me or the ingrained belief in third time being lucky. I can't help comparing myself with pregnant work colleagues and feeling envious of their little bumps. One even has a due date within a week of when my baby should have been born. It's tough to watch her bloom in front of me. Of course, she has no idea what I have gone through and excitedly tells me about what it feels like when her baby moves around inside her. I make the right noises but inside I'm unjustly screaming at her to have a bit more sensitivity. I remember how I could barely wait for my twelve week scan and now it should have been my twenty week one coming up, I could have found out if it was a boy or a girl by now. Tasha and Gin are off on holiday after the last part of the procedure and I'm relieved not to have two weeks' worth of interrogation this time around. I can just chill out and do my pregnancy test the day after they arrive home. I have to admit it will be nice to have the flat to myself too and to get away from me will remind them that they are a couple, without the spare part hanging around. I'm moving out so soon that it will be good for all of us to have some time getting used to being apart. Tonight we are heading for a big night out; it may be the last for a long, long time so I plan to enjoy it. Being so busy at work meant that we never got a chance to get out and spend the money Evelyn gave me for my intervention with my nephew. He still hasn't earned back his iPhone and laptop in good behaviour. Evelyn is very smart; she's chosen probably the best possible punishment for a young teen. Once his general attitude has improved and he can keep it up for two weeks, his items will be returned to him one at a time. She has seen an improvement in Chris and Matty's behaviour, however, there's nothing like a technology ban to make kids take notice. It was a smacked arse in my day; we didn't have much to take away. For me, the biggest punishment would have been losing my sketch pad and felt tip pens; not quite the same as a mobile phone.

We head out at 7pm to our usual Italian restaurant on the Bridges; all of us are off work tomorrow so it's probably going to get messy. This is the last night I will be drinking as I'm back on the baby plan from Monday. Ginny and Tasha fly out to Greece on Tuesday and they are buzzing from that feeling of knowing that you're getting away from it all for a week. There's a real sense of celebration to our evening. Not even spotting Will from the top deck of the bus can dampen my spirits tonight.
'Hey look, Ivy,' Ginny yells for all the bus to hear, 'your ex has a massive bald spot now.' I lean over her to look out the window seat, he does too, I see his face as he glances up at the pub names, he's out of his usual stomping ground but I'm still surprised he doesn't know them all by heart. He looks old and tired; I wonder if that young thing is taking it out on him, in monetary terms as well as beneath the duvet. Maybe it's just all the years of drinking taking its toll. Whatever it is he looks rough as arse and to think, I should be married to that right now. We ring the bell at the next stop and skip jovially down the stairs and out into the warm evening. The air had turned cool for a week or so and all of a sudden we've had this Indian summer sprung upon us. Ginny had commented how typical it was that they were off on holiday and missing out on this last burst of sunshine. It was clear that everyone had dug out their winter woollies during the cold snap, as one girl at work had clearly not shaved all week and appeared to have what resembled a squirrel under each arm. Because of her name, Mary, she would now be forever known as Hairy Mary in my place of work. My moniker of their choice was Poison Ivy after I picked up the boss a sandwich from our local deli and he was off sick with the shits for three days

after. Not my fault, of course, but it excluded me from the sandwich run every day after, just in case.
Marco greets us like old friends as we walk into Ciao Roma. He ushers us to our seat before getting all our gossip from the past two weeks, since we saw him last. This is undoubtedly one of my favourite restaurants in the world. Ordering is no longer necessary as we almost always have the same thing every time. In addition, our usual wine is always chilling in an ice bucket in the centre of the table, he even knows to switch Ginny's cutlery around the wrong way due to the quirky way she eats.

The wine flows, as does the banter. I can't remember having such a fun night out with my two best friends. All I've done for weeks is work and sleep. It's such a nice feeling to spend some time and money with good company. Evelyn's cash gift almost covers the meal and on a whim we decide to hit the karaoke in our old local. Ginny and I used to have a flat around the corner and we like to go back to the pub of our Uni days as much as we can. Tash heads to the bar as Ginny and I flick through the song choices. She will be up straight away but I'm a three drink kind of girl; it takes me that long to pluck of the courage and stop caring about making a tit of myself. So far I've only had two at the restaurant. Eventually, I feel brave and tanked up enough to have a go. We murder a few tunes before the karaoke guy 'loses' our next few choices in favour of more talented people that want to sing. We sit in the corner pretending to be X Factor judges and crack up at Ginny's camp portrayal of Louis Walsh and comments such as, 'you remind me of a young Gary Barlow,' to a rather masculine looking woman. Natasha does a fantastic, flamboyant Sharon Osbourne and I do my best Geordie accent and hair flicks to be Cheryl Cole or Tweedy, or whatever she's going by these days. Ginny has just returned from her turn to get a round in, when she grabs my arm and points in the

direction of the door. Will staggers up to the bar with a couple of his mates and has a bit of a heated discussion with the barman; probably over the fact that he's actually not had too much to drink to get another.
'Look at the nick of him, Ivy; can you imagine if you were married to that? He used to be gorgeous too, and that's coming from a lesbian.' Yes, he looks scrawny, with sunken eyes and is most definitely balding. As if he senses us watching, he spots us across the room and works his way through the crowd, slopping the beer he has managed to persuade the barman to serve him, over a young woman. She rages at him for spilling on her new, suede boots. They argue for a few moments before he pulls a few tenners out of his pocket and pushes them into her hand. She gives a loud cheer and counts them out in front of her awestruck gaggle of friends.
'Hey ladies,' he slurs, 'anyone fancy doing a duet with me?' Ginny tuts and steps past him on her way to the loo. She can barely bring herself to look at him. 'Hey, Ivy, you're looking nice. You been missing me?'
'No!' I roll my eyes at Tasha, who stares at him in disbelief.
'Me an' Sash broke up. She was still bonking her ex and you know me, I can't stand infidelity.' I snort in derision at his comment. The cheeky bugger! How dare he? He only hates it when it's being done to him. Welcome to my world. Idiot!
'Will, we are having a nice evening here; I think maybe you'd be better off rejoining your mates. They're doing shots,' I add hopefully.' Will waves a dismissive hand in the direction of the bar.
'I was thinking the other day how good me and you were together. We would nearly have a baby now if things hadn't gone tits up with you. What would you be? Eight months?'
'Nowhere near, Will. Look, I'm really not interested in getting back with you, I have my own plans now. Too little, too late.' Ginny flops back down and leans forward towards Will.

'Look, matey, no offence but do you fancy getting to fuck. It's a girl's night out; we're having what's known as a good time. You're cramping our style, so do one!'
'Ginny, this is between Ivy and me, nothing to do with you. We have a lot to discuss.'
'Next up this evening we have Ivy, Ginny and Natasha, *again*. Come on up girls.' I look from Ginny to the karaoke host in confusion.
'I thought we weren't allowed to sing anymore?' The karaoke guy raises his pint to cheer Ginny and the penny drops. 'That's karaoke prostitution,' I stammer out with difficulty.
'Who cares, it worked,' Ginny shouts over the music as she jumps up from the table. We take our places with our microphones and look expectantly at the blue screen. As the title comes up I dissolve into uncontrollable laughter. Oh perfect, I couldn't have put it better myself. Will gives Ginny a thunderous look as he downs a shot at the bar. We shimmy Beyonce style as we sing along to 'Single Ladies' With Ginny altering the lyrics to Will wishing he'd put a ring on it. I so love my best friend right now. Will has left by the end of the song after a parting shout of, 'you're all shit, get off!' To which Ginny turns and sticks her backside out at him in a 'kiss my ass' manner.

By midnight we are in our local takeaway for some chips and cheese to soak up all the booze. Reluctant for the night to end, we pour another three glasses of wine at home, you know the ones, they never have more than an inch out of them in the morning as you wake up, roll over and groan when you see the glass. The flat, by morning, will look like and explosion in HMV, as we had dragged endless CDs out to play our favourite songs. This had gone well until the hammering on the wall started at 4am and the piercing shriek of next door's toddler kicked off. Ginny's loud apology through the wall didn't help matters as a tirade of expletives was the response.

I don't remember anything after that until I hear next door's revenge at 6.30 am as they vacuum their rooms adjacent to our bedrooms. I can't be annoyed, it was totally deserved and because I'm so hungover it reminds me to sit up and down my pint of water and take two paracetamol before falling back to sleep.

I awaken again at 2pm as the smell of a Sunday roast wafts down the hall. Tasha is an amazing cook and due to the fact she never suffers from hangovers, has been up since ten and has been down to Sainsburys for shopping, while Gin and I slept through our pain. She has even tidied up and put away our casually tossed about CDs. We haul ourselves out of bed and I do feel much better after a shower and a change into clean jammies. We chat over Sunday lunch, laughing about the antics of the night before, in the scattered order that we begin to remember them. Tomorrow is the big day, baby attempt number two and our conversation turns to this. Ginny apologises that she and Natasha won't be around to offer their support in the dreaded two-week wait. I try not to look too relieved at the prospect of peace and quiet and being able to keep the details of my menstrual cycle to myself. We sprawl around the sitting room watching movies for the rest of the day; one of those amazing, lazy Sundays that top off a perfect weekend. Lucky for me I'm in that inevitable 'never drinking again' zone. I'm not going to miss not drinking at all for the next couple of weeks. I'm planning nothing more strenuous than bubble baths and early nights as the other two party out in Rhodes. It's the last month I need to put in this crazy amount of overtime, by the end of the month I will be flat-hunting for my cosy two-bedroom property for me and the baby. Even if it doesn't work out this time, we still have a left over embryo to implant for a third try. After that it's back to egg collection again. I have to think positively, this attempt is pushing us a bit financially. Frozen embryos have a slightly less chance of making it, or so Dr. Google informs me, but going through the whole process of injecting, harvesting eggs and the general anaesthetic for collection doesn't appeal too much to me.

Monday morning arrives and the weather has turned cooler again overnight. Our appointment with the consultant starts at 10am; Gin has pushed back all her jobs for today, until after lunch and I've taken a lieu day so I don't miss out on any pay. I shiver in the passenger seat of Ginny's van as we work our way through the traffic to the clinic. I instinctively look for Conor around and about in Edinburgh, just in case he is still around. Surely if he was living here he would have at least dropped me a text to meet up as friends. It's what we were before, although his flirty behaviour made me feel that he wanted more. Some people are just natural flirts and would act that way with your Nan. I didn't know him all that well to make a judgment call on that. Maybe he has a girlfriend now; he's not the type of guy that would be on the market for long before being snapped up. Tash's IT friends hadn't come up with any suggestions that we hadn't already tried, so I was no further forward in my quest to find him.

We pull up into the car park as Ginny mutters under her breath about how ridiculous it is that patients have to pay for parking in the clinic grounds. I fish for some change in my purse and she takes a couple of pound coins to add to the one she has.
'Right, Babymomma, let's go get pregnant.' This time we manage to remain semi-sensible in the waiting room. I distract myself by flicking through the year old magazines before discovering today's paper in the pile and making a grab for it before Ginny can. I read the headlines and first couple of pages, growing increasingly disillusioned by the

sensationalised, bad news. I flick to the film reviews to see if there could be anything on at the cinema that I'd like to go to, while I'm left on my own. It's been ages since I went to the movies. The fact that Gin and I had gone for a supposedly cheap night out and still managed to spend fifty quid between us meant that we now waited until things came out on DVD or Sky. I skim past a few of the much hyped new action type ones before settling on the latest Rom-Com starring Reese Witherspoon. This one sounds promising; I could do with a good laugh, Saturday night has reawakened my hunger for fun.

'Ivy Efferson?' the consultant shouts cheerily. Ginny nudges me from my trance as I stare transfixed on a new section of the newspaper that I've turned to. The latest book reviews.

'Oh my God, Ginny, *look!*'

'Come on Ivy, it's our turn, show me later,' she urges. I glance over a few more words before scurrying down the corridor after her.

'Conor's book, it's been released.' Ginny looks at me in confusion, as we walk into the clinic.

'Conor? Your man that you've now decided you fancy after spending weeks blowing him out, Conor?'

'Yes, I nod enthusiastically. He was writing crime novels and he's had one published. This is perfect, I can track him down now via his agent. I need to find out who his agent is; you'll help me, right?'

'Let's just get this over and done with and I'll help you, Ivy. The consultant is waiting.'

We both turn and smile apologetically before taking our seats at the desk.

The procedure is over very quickly and this time I'm not too uncomfortable about Ginny being in the room when it's taking place. She will be present at the birth anyway so I have to get used to having my bits on show. I could have done without the male trainee though. I'd thought it would have been all right when we were asked about him being present; he's a professional after all, but I couldn't help feeling like a centrefold in Playboy for those twenty minutes. The look on Ginny's face as she stared him down set me off with nervous giggles; she is slightly suspicious of any male that takes an interest in anything in the world of gynaecology. Of course she knows she's being ridiculous but it's not the most comfortable of experiences trying not to laugh with a catheter tube up your hoo-ha. After a telling off from the doctor, I finally calm down. I lay back and squeeze my eyes shut so I can no longer see my friend's face. It's a delicate procedure and I don't want to jeopardise our chances by acting like a schoolgirl.

Ginny has told her Mum and Dad about our IVF. We hadn't planned on telling anyone but I know she was just too excited and couldn't contain herself. I had known it wouldn't stay a secret from them for long; it's more my family knowing that I was concerned about. My mum will freak, but given my history of being pregnant before, I can shut her up with concerns over my stress levels. I have decided to tell them snippets of information. I will start with, 'hey, guess what? I'm pregnant.' I will then dodge all questions regarding the other parentage for about a week when I will further tell them it was by a sperm donor. Then, when Mum comes round from the inevitable faint, I will discuss the merits of being a parent without the influence of an alcoholic, cheating shit of a father this time. I'll wait, oh, probably a month after that and then tell them that Ginny kindly offered to co-parent with me and how two good mums are even better than one. Then I'll likely move house and leave no forwarding address. Ginny's parents, however, were over the moon. To them I was just another member of their family, and they too were joining the ranks on our happy, family holidays. They came out with some way-out hippy kid's name suggestions and were already referring to themselves as Granny and Grandpa. Ginny is their only child, they had tried for more but it just didn't happen. They had always hoped she would have children, naturally or adopted, and either option was just as good to them. I always envied Ginny her laid back parents; Jemima, with her long tie-dye dresses and whimsical nature, Ralph, with his calm, soothing tones. He never told Ginny off, simply sat her down and calmly explained that her actions had consequences and he would help guide her to make better choices in the future. This covered everything from bunking off school to getting pissed underage. There was never an issue to Ginny 'coming out,' they had been so open their whole lives that they knew pretty much as soon as Ginny did.

The appointment can't be over soon enough for me, and I race back to the waiting room to find the article on Conor again. I don't think I took in a single word of what was said in there today. My mind whirred over and over about the possibility of getting back in touch with Conor.

'Ivy, wait,' Ginny stops me mid stride as I speed back down the corridor. 'If you're serious about being with this guy then we really shouldn't be trying for a baby on IVF. You should be keeping your life as uncomplicated as possible. Will Conor really want to get together with a woman who has a baby with a lesbian and some anonymous donor? Really?' I hadn't thought of this, I hadn't thought of being with Conor as an option, given that I had no way of contacting him until now.

'Well, I don't know, it's not like I'm expecting him to be financially responsible and we made a deal; this way you and I both get to be parents,' I shrug.

'Well, only if you're sure. I'm happy to support you in all this but I don't want to deny you the chance to be happy in, let's face it, a more conventional way. Also, another thing to consider; you blew him out months ago when you came home pregnant; he thinks you're back with Will. What if he thinks you're only interested now he has a book out?' I groan inwardly. As usual, Ginny's right. This is going to make me look so superficial and that's so not the case. I've been trying to find him for ages.

'Well, I still need to get that newspaper so I can read his review at least. He did it, Ginny, he finally did it.' I squeak. We walk purposefully back into the waiting room and I rush over to the pile of magazines. 'It's gone,' I wail, 'Ginny, where's my paper?' Ginny scans the room and indicates to a man sitting in the corner, glancing shiftily over the sports page at me.

'Excuse me, Sir, but I need my paper back,' his wife stops reading a three year old Bella and stares at me curiously.

'This is mine, I brought it in with me,' he replies dismissively and looks back to the football results.

'Don't lie,' I shriek, in a sudden flare of temper, 'you know fine well that you didn't, that newspaper is mine.' Of course it's not, but he doesn't know that. I hold out my hand, waiting for him to hand it over.

'Listen, love, I bought this from the newsagent on the corner before I came in here, this here is my property. Now are you sure you're in the right clinic? Because you strike me as needing a completely different kind of treatment altogether.' I glower at his wife who gives a loud snort before stifling her giggles with her hand.

'Ivy, just leave it. I'll buy you another paper,' Ginny tugs on my coat sleeve.'

'No,' I declare loudly, folding my arms to stand my ground. I'm not sure quite what's got into me but it's probably some symbolic rant emerging from Will deleting Conor's number. I'm not giving in; this is my only link to finding Conor after months of losing him. What if we can't get another one? The Scotsman is probably the best selling newspaper in Edinburgh.

'Hey, call off your bitch, won't you,' the man yells at Ginny, who raises her eyebrows in the incredulous manner I recognise as being the first sign of her launching into battle. By the time the consultant comes to call in the next couple, she's stopped in her tracks at the scene in front of her; pages of the Scotsman strewn all over the room as I scrabble about the floor looking for the review page, Ginny and the man now puce in the face screaming at each other as his wife tries to pretend she has no idea who he is and reads the same line of her magazine repeatedly.

'Please! Enough!' the consultant screams over the racket. I hold up two halves of a page triumphantly.

'Got it!' I announce. I smooth down my dress and pull my bag back on to my shoulder. Ginny helps me to my feet before turning to the man, who is now glancing sheepishly at the consultant.

'Keep the fucking thing,' she spits out, before turning on her heel and dragging me down the corridor. Back in the van, I stare dumbly out of the window, trying hard not to laugh. Ginny eventually breaks the silence with a loud snort.

'Well, we better hope this fucking attempt works. I'm not sure how welcome we're gonna be back in there,' and the car rocks with our laughter, all the way back to the Bitchelor pad.

Chapter Fourteen

My friends have left before I'm up for work the next morning. I vaguely hear their excitable stage whispers from my slumber and I mean to call out and wish them a lovely time but I doze off again. By the time my alarm goes off the house is in silence. I sigh at the thought of a twelve hour shift; I really can't wait until this month has passed. Gone will be the overtime and I may even book myself a week of annual leave and pop down to Richmond to see Granddad. I've barely spoken to him these past few weeks; I've been so busy at work. The last time we talked, he said his cough was much better and he certainly sounded chirpier. He hadn't been surprised that I'd left Will after I lost the baby, but as I already had a job here, he had understood that it would be irresponsible to chuck it all in and go back to London. I still thought about my other life from time to time. How different things would have been being in London, working with Amelia and hanging out with Conor. At some point I would have realised I wanted to be with him. In some other world I would be the arty girlfriend of a successful writer, hanging out at book launches and hobnobbing with the big chiefs of the literati, maybe even the odd celebrity. Instead I'm looking forward to renting some run down flat and working my ass off to buy things that would make it appear a little less shabby. I know all I'll be able to realistically afford is a bit of a dive in one of the less des-res areas of Edinburgh. At least I have my table and chairs, it's a start, and somewhat symbolic to me in that I'm not a complete failure. They are currently in Mum and Dad's garage awaiting their new home. Well, there's no point on dwelling on the 'Sliding Doors' version of how my life could have been, there is work to do to pay for my dump of a soon-to-be flat.

I walk into work at 9am and straight into a forecasting

meeting for our new sales quarter. I'm not usually included in these, so I'm assuming I'm taking the minutes. I did this a few months ago and the boss was pleased with the results. Nobody could decipher the last woman's shorthand when he passed it on to his assistant to type up; even the woman herself struggled to make sense of it after the meet.

'Coffee, Ivy?' Steve, my line manager holds up a cup in my direction.

'Er, yes please,' I'm rather confused; normally he's the one asking me to fetch him one. Come to think of it, everyone is being rather smiley and chatty with me this morning. Oh, dear God, I'm about to be fired. Why is this happening again? My sales have been fine, mostly on target and I was asked to mentor a couple of new recruits last week. I'm going to end up unemployed and pregnant, *again!* I'm not even being trusted to take the minutes; I throw a cautious glance at Gail, Steve's PA at the other end of the table, impatiently tapping her pen against her teeth, clearly itching to get back to her Facebook profile or next level of Candy Crush, no doubt.

'Here we are, Ivy,' Steve smiles as he plonks down a milky coffee in front of me.

'Thank you, Steve,' I swallow nervously, my eyes flitting around the sea of smiling faces.

'Hi everyone,' he's back on his feet next to me; 'I'd like you to meet Ivy, for those who haven't had the pleasure, yet. She has been with us for a few months now and we have been really impressed with her work.' Steve gives me a grateful smile and a faceless, male voice from halfway down the table mutters, 'well done, dear.'

'Over the past two weeks I have slowly introduced Ivy to a higher level of responsibility, mentoring a couple of new recruits and dealing with a few of our more valuable accounts. I'm pleased to announce that she has stepped up to the mark and I had every faith that she would.' I stare up at Steve in disbelief, so this was what all the cloak and dagger stuff had

been about. The occasional crisis call that Steve had been too busy to deal with that he'd passed on to me, it was a test, and I passed. Get me! I'm not useless after all.
'So, Ivy, if you would like to, we want to give you the opportunity to manage your own small team in our sales division. We think you could go far within the company; we already have seen great results in sales from the two people that you've been mentoring.' I glance around the room looking for the first person to burst out laughing and shout, 'Joke! Actually, you're fired.' But it doesn't happen.
'Ivy? What do you think?' Steve asks encouragingly.
'Wow, this is a total shock. Do you really think I'm up to a promotion?'
'Ivy, have you ever known me to make a bad decision?' Steve laughs.
'Well, you did send me out to get you a sandwich and look where that got you,' with horror I realise what I've said and clasp my hand over my mouth. The laughter starts of as a small trickle and then spreads all through the meeting. Even Steve himself joins in, once he's recovered from the fact that his secret has been company-wide knowledge all this time.
'I'm so sorry,' I stutter, 'it's just the shock.'
'It's fine, Ivy,' Steve coughs, 'I've always admired your honesty even if I've not been keen on your choice of Delis. '

So, as of one week today, I'm a team leader. The rest of this week will be spent shadowing the current one, nine until five, then back in my old position for my overtime shift. I have to attend some staff leadership training next week. It hadn't gone unnoticed, all this extra work I've put in. I do feel rather guilty that they've assumed I've been trying to further myself in the workplace when in reality I was about to stop it all at the end of the month when I have enough money for my flat. Luckily, this is one thing I manage to keep to myself, given my most recent outburst, which I know Steve will be good-

naturedly plotting some kind of revenge on.
I'm paired up with Michelle, whose position I will be taking over. She is off to work in events management; she has only been in the position for six months and with the company for fourteen. Michelle is easy to work with and has a motivational approach to her team leading. They do seem like a great bunch that she manages. They even go out for after work drinks to celebrate the particularly good sales days. I discover I'll be on an extra £1.50 an hour and this just tops the day off for me. The pressure of running the third top team in the company is really quite daunting and although Steve is confident I will take them to the number one spot, I'm not so sure. My last job has knocked my confidence a fair bit. Mr. McLeod had said I wasn't a sales girl, how the heck am I to be expected to manage a whole team?

My shift flies by, even the overtime, and before I know it I'm humming happily to myself on the walk home. I decide to pick up a pizza to celebrate and watch a movie before bed. I listen to an answer phone message from Evelyn inviting me to dinner tomorrow evening to celebrate my niece's birthday. Finally, I have some good news to tell my family. I'm sure they hear me utter the words 'I have something to tell you,' and die a little inside. It's been nothing but shit for months now and finally things are turning around. Even if I am pregnant, it'll be around eight months until I go on maternity leave, and the extra pay is a huge plus. Perhaps I can even upgrade to a marginally less shabby apartment. We could be talking an extra couple of hundred a month after tax. I hug my fleecy pyjamas to me and help myself to another slice of pizza, I raise my can of coke a give a spur of the moment toast. 'Up yours, Will. I'm doing just fine without you."
The only downside to my good news is that I'll have to put my idea of a holiday on hold for a few more weeks. Mind you, even cutting down to thirty-five hours per week would

feel like a holiday at this stage
Day two of shadowing, and I deal with a few of the calls from people that ask to be passed on to a senior member of staff. Michelle sits next to me and smiles her encouragement.
'Hey, who needs a week's worth of training? You're a natural. Steve made a good call with you, Ivy.' My confidence soars; it'll be so nice to go along to my sister's house this evening with some kind of achievement to report. My team have responded well to my amateur coaching; I find it uncomfortable taking an authoritative role, I'm so used to just being friends with everyone. The shift ends and I walk down with a few members of my old team to the bus stop. They're a little hesitant around me these days; I'm one of *them* now. Although that makes me feel a bit sad, I know that I'd be happy if it was one of my colleagues who had been promoted, maybe it's just a bit of sour grapes on their part. I catch the bus along to Corstorphine and glance in the shop windows as we go by. I could even treat myself to something new with my pay rise. My summer wardrobe had a bit of a facelift down in Richmond but my winter one is full of last year's holey cardigans and baggy jumpers, I need a new look for the new me. Team leader, I still can't believe it.

I arrive at Evelyn's to a rather tense atmosphere. She and Gerald have clearly been arguing. I glance over at James who is engrossed in something on his iPhone. Clearly not over him, at least, I wonder what he had to do to earn it back. With a shriek, my niece catapults herself down the stairs towards me. Head to toe in pink, right down to her little trainers, feather boa and make-up. She looks for all the world like something Barbara Cartland threw up.
'Happy birthday, Matty girl. Have you had a good day?'
'I had school, which was sucky, but the dinner ladies sang to me and put a candle in my sponge pudding. Is that for me?' she indicates to the shiny parcel I've put down on the table.

'Nah, I have another party after this, that's for the little girl there.'
'Shut up!' she laughs a gives me a gentle shove.
'Go on then, I suppose you can have it.' She rips open the paper expertly and squeals in delight at the ballerina jewellery box I have bought her, complete with twirling dancer inside and a few trinkets I picked up in the market.
'Oh, lovely, Matilda. Mummy had one just like that when she was little. Wine, Ivy?' Evelyn holds out a bottle of Chablis towards me.
'No thanks, Evelyn, I have an early start tomorrow.' She shrugs and pops it back into the fridge. I'd love nothing more than to celebrate my good news but I may be pregnant, I'm not ruining our chances.
'So what do you think of my daughter? Yesterday an innocent child, today a two-bit hooker.'
'She looks...cute,' I offer, for want of a better word. 'Hey, I have good news, I...'
'Ev! Where do you want these canapés put?' Gerald hollers from the utility room.
'Bend over,' Evelyn's voice is barely audible.
'What's up?' I mouth at her. She shakes her head and glances over at Matilda, who is trying to copy the ballerina's pose and twirl.
'I'll tell you later,' Evelyn rolls her eyes. 'James, answer the door, please. That'll be Gran and Granddad.' James jumps to attention and I shoot him an impressed smile.
'Well done, Ivy, you broke him with that four hour DVD. He's now a desensitised, obeying machine.' I doubt that very much, Evelyn will have backed up my paltry repeat of her punishment with something far superior. I'm scared to ask what she came up with but whatever it was, it has worked.
'Evelyn, darling,' Mum floats in on a haze of Estee Lauder and air kisses my sister. 'Where is my Granddaughter? Oh look at you, my lovely, a vision in pink.' After greeting Gerald, James

and even walking down the hall to knock on Christopher's door, Mum finally says hello to me. I'm so used to coming last that normally I'd not even notice, but today I'm itching to share my good news. Matilda is showing her Grandfather her ballerina jewellery box; bending the dancer into new positions that make me realise that my gift won't last the day. I make a mental note to leave before then, but say nothing. I'll only get told off from Mum for 'being mean' to Matty on her birthday. I learned that the hard way after 'ruining' James' birthday by suggesting he may not want to practice his golf swing right next to a then two year old Matilda. Three hours sat in casualty with a hysterical toddler with an egg on her head an hour later didn't ruin his birthday, not at all.

'Ivy, how are you?' Mum smiles and immediately looks away towards her Granddaughter again. I take a deep breath.

'I'm good thanks, Mum. I had some good news at work today, I've been promoted to a team leader at work and start next week, I...' every pair of eyes in the room turns towards Matty, as she crumples to the floor with a blood-curdling wail. Well, not every pair of eyes, James is clutching one of his in agony. I spot the ballerina over on the floor by the sofa. Evelyn rushes to James as Mum runs to Matty and scoops her into her arms.

'Granddad will fix it, baby girl, don't you worry. Ivy! Why didn't you get her the one from Jenners, like I told you? This would never have happened if you did,' Mum snaps. Oh, of course, the fact she was formerly a ballerina and latterly a contortionist *would* be my fault.

'Actually, it was from Jenners, *mother*,' I lie, 'it's exactly the one you suggested I get; £34.99? Yes?' A rare moment of bravery coupled with being sick to death of always being in the wrong has driven me to make my statement. My mother shoots me a sceptical look and pulls Matty onto her lap. The box from the market was beautifully hand crafted and only twenty quid; I'm not made of money! Luckily I'd remembered the price of the one that Mum had suggested. Evelyn has prised open James' eye and declared him 'at it,' which is her way of saying there is nothing wrong and he's acting up for attention. He clutches his eye for another minute before giving up on the amateur dramatics. He has a red spot on his cheek so it clearly hit him, just not where he said it did. My sister's children love nothing more than getting the others in trouble, whilst making themselves look like innocent victims. My Dad looks from the ballerina to the jewellery box and scratches his head. Gerald comes over with a tiny spring he found by the fridge and sets about trying to reassemble Matty's gift.

'God, I need a drink,' I mutter aloud.

'Well done on your promotion, lass,' Dad has left Gerald to his far superior surgical skills, and has come over to the breakfast bar to congratulate me, where I am clenching my fists and wondering how the hospital had made such a major error on clearly mixing me up with another baby.

'Thanks, Dad,' I shrug. 'At least someone was listening. 'Look, I think I'm going to head soon, I've been doing a lot of overtime and I'm kind of supernumerary here anyway.'

'Not to me, you're not, but I know what you mean. Want me to fake call you?'

'Yes, please,' I smile my gratitude to my father, as he heads off to the bathroom with his mobile phone. I discreetly turn mine up in preparation.

'Hello? Oh, hi Steve,' I pause as Dad tells me about an urgent Team Leader meeting that I need to attend, whilst doing a pee in the background. 'Wow! It must be an urgent meeting, it's...' I glance at the clock, '6pm. Ok, no problem. Yes I understand the extra responsibility will mean working late at times. OK, I'll see you in twenty.' I hang up, slip into my coat on and grab my bag. Dad flushes the toilet and walks out of the bathroom, shaking his hands.

'No towel in there, Evelyn. Oh, Ivy, are you off, love?' He

gives me a discreet wink.
'I don't see why a sales girl would need to be called into a meeting at this time of the evening,' Mum's tone is scathing.
'But she not a sales girl, are you, Ivy?' Dad smiles knowingly, 'she's a Team Leader now, and a bloody good one too from what I hear.' I kiss Dad on the cheek and pick up my bag. I ruffle Matty's hair as I pass.
'Save me some cake please, Matt. See you later all, thanks for a fun time.' I close the door behind me and lean back on it, with a sigh of relief. Good old Dad. Nobody understands me as much as he does, on how alien it feels to be in this family. I skip down the path, swinging my handbag and take a right turn towards the bus stop and plan my evening: Chinese takeaway, movie, bath, and bed...bliss.

Chapter Fifteen

The rest of the week at work goes well. Now it's Friday and I have my end of trial appraisal. For once I'm feeling reasonably confident in my abilities, Michelle has already given me some positive feedback and beams at me as I walk into our meeting with Steve. We sit in a circle around the table, with our coffees and the usual untouched plate of biscuits in the centre. It can't just be me that always wants to reach out, take one and dunk it in my cup. Nobody ever picks up one of these 'show pieces,' they're probably the same ones we had at the last meeting come to think of it. Steve officiously piles together his papers and uses the table to tap them into a straight order. My attention is pulled away from the plate, to him.

'Have one, Ivy, you have a tendency to think outside the box and be original, so have a bloody biscuit.' I glance at Michelle who nods her encouragement. 'You may as well,' Steve laughs, 'we're going to have to chuck them anyway now you've drooled on them.' We all laugh at this and in one sweeping motion I pick up a chocolate digestive and dunk it in my cup.

'Atta girl,' Steve laughs. 'Now, your appraisal, Michelle has informed me that you followed her lead very well for the first part of the week but it was the latter part; working on your own initiative, that you really impressed her. You were helpful to the staff whilst encouraging them to think for themselves. You were pleasant and polite when calls were passed on to you, as a senior staff member,' I blush a little at Steve's praise. 'You passed your test call with the senior manager too, well done on that; he is not an easy customer, quite literally.'

'No way! That guy who shouted and swore at me after he asked to speak to the Team Leader?' I give an amazed laugh.

'Yes, that's the one. But you remained perfectly professional

whilst asserting your authority. Your comment about the fact that you were trying to assist him but you would appreciate it if he didn't raise his voice or swear at you, was entirely the right thing to say.' I give a shocked laugh.
'I had no idea he wasn't a genuine asshole.' Steve snorts out coffee and wipes the front of his shirt with a napkin.
'You mustn't tell anyone about the test call, though, Ivy. It's a company secret to weed out the ones who may need additional customer relations training. I shake my head seriously.
'Of course not, what a genius idea though.'
'Thank you, Ivy. Mine, of course,' Steve gives a mock superior look. 'So, there isn't anything else to say really, other than well done. We have a forecasting meeting in an hour and a half that I'd like you to attend. Here is your itinerary for next week. You'll be with your team nine until three then some management paperwork training until five. It's not long but can be quite a full-on, classroom type experience, including some homework, so you may want to take a week off the overtime.' Steve glances at his watch, 'you may as well go for lunch now, Ivy. You'll never get one if you go back to your team now. Michelle can handle things from here.' Thank goodness for no overtime next week. I had been keeping up the extra hours in an attempt to show that it wasn't all for the purpose of a promotion, but I am exhausted and not too worried about finances now that I know I'm on so much extra per hour.

I head outside into the low, Autumnal sunshine for my break. All around me the leaves are changing into beautiful, deep reds and golds. This could be my favourite ever season; the drastic change in colour, but also the slight chill in the air, and the promise of long, cosy nights in by the fire. I walk through the park, marvelling at the colourful display. A small cluster of children play in the leaves, throwing them over their heads and squealing in delight. Evelyn and I were never allowed to do this, just in case a dog had pooped in them, according to that endless, imaginary rule book of Mum's. I do remember Nanny and Granddad allowing it in Terrace Gardens, however; declaring it was highly unlikely and would wash off anyway. Kids needed to be allowed to be kids. I smile at the children and scoop a handful up too, throwing them up in the air. One little girl turns to laugh, before turning her attention back to the group. Today I'm treating myself to a sit-in experience of the posh looking, new deli, on the other side of the gardens. It's rustic, chalk written sign outside promises the best lunchtime experience in Edinburgh. Offerings such as salmon and brie on ciabatta and prawn and avocado salad with focaccia have been tempting me on every trip into work. Instead, I had gone to the canteen for a cheese toastie or baked potato and beans every day, to network with Michelle and the team. But today, I made an excuse about collecting a prescription from the chemist and decided that, for once, it was all right to be a little selfish. The weekend stretches before me, long and lazy. I plan to catch up on some neglected box sets I got for Christmas, that everyone has raved about, but I've never seemed to find the time to get around to watching. The new deli doesn't disappoint, even if my lunch break was a little rushed, it had taken me forever to read through the menu, let alone make a choice at the end of it. I sat outside enjoying what could be the last of the sunny weather and observe the busy, city life as I tuck into the best sandwich I've had since Granddad's picnic. All too soon it's time to leave for the afternoon stint. I'd been eyeing up some homemade carrot cake that I didn't have time for, so I decide that I'll come back on Sunday, with the newspapers and all the time in the world.

On a spur of the moment, on the walk back, I decide to call my Grandfather. It's been ages since I've spoken to him and I

don't want anyone else to get in first and tell him about my promotion. I doubt that they will, to be honest. Dad definitely wouldn't as he would know how important it is to me to share my good news first. Evelyn and Mum haven't spoken to Granddad in, I don't know how long. If I call him now he will be back from the allotment and preparing lunch. I know all the ins and outs of my Grandfather's day.
'Hi Granddad,' he answers on the third ring.
''Ello, Ivy, love, 'ow's me girl doing?'
'I'm good thanks, Granddad. How is your cough? Are you keeping well?'
'Oh, yes. That latest dose of antibiotics sorted that out. I do listen to you, you know.'
'Ah, so it is possible to teach an old dog new tricks?' I laugh. My Grandfather is one of those rare people who can make you happy just by hearing their voice. In my case, even happier than I already feel today.
'I have some news...' I pause for dramatic effect, 'I'm a Team Leader now,' I practically squeal out the words.
'Congratulations! Well done, my lovely, I had every faith in you, of course, so I'm delighted, but not surprised. '
'They said they've been really impressed with my work, especially over the festival period and my mentoring of two of the newbies. It was totally unexpected; I actually thought I was being very publicly fired in a board meeting. I just can't believe how wrong I got it, I've got my first ever promotion.'
'Well, when you're not being too busy and important, you come down and let your old Granddad take you out for dinner to celebrate, you have any holidays booked?'
'No, but at this rate it's going to be the end of the year. Maybe I can come down for my Christmas shopping; I've always loved Richmond at that time of year, how does that sound?'
'That sounds ideal. The boys miss you as much as I do.'
'Aw, I miss them too. Give them a head rub and a tummy tickle for me. Look, I'm going to have to go, I'm about to go

into a meeting soon but I just wanted to touch base.'
'Oh, listen to you and your fancy talk, Ivy Efferson,' he laughs, 'go get 'em, tiger, and don't stop until you're CEO!'

I head back into the call centre and take my usual seat next to Michelle, at the end of the line.
'Oh, I'm glad you're back a bit early, how do you feel about dealing with your first disciplinary?' I look at her aghast.
'You'll be fine, I'll be there to support you; I have to say, it's a first on this team and it's only an alleged offence. We are looking into the call recording right now but we need to ask Pete's version of events first. She hands me a note with the customer complaint on it.
'Are you serious?' I try not to laugh, 'is this like my mystery customer that I had to deal with? It's not really a complaint, just a test, right?'
'No, unfortunately this is genuine. Arguing with a customer is a definite no-no, but to tell them to go fuck themselves is serious shit. Come on, we have half an hour before the meeting, we may as well get this out of the way.' My stomach churns all the way to Pete's chair, he's on a call at the moment so I hang back and let him finish. This is the side of management I really will not like; a few days ago we were laughing and joking in the canteen and now I have to discipline him. He finishes his call and turns to face me.
'Hi, boss lady, how are you getting on? Hey, I was going to ask if you fancy karaoke at the pub across the road tonight. A few of us are going out after work.' I close my eyes and die a little inside.
'Er, I'll see Pete, I'm kind of knackered. Look, I need a quick chat with you, if you don't mind.'
'Sure thing,' he takes off his headset and follows me down the line. Michelle leads us to a small office down the corridor and we all take a seat. My heart is pounding so much that I'm sure they can both hear it.

'Pete, I need your side of a story regarding a customer complaint. Now, we're not accusing you in any way but have you had any run-ins on your calls this morning?' Pete's poker face gives little away; just the slightest flicker of recognition passes through his eyes.
'Well, I had one guy call me a prick for waking him from his sleep. He's on nightshift. I asked if there was a more convenient time that I could call and he said 'try never.'
'OK,' I nod in understanding, 'we've all had calls like that. What happened next? '
'I offered to take him off the call list and he muttered something that I couldn't quite hear, so I asked him to repeat himself, this seemed to annoy him more for some reason. Then he called me a minimum wage loser and maybe if I'd stuck in better at school I wouldn't need to be harassing people for a pittance in a dead end job.' I purse my lips and take a deep inhalation. Comments like that stung, I've had a couple of those types too. It's difficult to keep your trap shut but generally I enjoy being extra pleasant as it seems to piss them off more.
'I can see how that would have made you angry, Pete. What was your reply?'
'I think I may have told him that...I wasn't the sad loser. I mean working nightshift? That's even more shit than a call centre job. No offense, sorry! I am grateful to have a job at all, in the current climate,' he babbles on as I patiently wait for him to finish. 'By that I mean I actually have a life, I can go out in the evenings and weekends,' he trails off, shrugging defensively.
'You have to be the bigger person, Pete, if someone is being offensive we can politely say that it doesn't appear to be a good time to talk and thank you for your time and hang up. Did you tell him to go fuck himself?'
'Well, yes, but only after he told me I had such a tiny cock that it was actually a mangina.' I want to laugh, I so want to laugh.

I look at Michelle who is taking this very seriously indeed. Her expression sobers me.
'OK, Pete, well IT are checking through the recordings so we'll take a listen and get back to you. Have you had your lunch yet?' He shakes his head humbly. 'Right, well go get it now and we'll chat again later this afternoon once we've listened to the conversation. It's the first time we have had to chat about anything like this so maybe I can see if we can get you on to a customer service training course. It's probably going to mean a warning for you though.' I do sound very apologetic and I know Michelle won't like this. This transition of being friends to a senior staff member is not going to be easy. Pete stands to leave and just to try and smooth thing over a little and diffuse the situation, I can't stop myself from blurting out,
'the deli across the park is nice if you're wanting to get out of the call centre for a bit. I was there earlier, great sandwiches, 'I finish lamely.
'Ummm, yeah, thanks,' and then he's gone, couldn't get out fast enough. Something tells me my invite to the karaoke bar may be retracted; I can imagine them all trying to sneak out without me noticing later. I wouldn't have gone anyway; there would be too many awkward questions about why I'm not drinking. A little bit of the old me leaves with Pete; I'm not like them anymore. Well, in my opinion I haven't changed, of course but to them I have, I exhale loudly and turn to look at Michelle.
'Not bad, but just a little bit too chummy. I didn't expect a firing squad from you but I could tell you were struggling there.' I nod my agreement with a grimace.
'That was awful; I hated every second of it, maybe I'm not right for a Team Leader position. I was one of them just last week.'
'You did absolutely fine, Ivy, don't doubt yourself. As Steve says, he never gets things wrong. You're doing fantastically well in every other way; it's only the discipline side of it you

need to brush up on. Most of us struggle with that, it's what separates us from the assholes. Only they get off on the power of pulling rank. Luckily, I've yet to come across one of them here.'

I arrive to the meeting with five minutes to spare. Steve chats animatedly to a gray haired, suited man that I've never met before. I head over to the urn to make myself a tea.
'Ah, Ivy, come and meet Mr. Jones, I've just been filling him in on your progress and he's decided to pop down for the meeting to see our newest TL recruit.' I abandon my cup and wander across the room with Steve.
'Ivy, lovely to meet you,' Mr. Jones shakes me warmly by the hand. 'I like my new title, by the way. I always hoped to succeed in not being a genuine asshole.' His laughter booms over the room as I flush a deep red.
'Steve! You told him! I'm so sorry, Mr. Jones,' I stutter, 'great acting on your part, I feel totally prepared to deal with anything now,' I finish with an embarrassed shrug. We take our seats with our brimming cups. Steve smiles at me before reaching across the table, picking up a custard cream and dunking it into his tea. The others stare at him in shocked silence. Mr Jones gives a thoughtful 'hmm,' as if the option had never occurred to him, before reaching out himself and doing the same with a digestive. I watch as a few fingers flex around the table but nobody else follows suit, I'm tempted to join in but I'm still stuffed from lunch. Steve begins the meeting with news of the last quarter's forecasting successes and what we can learn for next year's Edinburgh Festival with regards to staffing levels. The pace moves quickly and I glance around the room to see most of the others frantically scribbling notes. It hadn't occurred to me to do this and I suddenly feel a bit out of my depth. I catch Michelle's eye and she smiles her reassurance. She isn't taking notes either, but I'll check with Steve later to see if this is required of me, for

future reference. It's actually really interesting to hear the projections; I've never been involved in something like this before. It makes me feel very corporate and important. Judging by the bored looks on some of the faces around me, I may not always feel that way. Halfway through the meeting, there is a tentative knock on the door.

'Come in,' booms Mr. Jones, looking irate at the disturbance. Gail, Steve's assistant sheepishly puts her head around the door, as if she's too scared to come all the way in.

'I'm so sorry to disturb your meeting but I have an urgent call.' Mr. Jones stands and manoeuvres his way around the table.

'Oh, I'm sorry, it's not for you Mr. Jones, it's for Ivy Efferson. A panic swells in my chest. None of my family or friends would ever call me at work. They'd text, or leave a voice message which I'd pick up on my break. My first thought is that something has happened to Granddad. I know I have just spoken to him, but you never know. I'm on the school emergency contacts list; it could be about one of the kids, if they haven't been able to get Evelyn or Gerald. Yes, that's what it must be. I run down the corridor to Steve's office, at this stage not even caring about the fact I've been called out of a meeting and how unprofessional that may look. I may moan about my family but still, no job would come before them. I snatch up the phone,

'Hello?' I'm breathless due to my fear and the sprint down the hall.

'Ivy, *we can't find her!* We've tried *everywhere...* even the rescue helicopters are out.' The voice on the other end of the phone sounds familiar but I don't quite recognise it through the hysteria.

'Who? Matty? Where is she? When did you last see her?' I babble, incoherently.

'No, Ivy, its Natasha...Ginny went out for a swim in the sea and she hasn't come back!'

Chapter Sixteen

I sit in my First Class seat and stare blankly down at Edinburgh disappearing beneath me. When I had got off the phone to Natasha, Steve was there, by my side. I crumpled into a hysterical heap and he hugged and shushed me until I calmed down enough to tell him what the call had been about. There was no question of what would happen next. I said the words, 'I need to be there,' and he took over the rest. His assistant ran off to fetch my bag and coat while Michelle's new assistant tried to book me on the next flight to Rhodes. This is why I'm in First Class; it's all they had left. The meeting had pretty much rounded up after I left anyway; at least that's what Steve said, but maybe he was just trying to make me feel better. I don't remember much about the journey to Ginny's flat, to pick up my passport and a couple of changes of clothes, but I do remember picking up a framed photograph of us in the hall. It was taken at our sixth year leavers' disco; all big hair and toothy smiles. We didn't do proms in those days, just the gym hall, some loud music and a few sneaked in bottles of Strongbow cider. We were hammered in that picture; I threw up outside school while we waited for my Dad to pick us up. He hadn't said a word about the vomit all down my white vest and khaki cargo pants, our staple uniform in those days when we all wanted to look like someone out of the girl group, All Saints. Dad had just silently pulled over for my encore, dropped Ginny home and snuck me in the back door and up the stairs. He waited patiently outside my room as I stumbled and toppled over several times, trying to put on my pyjamas. He then took my soiled clothes away and I heard the rumble of the washing machine as I fell into my drunken slumber, Mum never knew a thing. Evelyn was Uni by then, thankfully, she loved nothing more than to snitch on me to Mum. I had awoken the next day to see a basin by my bed and a pint glass of water, which I had downed gratefully in one. All this flashed through my head in the thirty seconds I must have been standing there.

The air steward smiles as she passes by and offers me a drink. On noticing my pallor, she asks if I feel all right and if there is anything she can bring. I order some water and wish it was possible to get a phone signal up here, I so need to hear if there is any news. Once I had managed to calm Natasha down, she had told me that she and Ginny had decided to have a day on the beach in Faliraki. They had booked without realising the extent of wild nightlife that went on in the party capital of Rhodes. Actually, even during the day it seemed to be one big party too. The words 'lively resort' have a whole different meaning in travel agent talk, it appears. I pieced together as much as I could from a barely coherent Tasha. They had arrived at the beach around ten and the water had seemed calm. They'd taken lunch but had not long had breakfast, so Ginny had decided to go for a swim first. Tasha had wondered if Ginny had suffered a cramp in the water and got hysterical again over the fact she had let her go in alone. I reassured Tasha as much as I could. Ginny is a great swimmer, she had swam for our school and travelled all over the country taking part in competitions. She had likely been carried off by the tide and swam to the nearest piece of land that she could see. She was probably at this moment on a bus back to Faliraki in her swimsuit. Tasha had choked out a laugh at this before it turned back into wracking sobs again. That's when I knew for sure I had to go, that and the fact this had all happened over four hours ago. I look helplessly at my phone screen; it's switched off, of course, but I will a message to appear to say she's been found, safe and well. I've heard that some planes have Wifi now but unfortunately, this isn't one. Even an email to say that there was no news would do; the agony was in knowing nothing. Tasha had tried to call Ginny's parents but they were off on some hiking trip in the

Alps and weren't due back until next week. They had no idea their daughter was missing and don't 'do' mobile phones.
The flight is just short of five hours but seems to take an eternity. My mind flicks endlessly through possible explanations but always comes back to the worst case scenario. I just can't make any other possibility seem plausible. It's so painful to think that my friend could have drowned, that she was struggling and calling out for help and no one was there for her. Even if Tasha had gone out too, it could have been both of them gone. Ginny is still so young, her life can't be over yet; she has such presence and is so full of positive energy. The thought that she is dead is just too awful to contemplate.

The second the seatbelt light is switched off, I grab my hand luggage from the overhead locker and barge my way through a few meandering people, towards the exit. I race down the steps and into the airport to catch a cab to Faliraki. I wouldn't even attempt to drive in Greece, even if I knew where I was going, but also, I want my hands free to stay on the phone to Natasha all the way. As I wait in line, I switch my phone back on and impatiently wait for a signal to appear. There will be a text saying that they've found her and I can have an amazing weekend and a good laugh about all this with my friends, before heading back on Sunday night for work on Monday. Eventually I get my signal and call Tasha, who answers immediately.
'There's still no news, Ivy. The local guys have been out on their speedboats too but it's really choppy out there now, they've put up the no swimming flags.
'I'm on my way Tasha, I'm at Diagoras airport now and I'm just waiting on a taxi. Hang in there; you'll just have at most another hour on your own.' Finally, I'm next in the queue and I jump in the back of the cab. Scots, at the best of times are difficult to understand to other nationalities; but a borderline

hysterical one even more so. Eventually the driver understands where I mean and we take off at a speed that would put the aircraft I just got off from to shame.
From the back of the cab I type, delete and re-type an email several times, to Ginny's parents. They do have email, to keep up to date with their fellow animal rights activists and are bound to check at some point on their trip. I end up settling for a brief, but urgent, message stating that they should call me the moment they receive this and that Ginny may be in some trouble. I can't think of any other way of wording it. I can't say exactly what has happened in an email but they need to know to call me immediately. I send it to both Jemima and Ralph, in the hope that at least one will get it. We have no idea where they are staying for their trip; it's all I can do. It's now around nine and a half hours that Ginny has been missing. I can't even pretend this isn't serious now; although I'm trying desperately to keep a positive frame of mind. It'll be dark soon and they will have to call off the search. I groan as a wave of stomach cramps wash over me. No, this can't be happening; I'm not even due my period for a few days yet, although it's true, my cycle has been out of whack for months now. It doesn't look like this much wanted baby is going to happen. Another cramp kicks in as I spot a green cross on a building, I ask the driver to pull over so I can run in for some supplies. We have another try yet; it will be all right, everything is going to be fine. I repeat this like a mantra in my head, for reassurance more than anything else. I haven't even had time to arrange any currency so I put my purchases on my 'emergency only' credit card, which also has covered my flight and cab to the flat and airport. I dash back out to the taxi and notice the heat for the first time since I arrived. All along the street, people wander around, picking out postcards and keepsakes, they look happy and relaxed. Probably exactly how Ginny and Tasha have looked all this trip. They still had over another week to go; they should be enjoying their

holiday, laughing at all of us back home in the increasingly chilly weather. Not like this, this too horrible to be true situation. The taxi finally pulls into the resort and with a panic I realise I haven't even thought about how to pay.
'Cash point, I need a cash point!' The driver mutely points to an ATM outside a shop and I dodge traffic across the busy road to get his fare. Luckily he turns the car and pulls up by the ATM, I didn't fancy my chances trying to cross again.
'Which way is the beach?' I practically shout as I hand him a bundle of notes. He looks down at his hand and smiles.
'I take you,' oh, suddenly he's friendly when an overpaying customer comes along. It's as we drive down a dirt road, which I would never have found, that I first notice the helicopter, it hovers over one spot before moving along around fifty feet.
'Thank you,' I shout as I exit the cab. I can see a crowd on the beach and a few police cars dotted along the coast line at various spots. A few people are blatantly ignoring what is going on and continuing with their sunbathing. I scan the crowd frantically for Natasha before finally spotting her crouched on the ground next to some police officers. I run towards her, shouting her name but she doesn't hear me. The officer next to her is talking into his radio, whilst glancing up at the helicopter. The sea looks wild and the wind has picked up, with some darker clouds heading our way. I give one final shout to Natasha and she stands and turns towards me. She look completely broken as she falls into my arms. She clings desperately to me and sobs into my hair. Finally she pulls away and roughly scrubs at her eyes, the way small children do.
'They won't say what's happening but the helicopter has been hovering over the same two bits for an hour now, there must be something there.'
'Please tell us what's going on,' I beg to the officer who has clipped his radio back onto his jacket.

'You are?' He gives me a slightly suspicious once over.
'A good friend,' Natasha says, 'a very good friend who has just flown from Scotland to help,' she gives me a watery smile.
'We don't know, Madam. The waves are very high today and a storm is coming. We have poor visibility out there.' A police speedboat zooms by. 'As you can see, we are doing all we can.'
'Why does it keep hovering over the same bits?' Natasha nods frantically at my question.
'It could be anything, rocks, fish, we don't know. But they thought they saw something and are trying to get a closer look. Maybe you should head back and get some rest. You've had a nasty shock; we can come and let you know if we have any news.' Natasha shakes her head violently and stares back at the sea. I agree with her; we are staying put here to find out any information as it happens.

The evening passes with no more news but Natasha and I still shiver on the sand. I have never seen rain like this. At some point we are going to have to leave the beach but I don't know how to suggest it. I suspect Natasha would stay here all night if I let her. Unfortunately she's not in the best position to understand her own needs right now. I'm going to have to go against the grain and take control of the situation. Luckily the police officer takes it out of my hands.
'I'm afraid we are going to have to call off the search for tonight. We will be out again as soon as the sun comes up but we can't see anything at all now, it's too dark.' Natasha chokes out a sob.
'Come on, Tash. Let's go get dried off and get something to eat and have a sleep. She is surprisingly compliant and we all walk back up the beach towards the track. The police kindly offer to drop us off at the room. Natasha sits on the bed in her wet clothes and stares into space, whilst I search through the drawers to find some dry clothing and turn on the shower for

her. I walk over to the bed and gently take hold of her hand.
'Come on, Tasha. Go have a hot shower and get changed. We can't do anything more tonight and Ginny needs us to be strong.' I feel anything but strong, I feel utterly terrified and sick, but I have to be brave for Natasha right now. She can barely function for herself.
'You know, she said I'd changed her mind about marriage. She said she just hadn't met anyone like me yet.' Natasha stares into space as she talks. I cringe at the past tensing but I let it go. If the unthinkable has happened, which as every hour passes seems incredibly likely, this is how she will be talking about Ginny from now on. It's a step away from denial, which may be useful in her recovery.
'Come on, love,' I soothe, and put my arm around her waist. I hoist her up and we walk to the bathroom. She closes the door and I allow myself a few minutes of selfishness as the worry and upset pours out of me. Before long, I hear the shower stop and with a loud sniff, I pull myself together. Luckily, one of the officers put my bag into the police car when the rain had hit us. Otherwise, all my things would be drenched. I lay out some clothes for Tasha on the bed and she emerges from the shower, looking like the water has washed all the colour in her away.
'Here you go Tash,' I indicate to her clothes on the bed. 'I'll be ten minutes tops.'
The hot water seeps through the chill on my skin but it can't reach the one in my heart. This does not look good at all. If she had made it to land then she'd be back by now. The best we can hope for is that she's clinging on to a buoy and wishing the storm would pass; but I saw that sea for myself. The realisation that all may not be well is hitting home. A thousand images flick through my mind of Gin and our time together. So many funny, silly memories; I can only remember us laughing. We were lucky in the fact that no matter how pissed off the other was, we always managed to

see the funny side in something. What would she say to me right now, I wonder? What could possibly be amusing about the fact I may have lost my best friend? She'd probably something along the lines of how lucky she is for not having to go to work a week on Wednesday. That she'd be standing by laughing at all us suckers for still being part of the rat race. Or perhaps, 'your Nanny says hi, I've only been here a few hours and she's already knitted me a cardi and matching hat.' In spite of the absolute devastation I feel, the laughter, or perhaps hysteria begins. Before I know it I have my face cloth stuffed in my mouth and I'm collapsed on the floor of the shower. That's exactly what she would say. A fresh wave of cramps, knocks the wind out of me and stops my laughter as suddenly as it started. I look down to see a trickle of blood pooling with the water. Fuck, the few hours of respite I had from my stomach pains dissipates. There will be no baby. Normally with me there's a buildup of a few days of cramps before the bleeding starts. Could it be the shock? Please don't tell me I was pregnant and lost it, this has many more similarities to my miscarriage than to my normal monthly cycle. I'm best not to dwell on this fact as there is nothing I can do about it. In theory, one of those really early predictor tests may have told me up to four days before; but would I really want to know? I feel horrendously guilty for some reason. Guilt that I couldn't make it work again for Ginny's sake, probably. Where are you, Ginny? I try to mentally connect with her like we used to do when we were younger. Years ago at Christmas, our teacher had brought in some Zener cards for us all to try out, for the end of term Friday. She had been amazed that Ginny and I had remarkably high scores sending these picture cards to each other, supposedly telepathically. After that, we arranged to do an unscheduled phone call to each other at some point over the coming week. We were startlingly accurate with that too. Our conclusion was that we most definitely had the gift of ESP, the reality was that I knew she would call just after Neighbours finished in an attempt to get out of the chore of homework. It wasn't too difficult to narrow down to a day either, since we spent most evenings either at each other's houses, swimming or at youth club. It was bound to be the one day I wasn't seeing her. I concentrate hard and try to send the thought that we miss her and are doing everything we can to find her. I finish my shower, wrap myself in a towel and walk out into the bedroom. Turning my back discreetly, I pull out a tampon from the pack in my carrier bag. I momentarily think I've managed to hide it but Natasha notices and a fresh batch of sadness envelopes her.

'Shit, Tash, I was trying to not let you see this, I'm sorry.' A baby would have at least been something positive for now. God knows we need it. I scurry back to the bathroom and dress as quickly as I can.

'Come on, love, let's go get something to eat and try and think positive for now. We will set our alarms for 5am and get straight back out there, I promise.'

'I'm not hungry,' Tasha voice is barely audible.

'Me neither, but we need to keep our strength up, for Ginny.' Tasha stands and I put a cardigan over her shoulders. At least she's warmed up a bit after her shower. A quiet meal and a couple of wines should help her sleep, and tonight, I'm bloody well joining her.

Chapter Seventeen

We walk wordlessly down the main street amongst the partying throng. I know that all Tasha wants to do is go and sit on the sand, looking out at the black of the sea and willing Ginny to walk out and say it was all a silly misunderstanding. I noticed her glancing towards the beach when we came out of the hotel. We walk past a few restaurants but Natasha seems to know where she's going. We walk on wordlessly with our arms linked in mutual support. Now and again Tasha lets out a loud sigh of helplessness and I give her arm a squeeze. I'm not convinced I'm going to manage to get her to eat, but I have to at least try. Eventually we arrive at a pizzeria with a large, outdoor seating area. Fairy lights adorn the trees and cosy tables are spaced out a respectable distance from the others; one of my own personal hates is eating whilst practically sat on someone else's lap.

'Here,' Natasha stops in her tracks, 'this is our favourite place. We come here every night, just about.'

'Here it is, then,' I force a smile.

'Natasha,' the waiter walks over with a beaming smile and pulls a chair out for her to sit. 'Ahh but who is this new woman? What will Ginny say when I tell her you...' the waiter notices me shaking my head and the panicked look on my face. He stops mid-sentence. Wow, they really did come here all the time. They're known by name and relationship status. Tasha seems to have not even noticed and stares at the chequered table cloth.

'Tash, I'm just popping to the loo, will you be OK for a minute?' She nods mutely. The waiter follows me into the restaurant, sensing that I need to talk to him.

'Ginny's missing,' my voice wavers saying it out loud for the first time. 'She went for a swim and...' The waiter looks shocked and points towards the sky over the beach. 'Yes, that's why the rescue helicopter was out. We still have no

news.' I finish with a helpless shrug. He grabs my hand.
'I am so sorry, my dear, I had no idea. '
'I know,' I nod, 'I've made her come out because she needs to eat , so, I guess you could just bring her what she would usually have, and I'll just have what she's having. I don't think we will eat much but if it's in front of her, she might.'
'My name is Christos. You need anything, you ask for me.'
'Thank you, Christos. Bring a bottle of their usual wine too. It may help her sleep.' He nods his understanding and I head back outside. Christos clearly passes on the news to the other staff as we have a few sympathetic glances coming our way and a table of rowdy twenty-somethings are told to keep it down. The atmosphere is sombre amongst the staff, clearly the news has shocked them. Within five minutes Christos appears with two pepperoni pizzas. Natasha has downed her first glass of wine and looks increasingly tearful. I've only have had a few sips but already I can feel my head spinning.
'Tasha, please eat something.' She looks up at me with brimming eyes. They have the best pizza here, Ivy, Gin says it's almost as good as Marco's. She always got the seafood one, I wouldn't kiss her after,' she looks sadly at her pizza.
'Ewww, anchovy breath, I'm not surprised. Maybe she chose that one because she didn't want to kiss *you*. You never thought of that, huh?' Natasha gives a small laugh and picks up a slice of pizza.
'Maybe...'

Tash manages just under half her pizza, which I'm more than happy with. Unfortunately she ordered another bottle of wine and by the time we leave she is absolutely hammered. I help her along the street as a small crowd of teenage boys cheer her on loudly. Christos had refused to take any money for our dinner. In some hushed up agreement the staff had decided to take it out of their tips for the evening. He had hugged us both before we left and told us that he would pray that tomorrow would bring good news. By the time we get back to the room Tasha is bordering on hysterical. I had to practically carry her upstairs and thanked God that she was only a size ten. I lay her carefully on her side in the double bed, setting both our alarms before crawling in opposite her. In spite of all the wine we've had, I cannot sleep. Any time I do manage to doze off, I wake up with adrenaline filled jerks and the horror of the situation hits me once again. Eventually I drift off into a deep, dreamless sleep and awaken to the alarm clock ringing by my side. I roll over to see if Natasha is awake but she isn't there. A warm breeze blows the curtains into the room and I wander out to the balcony.

'Where *is* she, Ivy?' I have nothing to offer so I just sit down on the seat next to her.

'Let's get showered and go down to the beach, Tash. We can let the hotel staff know where we are in case there is any news.

As we walk back down to the sea front, we notice the helicopter hovering further along the coast. The police speed boats are back out and they zoom across the water at regular intervals. We sit on the sand and I hand Tash a bottle of water, she looks awful, her skin is clammy and white, her eyes appear sunken in her head, I noticed a similar look on myself earlier. The stress and worry is etched on both of our faces. Tash stands and looks up at the helicopter before walking down to the water. With her out of earshot, I take the opportunity to call home.

'Hi Dad. It's Ivy. I just wanted to let you know that I'm in Rhodes. Ginny went missing in the sea about ten yesterday. I'm out here to support Tash and see if I can do anything to help...' I trail off as I hear my Dad's panicked voice.

'Barbara, *Barbara!*' My Mum's hurried footsteps echo in the background and I hear my Dad's worried explanation.

'Ivy! Oh my darling, are you all right?' tears prick my eyes at

some kind words from my Mum, for once.
'Not great, Mum. We just need some news now, it's been nearly twenty-four hours.' I hear my mother give an emotional choke in the background.
'Shall we fly out, dear? Do you need us there too? You may be supporting Natasha but what about you? Who's there for you?'
'Thank you, Mum, that's really kind but we'll be OK. The police are doing all they can but there's not really anything else we can do.'
'Please call me the second you hear anything. I can't believe it. Ginny feels like a daughter to me, God knows I've known her long enough. Give Natasha a big hug from us and I will let your sister know.'
'OK, thanks Mum. Look, I'd better go; Tasha is walking back up the beach. Can you let Granddad know too, he's really fond of Ginny. He gets upset that people don't want to worry him and leave him out of the loop.'
'Yes, of course. Stay safe, dear and do not go in the sea yourself. You stay on dry land.'
I hang up just as a police officer walks up to Natasha. I leave them to chat a few moments before going over.
'Ivy, the police have asked for volunteers to walk a few miles each of coast. To see if they can...' she pauses.
'I know, I know. Which bit shall we take, officer?'
'You can take this one, there are people all over the island walking along stretches, right now. I'm impressed with the turnout. I only mentioned it to a few resorts and they all rallied round.'
'See, Tash? See what everyone is doing for Ginny?'
Tasha gives a weak smile of gratitude and we set off along the beach; walking along the shallows in silence. We walk for what seems like miles, pausing every now and then when we spot a person in the sea.

By one, I am exhausted and dehydrated, so I suggest to Natasha that we get some lunch from the little beach hut we are passing, and she agrees. Even with my sallow skin tones I can feel the burn on my body. It'll do us good to rehydrate and reapply some sunscreen. Even although it's nearing the end of the holiday season in Greece, the nights are chilly but the days remain hot. To us, anyway, the Greeks are finding it cold and think we tourists are crazy to still be going in the sea and the pool.
'I can't believe that all over Rhodes people are giving up a day of their holiday to help,' I break the silence that has come over us again. We take our seats and order some food. The friendly, older, Greek woman bustles around us and I think how nice it feels to have a proper grown-up around. I still don't feel like an adult; especially in situations like this.
'Well, Gin is an attention seeker, I wouldn't expect anything less,' Tash smiles. '
'She's out there somewhere,' I glance out at the rolling waves, 'it's just knowing where that's the problem.'
Tash nods and takes a half-hearted bite of her sandwich, which the waitress has placed in front of us. I know all Tasha would have done today is kept on walking until she was exhausted. I'm glad I'm here to make sure she does at least the basics of eating and sleeping. I couldn't have stood being at home and waiting on a call; I may not be doing much but at least I feel I'm contributing in some small way. After half an hour, and three bites of her lunch, I relent and agree to start walking again, Tash won't eat any more and I suppose it's better than nothing. At least she's had some fluids. I can understand where she's coming from, stress almost always affects the appetite; unfortunately in my case it's usually the other way and I stuff myself silly. In this case, it's different; this isn't just normal everyday stress; this really is a life or death situation. As we walk along the beach, my phone rings briefly but when I take it out of my bag, the signal disappears.

It's an unknown number, which I wouldn't answer under normal circumstances, but it could be Ginny's parents. I swing around looking for somewhere I may possibly be able to get a signal. The nearest place is back where we came from.
'Tash, we have to go back, it's probably about a ten minute walk to that little village. I need to call this number back.' We turn back around and pick up our pace. I am dreading this phone call but I have to be the one to do it, Natasha is in no fit state and would only get hysterical. I've known them for so long; I really owe it to them to be as honest as I can.
We make it back in under five minutes and I scan my phone for a signal. Once it appears I call back the number. I assume it's a receptionist that answers as she gives the name of a hotel that I don't quite catch, and when I ask for Jemima or Ralph Haywood, she asks me told hold. They've just left but she can probably catch them up. I hang on for a good five minutes before I hear Jemima's breathless voice.
'Ivy? We just saw your email. Is Ginny all right?' I take a deep breath.
'We don't know, Mima, she went for a swim yesterday morning and hasn't come back. There are loads of search parties out and the police are being fantastic. I don't know what else we can do.'
'Oh, dear God,' I hear her reiterate all this to Ralph, 'Ivy, we will arrange flights to come out to Rhodes right now. Are you and Natasha OK?' This typical of Mima, she has such a big heart that even with all the turmoil she is going through, she still thinks of others first.
'I'm here for Tash, Mima, but we would love for you to be here.'
I don't have a blasted mobile either, look, we will be out of reach for a bit but I'll call again from the airport. Be strong, girls. We will be there as soon as we can.'
I stay put in the beach bar for a while so that I can have a signal when Mima calls back. Tasha decides she will keep on

with the search and heads off along the beach again. I make her promise not to keep going and to stop when she meets the next search party and come back. An hour passes and Ralph calls. They have managed to get on the next flight out in forty-five minutes. He sounds calm, but I know inside things will be very different; he will be putting on a brave face for his wife. I order a coffee and scroll absently through Facebook, now that I have a wireless connection. I find myself on Ginny's page and read through some of her updates. I haven't been on for days and there are some lovely holiday snaps of her and Tash. Her new profile picture is a selfie of both of them and her cover photo is a panoramic view of the beach at sunset. The caption she has chosen chills me. It simply says 'Heaven.'

Just over an hour later Natasha returns. I had looked along the beach but there was no sight of her. I thought it may be good for her to have some time to herself. Selfishly, I wanted some time to be alone with my thoughts too, and to reminisce. I felt maybe she had needed the same and that was probably why she had chosen to go off on her own.

'Let's walk back to where we started, Ivy. My battery has just died and the police won't be able to get me now, I need to know if there is any news. We head back towards the resort in the afternoon sun. Mima and Ralph will be in the air now; I feel better knowing that some proper grown-ups are on their way. I feel out of my depth in this situation and also, any news we get, I want them here for. Natasha glances along the beach and a realization dawns on her.

'The boats have gone, Ivy, so has the helicopter,' Natasha stares at me in shock. 'They've found her! I just know it. Come on Ivy, run!' I follow behind her as she sprints along the sand. We arrive, breathless and sweating, ten minutes later. A police officer straightens up when he see us run towards him and begins to walk towards us.

'Have you found her?' Natasha pants. I freeze at his solemn

expression that she doesn't seem to have registered.
'We're not sure yet...' he says carefully. A strange, guttural, wailing sound begins and it takes me a few seconds to recognise that it's coming from me. Natasha gives me the strangest look before realisation dawns.
'You've found a body,' Natasha stares at him intently, trying to read his expression.
'I'm afraid we have. A woman's body was found just outside the harbour in Rhodes Town an hour ago.'

Chapter Eighteen

Today is the day of Ginny's funeral. Although more spiritual than religious, these days, Mima and Ralph have decided to use the local minister because back in the day he christened Ginny. It just felt right to them to complete a full circle. She will be buried in the family plot alongside Mima's Mum, Dad and brother. There were three spaces left for the three family members remaining; this had always creeped Ginny out, to know where she would be one day. It had been a nice thought to all end up together, of course, but Ginny had commented that it now gave her the heebie-jeebies to walk through the cemetery and see her last place of resting. Of course, we all laughed about this; she wouldn't have to worry about that until she was at least in her seventies, and by then it may actually be quite comforting to know. None of us had ever imagined that this time would come so soon. I think about my flippant comment about how at least she would have the sun in the afternoon and not in the morning, which pissed her off in the old flat, as it woke her at 6am every summer morning. She based her purchase on the Bitchelor pad mainly on the fact that her bedroom remained in the shade until late afternoon. Mima shakes her head at the dug-out hole as I stand beside her.
'This isn't how it should be, Ivy. Ralph and I should be in this space first, not my little girl.' She chokes on the last few words and I turn to hug her. I have no useful words to say so I just hold on to her as she literally shakes with grief.

Ginny's death has completely heartbroken all of us; Both Mima and Tasha have been on valium since we got back from Rhodes. I think back to Natasha collapsing in the sand, the police officer had really not known how to deal with her. One of the older women sunbathing nearby had kicked into action. She was clearly a mother herself and knew exactly what to do with two, quite literally, hysterical girls. Arriving back at the apartment was a blur; but a bottle of brandy had appeared from nowhere, probably the woman's room. What was her name? Bridget, I think. She sat us on the balcony with a drink and busied herself with packing up the room, carefully folding clothes into the case and thoughtfully leaving out some warmer clothes for the flight home. I'm due to catch my already booked one back the next day and I want Tasha with me. We had no idea what we should do with Ginny's body in this situation but they did have insurance which covered repatriation. I've always found that aspect of travel insurance rather maudlin, I'd never have imagined in a million years that any of us would need to use it.

Mima and Ralph had arrived at the room a few hours later. Bridget had explained everything so that we didn't have to face it and then made a discreet exit. We never saw her again and I wish she could know now how grateful we are to her. We didn't even know what room she was in. Mima had, of course, expressed her gratitude and said that was enough; we had been in shock and to forget about not thanking Bridget ourselves. She and Ralph had already known in their hearts that Ginny was gone. The length of time that she had been missing, and the storm, had given them an early realisation; while Tash and I had clung endlessly to our hope.
Tasha had insisted that we spend our final night in their favourite restaurant; I think she needed some kind of closure on it all. Ralph said it was a beautiful way to remember Ginny and in spite of our grief, we should celebrate her life that night. He's a deeply spiritual man, the kind of peaceful presence that is very comforting to have around in situations such as these. Both he and Mima have a strong belief in the afterlife. Mima works in crystal therapies and Ralph in counseling. He was absolutely devastated at the loss of his daughter, of course, but is quick to tell us that we will all meet

again; nobody is ever 'lost.' We had showered and changed in almost silence. It was amiable and not at all uncomfortable, almost like a calmness had descended. We knew now, Ginny had gone and there was nothing we could do.

Mima had held Tasha's hand as we walked down to the restaurant; I think both had wanted the comfort and support. News had already reached Christos and the others. Ralph had taken himself off for a couple of hours to formally identify his daughter. We knew for now, for sure. It was all around the island that our friend had been the unfortunate one washed up by the harbour wall. We had drank and dined, hugged, cried and laughed at the endless funny antics of Ginny. We heard stories from her childhood that we had never known and reiterated ones that she had told us.
'She never was your usual common or garden little girl, and we embraced that,' Mima had laughed, 'her favourite toy was a tool set, no wonder she turned out to be a plumber.' I had been all frilly dresses and baby dolls; even at a young age my strong maternal streak had been evident. Ralph had arranged Ginny's repatriation and we all flew home without her. Tasha had wanted to be on the same flight as Gin but it just wasn't going to work. They said they would get her home as soon as possible but there was no way of knowing exactly when, we needed Tasha with us to provide her with support. She had desperately wanted to see Ginny's body but Ralph had dissuaded her, telling her to just remember Ginny how she was in life. I think that was his kind way of saying that she wasn't in the best of ways for Tasha to see.

The rain starts just as Mima and I walk up the hill to the church. The minister gently indicates for the other mourners to step aside as Mima approaches. Ralph takes her hand as the Reverend gives his condolences. As I walk into the church, I see Ginny's coffin at the altar. My knees buckle

slightly and I hold on to a pew for support. Across her coffin is a rainbow flag; the symbol of gay pride, which is present due to Ginny's insistence one drunken evening. We all moaned at her to shut up and stop putting a downer on things, she never got that way often with drink but occasionally she would come out with what we thought were morbid comments, after a few drinks. Everyone is dressed in bright colours, again a suggestion of Ginny's. She never wanted mourners in black, she wanted to lift their spirits and for her life to be celebrated. When I had told Mima and Ralph about this, they had thought it was a fantastic idea, she had never got around to mentioning it to them once she'd sobered up. For those that hadn't heard, Mima had some colourful scarves to brighten up the black. Natasha had even gone a step further and bought her and me a rainbow umbrella each, just to continue with Ginny's theme. After all, it's Scotland, if it isn't raining already, it probably will be later. I spot Mum, Dad and Evelyn in the fifth row and give them a discreet wave. I go to move into their pew but Ralph takes my arm.
'Oh, no you don't, young lady. You're family, front and central with us.' I sit down next to Natasha and give her hand a squeeze. She gives me a watery smile and then her eyes wander back to the coffin. I glance around at the brightly coloured, packed church and think how proud Gin would be at the turnout. She always claimed she didn't need many friends; preferring quality to quantity, but here we have a mix of family, friends and customers, the lives of whom she had touched in some way. Reverend Brown takes his position and a Snow Patrol song begins to play. That same drunken night, Gin had declared that she also wanted the lyrics to 'Chasing Cars,' blared out. She thought people would laugh, if she asked them to lay down beside her, should this situation arise, and sure enough, as I look around I see it evoking a few smiles and indulgent shakes of the head at her cheek. Tasha's brimming eyes remain fixed on the coffin for the whole song.

The music ends and the Reverend glances around at the congregation with a warm smile.

'I think we can all agree that was very typical Ginny, she wanted to make you smile today, and for her funeral to be a bright and colourful affair. Mima and Ralph, Ginny's parents would like me to thank you for respecting her wishes.' Ralph nods his approval and his eyes fall on his daughter's coffin, as Reverend Brown takes up his eulogy.

'At the family's request, today will be about celebrating the life of Ginny Haywood and will be as true to her as we can be. Twenty-nine and a half years ago, I actually christened Ginny in this very church and even then, she had a lot to say.' A ripple of laughter echoes through the church. 'Not only did she scream through the entire ceremony but she then vomited over my robe before I handed her back to her Godmother. Even then, her opinion of organised religion was evident. Several years later, at the age of five, she informed my wife that Jesus walking on water may have been a miracle but the fact that her Grandmother had managed to get her to go to Sunday school that day, was an even bigger one.' The ripple is a little louder this time; Natasha snorts out a laugh and turns to me in open mouthed amazement at the unorthodox words of the minister.

'Yes, Ginny was unconventional even then. The thirty years she has spent in this world have been full of fun, laughter and she has brought joy to us all. She was extremely proficient at her job; in fact just three weeks ago she unblocked the vestry toilet and had joked that I'd do anything to get her into church. I can only imagine what she'd have to say about having to be here today, probably something about me always having to have the last word.' Mima lets out a loud chuckle at this; the banter that the Reverend and Ginny have had over her non-attendance at church had been a standing joke for years. He goes on to acknowledge Ginny's life achievements and how happy she was to find love with Natasha. Unlike some views of the church, Rev Brown was happy to celebrate love in its variety of modern forms. Ginny's sexual preferences have never been an issue in his church, just her lack of presence at his sermons. By the time the collection dish comes around, the mood in the church is light, as people discuss their own happy memories of my best friend. The collection from today will go to an AIDS charity, at Ginny's request. My heart swells to see a lot of notes in the dish by the time I add my own.

As we make our way down to the grave side, the sun begins to shine. The rays soak through the leafless trees and bathe us all in light. It feels so appropriate that the sun would come out for her; she brought so much light into all of our lives. I take my cord at the graveside and try to stay strong as we lower my friend into the ground. The minister indicates for Natasha to come forward with her single red rose, which lands perfectly in the centre of the flag. I grasp Mima's hand as Reverend Brown utters the words to commit Ginny's body to the ground. We all seem to hold a collective breath at the finality of this. It's our last goodbye and the tears start to flow within the funereal group. There is no brushing over this part of the service, the jovial atmosphere has gone. Finally, it's all over and a few people walk over to the graveside to say a few final words to my friend. I hang back at wait my turn and think back to the minster's words. I'm impressed at the honesty of his service today. I can tell Ginny's parents are relieved that he went along with their rather unusual requests. The last few remaining have their say, which for me is just a simple,
'Thank you for always being there for me, Ginny. I love you and miss you. Until we meet again...'
We stand a little bit away as Natasha stays by the graveside, looking sadly down at the coffin. She'd found and lost the love of her in just a few, short months. It seems so unfair.

With a deep sigh, she turns and walks towards us and we climb in to the black car and head off for the wake.

We arrive at the hotel twenty minutes later; already the room is packed out with friends of Ginny's; some I recognise from school and others from the bars and clubs we frequented. Natasha has brought Ginny's iPod and she places it on the docking station. Today is all about Gin, even down to her taste in music. As I stand at the free bar that Ralph has insisted on, I spot my sister waving from a corner table. I hold up a glass to her and she gives me a thumbs up. Mima stands to the side of me chatting with Natasha. I inadvertently overhear some of their conversation and it seems that Ginny had been looking out for Natasha, even though they hadn't been partners for long or in the eyes of the law. The bitchelor pad has been passed on to Tash. Mima had waited until today to tell her as she had wanted something positive to say after such an emotional day; Ginny had discussed it with her parents a month ago and they had whole-heartedly agreed. They had actually planned to arrange a civil ceremony when they got back. Nothing was finalised in a will; who would have expected this to happen? But Mima and Ralph, as next of kin, would respect their daughter's wishes and sort it all out. She also made allowances for if she and I did manage to have a baby together. It would have gone 50:50 between Tash and me, to cover years of child support. It was our IVF treatment that had actually prompted the discussion with Mima and Ralph, Ginny had wanted to make sure everyone was taken care of. Tasha stares at the bar as she listens. I know this is far from the most important thing in her world right now but it gives me a warm feeling to know that she will have a secure home for as long as she wants it and one that reminds her of the love of her life. Gin had bought her flat at eighteen and had cleared her mortgage ten years later with hard work and lots of overtime. Mima glances at my glass of

wine and gives a sad little smile, there will be no baby, we all know that now.
'Never mind, maybe it's less complicated for you this way,' she smiles, giving my arm a little squeeze.
'She would have made a great parent, Mima. It gave her a real buzz of excitement over the last few months and I feel like a total failure, if it's any consolation.'
'Now you stop that, young lady. You are in no way a failure. It took us three years to even fall pregnant with Ginny, I know how difficult it can be.'
'We have one round left but I don't know if I want to do it without her now,' I shrug.
'There is no rush, my love. You take your time to decide, you're only young, yet.' I nod and glance over at Evelyn. 'You go, Ivy. Sit with your family. I'll get round to them to thank them in a bit. Such beautiful flowers they brought for my girl.'

'You OK, Ivy?' Evelyn smiles as I take a seat next to her. 'Brilliant service, so very... Ginny,' she takes a large gulp of her wine.
'It was, wasn't it? Hey, good of you to come along, I know you weren't exactly friends.'
'Oh, *that*. Ginny and I were fine; we just loved to wind each other up. She had a good heart.'
'So how are my darling niece and nephews? Is James behaving?' Evelyn gives a shrug.
'He told me the other day that I'm an embarrassment to him. I collected him from school but I wasn't in the Audi, it's a definite no-no to turn up in the Clio. So working class trying to be middle, apparently. I told him his life could be worse, he could live with an ungrateful, little shit who thinks he's the most important thing in the universe and me merely breathing would be an embarrassment.' I watch as she takes another large gulp and she catches me looking.

'It's fine, Dad's driving. Huh! As if the gin monster would be,' she pulls a face in Mum's direction.
'How's Gerald? Are you speaking again after Matty's birthday?' I ask cautiously. Evelyn gives me a curious look.
'You know, I think I may leave him, Ivy. You know he's having an affair, don't you?' I study a fallen sausage roll on the floor as I think of a suitable reply.
'Don't get mad but I did ask him about that after Ginny and Tash saw him in a restaurant with a blonde woman. He said you were having an open relationship.'
You mean a red-head, and no, we are not. Well I'm not,' Evelyn snorts.
'No, I specifically remember Gin saying a blonde woman.'
'Oh great so there was more than one, well that's just bloody *fantastic*!' A few people look around at my sister, who raises her glass, smiles and mouths her apology.
'Let me get you a coffee,' I move her wine glass a little away from her but she notices and grabs it back.
'No, I am fine with wine, thank you. If he can go out and have a good time then I can do the same.'
'But, it's a funeral, Evelyn,' I whisper, 'You can't go getting smashed, it's just not the right thing to do.'
'Of course she can,' Mima takes a seat on the other side of my sister, 'Ginny would want you all to get smashed, on her, and spend all day tomorrow swearing at her through your hangovers. Here, Evelyn, have another.' I groan inwardly as Mima tops up my sister's glass with the wine bottle she has placed on the table.
'Jemima, I am so sorry for your loss. All of our losses, actually, Ginny was such an amazing person. I wish I was more like her. She took no shit, didn't care what people thought of her and she was so, so funny.' Mima smiles indulgently at Evelyn's fond words for her only child.
'She was hilarious, wasn't she? When I asked her about Natasha's background she told me she was raised

conventionally Jewish. When I enquired if she went to synagogue she told me no, just like her, she'd rarely attended or paid attention to religion and for years had thought that Rabbi was the plural of rabbit.' Mima and my sister laugh until tears stream down their cheeks. I give a chuckle at the memory that I'd heard before but forgotten about. I head back to the bar for another wine; I may not notice how drunk my sister is after another one.

I work the room for a while and return to find Mima and Evelyn deep in drunken conversation.

'Leave him,' Mima hisses, 'You are better than that, Evelyn. He doesn't deserve you one bit. Put the house up for sale and split the proceeds. Get yourself a nice, little, city flat and start living for once.'

'Evelyn, should you really be discussing this with Mima, today of all days?' I interject.

'Of course she should,' Mima waves a dismissive hand at me. 'I haven't seen your sister for years, we are having a long overdue catch up, aren't we, Evelyn?'

'Mima, the Reverend is leaving now, would you like to say goodbye?' the ever gentle Ralph whispers to his wife.

'Oh, do excuse me, girls, I'll chat to you in a bit.' Mima negotiates the table with difficulty. I catch the almost empty wine bottle before it hits the floor and my sister gives me a mischievous smile.

'What? Why are you smiling like that, what have you done, Evelyn?'

'Oh, just got that guy's number over there,' she points unashamedly at a very cute, younger man, who winks at her.'

'Evelyn, *no!* You can't pull at a funeral, for goodness sake.'

'It was Mima's idea, actually,' she bristles indignantly.

'It was nice of you to say all those lovely things about Ginny. I think Mima appreciated that.'

'Well, they're true, she was fabulous.'

'But you never got along, you always looked at each other like

shit,' I whisper.
'Pffft! Shows you how little you know, Ivy. There was a reason we were like that. She hated the fact that I married Gerald.' I frown at my sister in confusion and she gives me a wearied look. 'Ginny always wanted *us* to be together. Her and I,' she clarifies.
'But...but you're straight.'
'Am I? Am I really, Ivy? Your best friend didn't tell you everything, you know.' I stare at my sister in open-mouthed shock.
'You and Ginny, you were together?'
'Well, not in the biblical sense but we went out a few times, had a few snogs and then I met Gerald.' I note that she's dropped the 'My.'
'So you're *not* straight?'
'I guess I am, what did Ginny call it...bi-curious?' Evelyn shrugs, 'trust me when I say that I am gutted about her death, we just had so much history that it came across as hating each other to the lesser trained eye.' She tries to tap just below her eye in a mysterious fashion but pokes it instead and blinks furiously. 'See, your man there that I got the phone number from is totally my type, but so is that woman over there,' she points to an achingly trendy friend of Ginny's that I recognize from the gay club. 'I always have had a penchant for hipster chicks,' she shakes her head dismissively and starts to chair dance along to a nineties dance track that comes on Ginny's iPod. I take a deep breath and try to take in the bombshell that my sister has just dropped. She takes off in the direction of Mima and to my horror, drags her on to the dance floor. Ginny's mother seems more than happy with this idea and starts throwing some exuberant shapes herself. A few people stare in muted shock, looking around at each other to check if this is appropriate. Hipster chick grabs her friend and joins in and before long, the dance floor is heaving with mourners, strutting their stuff. I smack my head off the table a few times

to try and wake myself up from this crazy dream, Mum slides in at the side of me with her gin and tonic.
'What on earth has gotten into your sister?' she exclaims.
'Ginny fever, it appears,' I raise my eyebrows, 'I think she would have approved of this, Mum. Don't be too hard on Evelyn; as funerals go, it's certainly lively.' Mum clutches her throat as Evelyn grabs Mima's scarf from her neck, loops it around Ralph's waist and pulls him onto the dance floor too.
'I think I'll tell your Dad it's time that we left,' she blanches as Ralph dips Evelyn, tango-style, on the dance floor.

By seven in the evening and with Mum and Dad long gone, taking my mother's shock at our inappropriateness with them, there is a full blown post-funeral party going on. Evelyn has obtained the phone number of Ginny's female friend too; who found her twinset and pearls ensemble 'ironic.' Evelyn had stated that it was actually moronic and not the real her at all. However, her kids were at a vulnerable age and she wanted to dress like this for now. Turning up at school in 'cool mum' gear would make life far too easy for the little shits. Actually, I'm loving this new and improved sister, who could not give less of a fuck. Far from being inappropriate, it is exactly how Ginny would have wanted things to be; lots of laughter, her choice of music and a shitload of booze. I can imagine her looking down on us all in Nanny's knitted jumper and laughing at all our antics. Even Tasha is up on the dance floor. She's not smiling much, of course, but she is doing her best in celebrating her girlfriend's life with the rest of us. We party on until around eleven, by which time almost everyone is ready to hit the hay. Mima thanks the bar staff at the hotel, for their hospitality. They look a little shell-shocked; never before has a wake gone past a few hours of cups of tea, a limp sandwich and a sausage roll or two. This is a first and the boss will be shamelessly rubbing his hands with glee at this bar bill. Mima and Ralph take

Tasha home to theirs for the night and on Evelyn's insistence we get some chips and go on to the gay bar with some of the others. She already called Gerald before school pick-up time and informed him he would not be working late, going on date or whatever the fuck he had planned for that evening. With a simple 'they are your kids too so suck it up, sunshine,' she had hung up on him and switched her phone off. I had gazed at her in wonder and admiration. She needed tonight, this catharsis of her unfinished business, and I was sure as shit going along for the ride!

Chapter Nineteen

I returned to my job the following week and was grateful for the distraction. My belated training went smoothly and I was thankful for the heavy, evening study I had to put in. I take to my new role as a Team Leader, like a duck takes to water. It's almost like because one of the worst things possible has happened that I no longer have anything to fear. Well not from a work situation anyway. After the funeral, I had mentioned to Tasha that she may want the flat to herself now but she had insisted she couldn't think of anything worse and would I please stay on. I was happy to, of course. I love the home that so reminds me of my best friend and I like being nearby to keep an eye on Tash. She still sleeps with one of Ginny's worn t-shirts and snuggles into her girlfriend's pillow. She was tearful about the fact that the smell of her was already starting to fade. I had no words of comfort so I just hugged her and then we cracked open a bottle of wine, ordered a takeaway and watched Friends re-runs. I don't mention anything that Evelyn has told me about her and Ginny's dalliance. It would only hurt Tasha's feelings and possibly devalue what they had together. Their relationship was true love, Evelyn was merely a fling.

The weeks fly by so quickly, mainly because my job takes over my life and seems to consume most of my time. I take home work that I don't get time to do in working hours, staff appraisals and forecasting to put forward in meetings for what I expect my team to achieve. The weekends seem to take forever to come around and are over in a flash. Friday nights I am too tired to appreciate and by Sunday, I'm raring to go out but I have work the next day. I feel I have one day only that I can fully appreciate the weekend, and that day, Saturday, is taken up with cleaning, shopping and cooking for during the week, when I'm too knackered to be bothered. Tash seems to

be coming to terms with Ginny's death a little now. She smiles a little easier and makes an effort to see friends, once a week. It may be baby steps but at least they're going in the right direction.
Far from being mortified about her behaviour that evening, Evelyn has been liberated. She has found a new flat for her and Matty, in Polwarth; a smart and affluent area much closer to the city than Cortstorphine. After they announced their official split, the children were given the choice of who they wanted to live with. The boys had chosen Gerald, for purely mercenary reasons; they want and Daddy indulges, anything for a quiet life is Gerald's style of parenting. Matilda had immediately answered that she was going with Mummy but would stay at Daddy's for the weekend. Although she had hoped that the boys would choose her too, this had much delighted my sister. It had totally put a pisser on Gerald's social life and his mistress had backed off a little now he was going to be a single Dad. She was only twenty-eight, she didn't want saddled with a couple of gangly, spotty teens and a rather precocious little princess with typical pre-teen attitude. Clandestine dinners out being replaced with fish fingers and chips at 5pm, was not her idea of fun. There were plenty of other married men out there she could move on to.

I saw them out one evening when I'd picked up Matty from after school club. Actually my niece had spotted them, sat in the window of a brasserie in Bruntsfield and had insisted on going in to see Daddy; I was happy to oblige. She was exactly the sort that a woman would spot a mile off, as mistress material. Her glossy, red, fashionable haircut, the tailored work suit that spoke of a high up position when really she was the assistant to the assistant. She was a classic, dress for the job you want, not the job you have, type. The sultry voice, saying hello to my niece with a fake, well-practiced smile on her lips that didn't echo the barely disguised ennui in her eyes. I had given her a look that said, 'kids, huh?' when Matty had enquired, 'Who is *she,* Daddy,' in a rather disdainful tone. She's the type that men would describe as, 'really friendly,' whilst women would reply, 'yes, but funnily enough, only with you and other men.'

Evelyn found a job in her old career of teaching French, in a very posh nearby school, that's named a 'college' just to show the parents that they are so ahead in their education that they are onto the next milestone for their children. Her hours fit in perfectly to pick up Matty from her after school care and take her home to their new flat. At the weekends she goes on dates; sometimes with men and occasionally with women. She refuses to categorise herself and says it's a personality attraction, not a male or female one. She takes the boys out for dinner every Thursday and on another evening of their choice they will often go and see a movie or go bowling. Their lives are busy and they often can't be bothered, but she insists they at least see her once a week. Gerald calls occasionally, when he can't cope with the boys, to ask Evelyn to go back. He wants to give Relate counseling a try to see if they can salvage their marriage. She says he should have appreciated all she did when she was there and no amount of counseling would make her put up with any more of his shit. She said she would be happy to let the boys know the real reason that she left if Gerald feels it would be helpful in their understanding of the situation. She wouldn't of course; she would never utter a bad word against Gerald for the sake of the children. I think the older ones have a pretty good idea anyway, by the amount of Daddy's 'friends' that stay over. Evelyn is pleased she can have a good, strong influence on Matilda, however. She wants to show her that you don't put up with bad treatment from anyone; men included, and instil in her a sense of self-respect that Evelyn herself has been lacking. Judging by the strength of character that my niece has, I doubt that is something that Evelyn will have to worry about. Her monumental strops make Gordon Ramsay look like a pussycat.

Today, it's exactly four weeks until Christmas. I walk through the chilly town centre that sparkles with frost and fairy lights. Princes Street always looks beautiful but never more so, than at this time of year. I take in the view; the picturesque gardens that slope up to the imposing Edinburgh Castle, the gothic looking Scott Monument that towers over me right now and the festive window displays in the stores. I stare in wonder at all the vibrant winter fashions that the stores are offering. Ginny and I loved this time of year; the exciting build up to the festive period, planning party nights out and trawling the stores all weekend looking for quirky and original gifts. We'd make home-made cards and bake Christmas cupcakes to give out to family and friends. The preparations for us started a good six weeks in advance. I don't know that Tasha will want to celebrate this year, let alone put the tree up, and I won't push the issue. I have a holiday to take next week and I'm keeping my promise to Granddad that I will visit and do my Christmas shopping in Kingston and Richmond. I love the buzz of big cities at Christmastime. There are more smiles exchanged, the bored looking shop staff are suddenly pleasant and eager to help. It's as if putting up a few lights transforms our personalities and we are all a little nicer to each other. Once I come back from my holiday I am moving on to managing a larger team of people. This week I have been training a new recruit, who has that familiar bug-eyed, I-can't-cope look that I had, just a few, short months ago. She will do an amazing job with my team; I have every faith in her. Next week is her trial to go it alone and she hasn't had the nasty call from the CEO yet, but I'm expecting it tomorrow. She will cope fine; I've already heard her in action with some of the trickier of customers. I've become numb to the workload; I sense that it was little league compared to what's coming next, for me.

The wind picks up and I pull my coat tighter to me. Last year's winter coat has a few lost buttons and has a large pull in the wool. I glance across at the shops and pause for a few moments. It would be lovely to go and splash out on a new coat. Since I never moved out of Ginny's flat, I never needed to use my deposit for my own place. My overtime pay that was going to be for my new furniture was swallowed up by my credit card bill, that I'd used for my dash to Greece. Not that I mind, I wouldn't have had it any other way. No, I'll hang off shopping for now; there is no fun in doing it alone. I like to have that all-important second opinion when choosing clothes. I pick up my pace again; just stopping for a few moments has allowed the chill to creep in through my worn-out boots. By the time I reach the corner of Lothian Road, a few flakes of snow have begun to whirl around me. I pass some advertising billboards and stop dead in my tracks, causing a woman behind me to crash into me with an armful of gifts. She mutters a few swear words in response to my apology and brushes past me with a loud tut. My eyes go back to the billboard and I wait as it rolls around and changes back to the original advert. There it is! I jump up and down on the spot. 'Love's bleeding heart,' by Conor Byrne. He did it, he made the billboards. So many times I have reread his book review once I'd salvaged it in the fertility clinic. I had Googled him but found out little more than he was with an Edinburgh agency. I knew then that he had probably come up for a meeting with his agent on the day that I saw him and now, his book has been released to the public. The critics had raved about it and I've been checking several times a week for news of its release. How could I have missed the launch in my searches? I dash back onto Princes Street and head for the nearest book shop. I could download it, of course, but I really want the book, it feels more real to me. I smart a little at the fact that he had definitely been in Edinburgh and hadn't called me. He's moved on, was what I had taken from that, and fair enough, I had left without an explanation or even a goodbye. But I could read his words and take pride in the fact that my friend had made it. That would have to be enough. I have to ask where his book is, I had expected at least a display in-store, if not in the window. The sales guy takes me to the alphabetical section and finds three copies under B. Who cares, he has a book out in one of the largest chains in the UK; that would be enough for anyone to dine out on for the next few decades. I race home with my copy and on an impulse, pop in for a pizza from the Italian restaurant downstairs from the flat, it's the best restaurant on Lothian Road and this is a cause to celebrate. I text Tash and when she replies, I order a pepperoni one for her too. I fidget anxiously in the queue, barely unable to keep my hands from stroking over the front cover and reading Conor's words. Finally, I trundle up the stairs with our pizza boxes and stumble into the kitchen, to see Tasha standing knee deep in tinsel.

'It's time,' she smiles, 'it's what Ginny would have wanted, for us to go on as normal.' With an indulgent smile, I set the pizzas down on the table. Of course decorating the flat will come first; my friend's recovery in the grief process takes precedence over anything right now. Tash opens a bottle of Prosecco and I wander down the hall to put Conor's book by my bed for later. I walk back into the room to see that Tasha has put on the Christmas music channel and I take a seat next to her at the table. We eat our pizzas straight out of the box and sip our fizz. A lovely contented silence falls between us but I know we are both thinking the same thing, that Christmas may look the same on the outside but will never be the same without Ginny. By the second glass, our spirits are higher and we singing along to songs of bygone Christmases and stand back to view our handiwork. We string the paper

chain that Ginny made in primary school along the fireplace and the room is complete. We switch off the lights for the official lighting of the tree; this had gone badly wrong last year when we realised the lights were broken and had to take them all off again. Normally I would plug them in whilst they lay on the floor, just to check, but Ginny had insisted that we live life on the edge. There was much swearing and a late night trip to Poundland via the offy after that, but we were sticking with our new tradition of life on the edge. We both gasp as the lights twinkle into action, Tasha puts on the real effect gas fire and flicks through the movie channel.
'Love Actually and a fuck-off slab of chocolate?' Tash smiles, she needs this tonight, it's the most open she has been since Ginny died and I'm all for it.
'I can't think of anything better. Well, apart from doing all that in our jammies.' We race each other down the hall and appear minutes later head to toe in fleece. I glance behind Tasha into her bedroom and note that she finally changed her bedding. She hadn't been able to bear doing it after Ginny died. It's a small but significant, personal victory for her.

I can't remember how many times I have seen this film, but every Christmas it feels like new. This year in particular, the funeral of Liam Neeson's wife fills us with sadness. The scene of Emma Thompson in her bedroom playing Joni Mitchell makes me think of Evelyn. So much has changed in the past year that the movie seems to have a new poignancy. Ginny had declared it soppy shite last year, before apologising once she saw our shocked faces, but we still watched it, as we had every year since we first saw it at the cinema the Christmas it was released. You don't diss Love Actually, it's like, sacrilege or something. By the end of the movie Tasha declares that she is exhausted and is heading to bed. I still have half a glass of Prosecco left so I put the music channel back on and read Conor's book by the light of the tree. The dedication is to someone I don't recognise; a friend it would appear, with RIP after it. I don't know quite why I needed to check that first; perhaps to see if he had a significant other by now. I consume each word with awe and admiration and I'm seriously impressed with the two chapters I've read so far. I'm more chick-lit than crime thriller, usually, but he has written it so that it's easy to picture the scene. The reflection through the window of the woman changing for bed, as the scorned ex-boyfriend watches from out in the darkening street. By the end of the second chapter, my eyes are struggling to stay open. I give in and creep quietly down the hall to bed. Testament to Conor's writing, I sleep with the light on. The killer struck his revenge after he saw the heroine's light go out.

'Conor, you asshole,' I whisper as I drift off into a nightmarish sleep, 'I haven't slept with the light on since I was five.'

I awaken the next morning before my alarm. Excited by the fact that it's Friday and also because this weekend I am catching the train down to my Grandfather's in Richmond. Normally, holidays in the festive season are discouraged but I am long overdue to take my annual leave. Work has been flat out for the last couple of months; I've either been training my new recruits or training myself. I may be on a lot more money now but they're definitely making me work for it, and I'm exhausted. I pick up Conor's book; I have enough time to read another chapter or two since I'm awake so early. I'm in awe of his talents; who knew there was so much going on under that scruffy, too-long hair that he has. I wonder if he has author Facebook page or a Twitter account. I'm torn between wanting to search now and reading some more. Searching wins and I type Conor Byrne author into Facebook. An older guy based in New York pops up and a few random Conors appear underneath, but not mine. I do the same with Twitter but can't find anything there either. Oh well, it was worth a shot, before long he is bound to have a website of some sort, I'm sure his agent will be pushing for all the multi-media side of things. He's a relatively new author, as far as the public are concerned. When I do find a way to get in touch, I'll just leave a friendly congratulations message for him and leave it up to him if he wants to get in touch. I finish chapter three and resist the urge to read more; I'm now bordering on running late and only have ten minutes in the bathroom now before I collide with Tasha's allotted shower time. When Gin was alive, we had an unofficial bathroom schedule so there were no hissy fits or people being late for work. Tash and I just stuck to it afterwards too. It helped make things feel semi-normal, I guess.

The last day at work goes surprisingly quickly and before I know it, the clock is telling me it's just after five. I had popped out at lunchtime to collect my tickets from the train station. Ten o'clock tomorrow morning and I will be on my way to London. I really can't wait, Richmond at Christmas, shopping and dinners out with Granddad and for once, money in my pocket to spend. I plan to be in bed by nine, just so the morning comes around more quickly. I arrive home and pull out my case from the back of the walk-in cupboard. I'm only going to pack a few items of clothing as I'm planning on buying most of my winter wardrobe down there. I pop my sketch pad in too, just for old time's sake. It'll be far too cold to sit out but I can always draw from photographs, taken with my phone and printed out on photography paper. Either that or I could sit in a café and draw the scenes outside. I am a little shy at showing off my work, however, so this doesn't appeal quite so much. By the time my large case is a third full, I decide that this is plenty and zip it shut. I wander down the hall to the kitchen and rummage in the freezer for something for tea. My choices appear to be a tray of ice cubes or a few frozen peas that have escaped from their bag at some stage.

The cupboard turns out much the same in the way of fare, a bashed tin of peaches, a jar of out of date pasta sauce or a battered and slightly torn cup a soup, of unidentifiable flavour. I grab a bundle of takeaway menus instead and wander through to the front room with a glass of wine to peruse them. Tasha is out tonight with some friends. I have noticed a change in her over the past week; she is slowly but surely moving forward from Ginny's death. The bedroom remains exactly how they left it before the holiday, apart from changing the sheets. Gin's laundry is still in the basket and she hasn't cleaned. But she put the tree up, that in itself is nothing short of a miracle. I call for a Chinese takeaway and change into my jammies. I do love living with Tash but it's always a buzz to get a night in to myself no matter who I am living with. I scroll through the channels and settle on the Christmas twenty-four one. A cheesy, festive movie will top my evening off nicely; I smile to myself and hug my fleece covered knees to me. For the first time in months, things feel more settled. It saddens me a little, how things carry on as normal, regardless of who has left us. I know it has to; Gin wouldn't have wanted it any other way. We go on with our lives as normal but with a hollow in our hearts and a huge Ginny shaped hole in our lives. The doorbell interrupts my thoughts and I grab my purse and head for the door. The delivery driver looks me up and down and laughs at my ensemble of fleece. Who cares, I'm cosy, I'm on holiday and I couldn't give a shit. Just as I'd promised myself, I'm in bed for nine. I read another two chapters of Conor's book and switch my light out and then back on again. Reading a crime thriller in an empty house was not my best move. I awaken briefly around eleven when I hear Natasha stumble in, and finally feel brave enough to embrace the darkness.

Chapter Twenty

I'm awakened by my alarm at 8am; sitting up sharply from the horror my nightmare and feeling momentarily confused as to where I am. That bloody book! In my horrific dream I was bound and tied in a cellar. A faceless man loomed over me with his knife glinting in the light of a match. He was tormenting me, mentally. He told me he had already killed Ginny and Tash, leaving their bodies on a beach. I was to be his next victim and then he was going after Evelyn. My fear slowly dissipates as I glance out of my window at the low winter sun. I've taken to sleeping with my curtains open, as the street lamp outside ensures that my room is never completely dark. I've never been a fan of scary movies and books, for this exact reason. If it wasn't Conor's book then it would be in the local Oxfam shop by now. I'm only sticking with it because he wrote it and now I've started, I'm intrigued. I glance at the novel on my bedside table warily. Maybe I shall stick to daytime reading from now on, these batshit crazy dreams are scaring the bejeezus out of me.

So, today I'm off to London; I give a little squeal and throw back my duvet. I can't wait to see my Granddad, it has only been a few months but it feels like the longest time. I know that it's only because so much has happened between then and now. Granddad had been so saddened by Ginny's death and shocked by Evelyn's abrupt ending of her marriage. He had hoped to come up to attend Ginny's funeral but I had put him off, due to it coinciding with a chiropractor appointment he had to attend at the hospital for his newest ailment, an increasingly painful back. Everyone knew he cared and he'd sent the prettiest bouquet to the church. His health had to come first and he had reluctantly complied. This recurring cough has been worrying us all too, but as it seems to improve with antibiotics, the GP hasn't referred him for a chest X-ray.

He has now had three courses of pills; the last ones were really hardcore, for treating superbugs and the like. He quit smoking thirty years ago so he isn't particularly worried. Also, he refuses to take the train as he can drive up for half the cost. We all hate the thought of him travelling up the M1 and M6, his eyes and reactions aren't quite what they used to be. He manages the fairly short journey from Richmond to his Dukes Meadow allotment, but even now he complains about the A316 and its heavy traffic.

My train leaves in two hours but I'm already packed and have my tickets. I pop Conor's book into my handbag and head off for my shower when I hear Tasha finish in the bathroom. I've just switched off the water when she knocks on the bathroom door.

'That's me off to work, Ivy. Have a lovely trip, see you next week.'

'Thanks, Tasha. I'll give you a tinkle midweek, for a catch up.' It's more that I want to check that she's coping on her own. I'm confident that she will be absolutely fine; it's probably even more so for my own peace of mind than Tasha's. I'm not convinced I'd be even half as brave as she is being if it were the love of my life, to be honest. Christmas will be tough for all of us this year; perhaps a week to reflect on things will be good for her. Every Saturday she goes down to Ginny's grave with fresh flowers and tidies away the old ones. I went with her once and she just sits cross-legged on the ground and tells Ginny all about her week. I had felt a bit intrusive and had left her to go on her own after that; it's her ritual and not one that I should be part of. Mima still calls a couple of times a week to check we were both OK; it's good for us to find out how they are coping too. Tasha has been round for dinner a couple of times; I'm so pleased that they're nurturing a continuing bond with their daughter's girlfriend.

I reach Waverley station with half an hour to spare. I pick up some food for the journey from the bakery and wait on my platform with a buzz of excitement in my stomach. I've already called Granddad and told him I will take the tube to his, I'll be heading into London around rush hour and it's less hassle for both of us this way. He sounds as hyper about the visit as I do and has booked us into a restaurant for dinner at seven. The boys are looking forward to seeing me too; I've missed the calming influence of the cats. I'd love to have one if we didn't live in on the busy Lothian Road, with no garden. I pick up a Metro newspaper from one of the stands, idly flicking through while I wait for the opening of the gate to board the train. I scan the headlines, yet more bad news. I quickly move on to the inside and read my horoscope, flicking on to the entertainment section. There is much hype in London over the long awaited tour of girl group, Slutz! They will be playing at Twickenham stadium on Saturday night. I'm not a big fan of their music but they are huge within the mid-teen age group; probably due to their rather controversial name as opposed to their music. I suppose you'd call them pop, although they class themselves as Indie Rock. Lead singer Marissa is renowned for her loud opinions and went crazy on a chat show recently where the rather antagonistic host had referred to them as pop-tarts. Well with a name like Slutz! you'd have to be prepared for some kind of comparison to other persons of ill repute. I scan over their attitude laden photo shoot; I can see why they'd appeal to a teenage market with their faces like a smacked arse. The boys all want to date them and the girls desperately want to be them. An image such as theirs can't have a long shelf life; I mean, their ages range from twenty-four to twenty-eight. Mardy isn't the best of looks by the time you hit your thirties. I'm about to turn the page when a smaller picture further down catches my eye, entitled 'Marissa out in Leicester square last week with author boyfriend, Conor Byrne.' I re-read the text in disbelief.

Really? Conor and Marissa? Obviously I don't know her personally but given her public persona, I would not have put those two together. Conor is just so chilled out and I imagine she would be a pretty high maintenance girlfriend. I gaze sadly at the photo; Conor a few steps behind while she graced the limelight, clutching his hand territorially. He's moved on, what did I expect? That he'd be pining for me and waiting for me to throw a few scraps of affection his way? No, of course not. I fold up the newspaper and tuck it under my arm, a little bit of my shine has gone. Well, at least he will be easy to look up now. Anywhere that she is, he will be, I guess.

The guard waves us through and I walk down the platform, looking for my carriage. I spent the first hour of my journey Googling Marissa. There's only one other reference to Conor in an interview for Heat magazine last week, in which she gushes about how talented he is. She hasn't read his book yet but he had admired her for so long that she's sure the lead character is about her. They both have blond hair, after all. She goes on to say how fed up she was of dating fellow musicians as she struggles with not being the star attraction in a relationship. 'My number one dating rule is they can't be more famous than me,' she had said. Typical believe-your-own-hype sort. Cheeky cow; how must that make Conor feel? She had only become famous by dating a variety of Indie musicians in the first place. She'd been a glorified groupie since she was fresh out of high school and was terrible live, so I've heard. Auto-tune can make anyone a famous singer these days. Gosh, I'm embracing my inner bitch today. This has unnerved me somewhat; not only could Conor do better, like...ahem, moi, but she's also taking the piss out of him very publicly. He will be famous on his own merit, not by any trail that she has blazed for him. I open up my sandwich and my bottle of water and start on chapter four of Conor's book. The heroine has now been replaced in my mind to some ratty

haired wannabe and this annoys me greatly. Before, she had been a polished, glamorous woman, ordinarily fearless of everything but scared witless by her unknown stalker. The new version has the lead character bad-mouthing her stalker to the press and him seeking revenge. I now find that I'm enjoying her fear instead of sympathising with the horror of the situation. With a sigh, I snap the book shut and place it on the table. Can it really only be Newcastle that we're pulling into? I wait until passengers leaving have alighted and the new ones boarded and head down to my case to dig out my sketch pad. Drawing is like therapy to me; I manage to completely lose myself in my art. I always have done, even as a small child I remember the soothing scratch of pencils on paper. Most of my pocket money went on art supplies and I prided myself on starting each art session with perfectly sharpened pencils. None of my family were ever stuck for Christmas and birthday presents for me. Whereas, Evelyn was a book worm and never out of the library. We used to sit in amicable silence in our local one. I would draw for hours until my arm cramped and Evelyn would relent and reluctantly traipse me off home. Our parents were keen for us to be well read and my sister and I had struck a deal; I would let her use my library card to satisfy her voracious appetite for books and she would tell me roughly what they were about for when Mum interrogated me about them. Evelyn tried to get me into books more by reading to me sometimes at night. We had differing tastes; her favourite was, and still is, Little Women. Mine was Charlotte's web. I had bought her the first edition of the classic for her twenty-first birthday and she was so delighted, she was nice to me for a whole month after.
I'm so lost in my thoughts, that when I break to order a coffee from the passing buffet trolley and glance back at my work, I see that I've drawn a sketch of Nanny standing over her chipped baking bowl in her apron, wooden spoon in hand. Her cardigan and slippers are the ones I remember from

childhood. It's a side view of her but it's my Nanny to a tee. On the floor at her feet, the kitten versions of Archie and Dave glance up at her; Archie, as ever, raising a curious paw towards her, in the hope of a taster. My Granddad is going to love this one. I may surprise him with it in a frame to say thank you for letting me stay. Mind you, the pressure is then on for him to put it up and he may not want to. I'll see what he says first; I can always buy a frame later. I place it in my file and on Conor's suggestion from months ago, I decide to do another 'Fundon' sketch. By the time we have pulled into Kings Cross station, I'm done. As suggested, I've drawn the Prime Minister in a jellied eel van. I'll work on Boris on the London Eye through the week. I pack away my pad and grab my case, before jumping off the train and heading towards the sign for the Underground.

I call Granddad from Richmond station and arrive at his house fifteen minutes later. He hears the bus rumble by and stands with a beaming smile at his back gate. I quickly look both ways before running across the road, I'm home, I'm really home. My Granddad squeezes me until I'm struggling to breathe, before holding me back to take a good look.
'You've lost weight, Ivy, and you look so grown up. Must be all the stress from that big, important city job you have now.'
You look great, Granddad,' I smile, and he does, he has the rosy glow in his cheeks back and has put on a little weight again. His chest doesn't have that rasping sound that it had in the summer. He takes my case and we walk up the path together, arm in arm. The kitchen is warm and bright after the darkness of the winter sky. Archie jumps down from the old rocking chair and walks over to me for a good sniff, Dave rolls over, opening one sleepy eye to check me over, before settling back down on the rug. I scoop up Archie and nuzzle into his soft fur. He smells of wood smoke and leaves. I have missed all my Richmond boys and immediately feel comfortable and

relaxed. Granddad ladles me up a mulled wine, as is our Christmas tradition and pops out a plate of warm mincemeat pies on the table.
'Right, me old china, we have an hour before we have to leave for the restaurant so I want to hear all about what's been happening with you. I don't know where to start. Ginny's death has been by miles the main thing that has been on my mind. We talk about it for most of the time we have to spare and over two glasses of mulled wine. Granddad shakes his head sadly as I tell him all about the awful trip to Greece but we have a good laugh over the Rev's words at the service and at Evelyn's antics at the wake. With a start, we realise we will need to leave in the next five minutes; so lost were we in our conversation we never even noticed the time. I slick on a bit of lipgloss and pull a comb sitting by the hall mirror through my hair. Granddad laughs when he informs me that it's his flea comb for the boys and at least he knows I'm clean now. I roll my eyes at my stupidity, shrug on my coat and grab my bag, ready to go. We wait in the chilly night air for the bus back up to Richmond. I really need to go shopping tomorrow. Every part of my body is freezing. Granddad is surprisingly good fun to shop with. He has the impeccable taste of a man who has seen many a timeless classic.
'Here we are,' he blows on his hands and the steam from his breath fills the air, as the bus rounds the corner. All the way through Richmond, I gasp at the six foot trees adorning the front windows of the grand houses. Oh to be able to afford one of these. As if reading my mind, Granddad leans in and whispers,
'One day, love.' I raise my eyebrows to say 'as if,' and he laughs. Life just doesn't go that way for the likes of me; Granddad may think I'll make CEO but I don't.
'I reckoned that after tea you might help decorate my tree with me. You have a good eye for detail like your Nanny. She would always rearrange the ornaments I put up,

apparently you should space the colours out and not have two the same together.

'She was right, too, yes, I'd love to help you. It's my favourite part of Christmas, I think. Oh, actually maybe the shopping, or wrapping presents.' Granddad gives a chuckle.

'You've always been the same; you love every part of Christmas. Even as a little girl you were the same,' Granddad smiles nostalgically as we make our way down the bus.

'So this new place, what kind of food does it do?'

'Pub grub, gastro pub, I suppose. Not as nouveau cuisine as a gastro pub but definitely not scampi in a basket, either.'

'Sounds good to me, but tonight is all about the company and the sparkling wit of my lovely, old Grampy.'

'Hey, less of the old. I'm still a fine specimen of a man. You haven't called me Grampy for a few years,' he ruffles my flea combed hair. We take our seats and Granddad perches his glasses on the end of his nose and holds the menu out at arm's reach.

'Jeezo, it better be good, look at these prices, Granddad,' I exclaim.

'Well, you're worth it, and anyway, tonight is somewhat of a celebration.'

'Yes, it sure is. I know it's not that long since I've been down but it feels like forever.'

'No, I mean your art sales.' I frown my confusion at my Grandfather, he smiles enigmatically.

'But I'm not planning on selling any, Granddad. Oh, that reminds me,' I pull out the file I grabbed from my case and stuffed into my oversized handbag. 'Look what I did for you on the train.' I hand him the portrait of Nanny and his eyes cloud over with memories.

'Ivy, I don't know what to say,' he tilts his head as he looks at it from all angles. 'You've captured her perfectly; I even remember those old slippers and cardigan. Oh, look at my boys!' he laughs, with more than a smidge of emotion. 'You

should be doing this as a career,' he says seriously. 'And the celebration is that after I'd scanned your lovely drawings, of course, well…I sold them.' I stare at my Granddad in shock.
'Who to? Who would want them? They're not good enough to *sell,* Granddad,' I whisper across the table.
'Well, this art collector thought they were. I got chatting to him in a pub in town and he wanted to take a look. He collects all things 'London' and he adored your 'Fundon' one in particular. Reckons you could put them in a gallery, or something.' The waitress comes over to see if we're ready and I'm in such a state of shock, I shrug and indicate to my Granddad. He laughs and tells her we will both have the steak and a bottle of Pinot Noir. Granddad, reluctant to tear his eyes from Nanny, flicks to my next drawing, the jellied eel van one with the Prime Minister. His laughter booms across the restaurant and a couple at the next table smile our way. He reaches across to show them my sketch and they laugh along with him.
'That's my Granddaughter,' he announces proudly, 'Ivy Efferson. Remember her name, you'll be hearing a lot of her.'
'No, Granddad, shush, *please,*' I beg, blushing furiously.
'Well done, dear,' says the man, 'Today Richmond Quadrant, tomorrow Tate gallery.' My Grandfather gives me a superior look.
'See, I told you you're a fantastic artist, Ivy.'
'So, who is this guy? How much did he pay for my scribbles?'
'Oh, just over a grand for the three. He wants more London ones though, so you best get to work. He will be back at the end of the week to see me. I told him that should be enough time to get some more together.' The wine arrives and I take a large gulp to numb my shock. 'Ivy, seriously though, you could make a living from this. I know they say artists are never rich until they die, but that guy, he really sees the same potential in you that I do. You don't need to make any rash decisions right now, but I really do think you should consider

putting together a collection to sell. Look at that,' he holds out my drawing, 'I'm actually holding an original Ivy Efferson sketch.'
'That she just scribbled out on the Flying Scotsman,' I laugh.
'Why do you think I told you those Richmond Hill houses were within your reach, Missy? So many people believe that their hidden talents should remain just that. Take a leap of faith and share them with the world. What have you got to lose? Bugger all, my love.' I nod mutely, looking around the restaurant as if the people in here represent the world. For the first time it months, the colours seem brighter. I feel like since after that day in the park, as I wandered happily through the autumn leaves, that I've been seeing in black and white. The world seems vibrant all of a sudden; perhaps it's the wine but at this moment, right now, I do feel like anything could be possible. I feel like I've been in a cloud of depression since I lost my beautiful, funny and gregarious friend and that nothing could ever be good again. Another promotion at work? Meh! Big deal, didn't they know I don't care about shit like that anymore? I'd developed a new found tolerance, if not love, for the more difficult members of my family, and it had paid off. Evelyn and I had grown close again and I was surprised to discover that under that lacquered hair and away from Gerald, that she really had been the same sister all along. Maybe she hadn't ever changed and it was just my perception of her that had. Perhaps it said more about my feelings of failure than what she had ever thought of me. She has chilled out so much these days and had even relented and allowed Matty her own Facebook page, which she monitors closely. She had made me laugh at some of the things she had learned about her daughter through reading her updates; particularly that she appeared to be in a relationship, with a boy in her class. When Matilda had changed her relationship status to 'it's complicated,' my sister had called me up in disbelief and asked how that could be possible. Had he pulled the head off

her Barbie, or something? I had laughed so much at that. Our steaks arrive and Granddad pours a generous amount of blue cheese sauce over his, before topping up our glasses.
'You've gone quiet, Granddaughter. Are you in shock?'
'Quite the opposite, Grandfather, everything seems so much clearer right now. I think I just needed to be home to feel it.' He smiles and gives me a knowing look.
'You have always been that way, you know. A Richmond girl at heart; any time you had bother in school I'd summon you. Your Dad always knew a trip down here would sort you out. You went home a different child once you'd been here. It's like your spiritual home, I guess. Maybe it's a past life thing.' I laugh and look at my Granddad in disbelief. 'What? I may not be religious but I'm spiritual, you know. Your Nanny hasn't gone far; she just can't nag me the same. I'll just enjoy the peace and quiet till she comes to fetch me and it all starts over.' We both chortle at this and clink our glasses together in an impromptu toast to Nanny. The food in here is amazing, it's like my taste buds have woken up from their deep sleep along with my colour vision. Granddad is so right, this is my home. If I thought for one second that I could make a serious living with my art, then I'd be down here like a shot. No more long shifts, grabbing a pizza on the way home and the most fleeting of evenings sharing a bottle of wine with Tash before we head to bed, only to rejoin the rat-race again tomorrow. Don't get me wrong, I adore Tash and living with her is fantastic, but we don't get the quality of time that we'd both like. Eat, work, sleep. Rinse and repeat. It's a constant hamster wheel of nothingness. Just imagine, my office could be the river bank, or Covent Garden, or Embankment. It could be wherever takes my fancy and only dependent on the weather. I look at my Grandfather in awe, what is it about him that makes me feel like anything could happen?

Chapter Twenty-One

We arrive back to Granddad's house and this time I had glanced out at my opulent surroundings with a new intent. If my Granddad believed I could do it, maybe I should try too. Sure, it would take a lot of thousand pound sales to save up for one of these but who knows. Granddad had suggested I move on from drawing and attempt painting and suggests we go to the art supplies shop in Kingston tomorrow. We drag in the Christmas tree from the garden and into the front room. He had it delivered earlier today and hid it as a surprise for me. He places it in the stand and cuts it from the restraints. The branches spring to life and immediately the room fills with the festive smell of pine. It towers way above my head and I gasp in admiration, now it properly feels like Christmas. Granddad puts on his beloved Classic FM and an instrumental version of Silent Night surrounds us. I grin in excitement and run to the kitchen for the remainder of the mulled wine. We sing along to the carols and I attempt to teach Granddad how to space out the colours properly.
'Just imagine that they are potato plants or pumpkins, Granddad. You wouldn't put them too close together.'
'Now, young Ivy, if Nanny had put it like that I would have known exactly what I was doing,' he looks at me in mock amazement. An hour later and the tree lights glisten in the darkened room. Granddad's boys come to investigate; sniffing the branches, pawing the baubles and playing hide and seek in the lower branches. I pick up Dave for an impromptu, drunken waltz to Vivaldi's 'Winter' and Granddad does the same with Archie. Eventually we flop onto the sofa and pick up our glasses.
'Granddad, you're a tonic. I can't remember the last time I had such a fun night.'
'I know what you mean, Ivy,' he scratches his bald patch thoughtfully. 'I haven't had this much fun since you were

down here last. Sure, me and the boys tick along fine but we were kind of lost without you.' With a pang of guilt, I think about Natasha. How would she feel if I were to move and leave her all alone in the flat? From three of us to one. It's a bit soon to be abandoning her like that. Granddad reads my expression.
'She'd be fine, you know, I managed when Nanny died. We are tougher than we look.' I nod unconvincingly.
'Yes, she probably would but I'd rather talk to her first if you don't mind. I can say you've suggested it and see what she says. But what about my job?'
'Well, that's something you have to decide on. Do you love it? Or do you just enjoy the fact that someone has recognised your worth at last? Because if it's the latter, then I don't consider you as losing anything at all. You've been good at all your jobs, Ivy. You just haven't had the praise and the opportunities that you deserved.' I nod my understanding as I mull this over, yes, I like my job but do I love it? Probably not. Would I give it all up to make a living from my art? Definitely! Take a leap of faith, hmm. I'm not a big leaper, to be honest. What foresight does my Granddad have that I don't know about? We finish up our glasses of wine and head up to bed. Archie trails behind me, as usual, and I notice he is finding it more of a struggle these days. My poor old men, as dad would say, 'old age doesn't come itself.'

I'm wakened by the low winter light streaming into my bedroom, at 10am. I smile as I snuggle back into the duvet, and the realisation dawns that I'm in Richmond. I listen as Granddad potters about in the kitchen, chatting away to Archie and Dave. Such comforting sounds. I swing my legs out of bed and put on Nanny's slippers, which I have unofficially inherited. I wander downstairs and hug my Grandfather good morning. He sweeps his arm out in an officious manner and I take a seat at the table. He places a

plate of scrambled eggs, bacon and toast in front me.
'Thank you, I'm so looking forward to today Granddad, I need a whole new winter wardrobe and painting materials, that's our shopping list. Oh, and I'm treating you to lunch today, no arguments.'
'That sounds good to me. Thank you. So, we never got round to talking about your sister. Is she enjoying her new single status these days? '
'Yes, loving it, she's like a different person, actually. She even mentioned coming down with me the next time I come and see you.' Granddad raises his eyebrows in disbelief.
'My, my, she really has changed.'
'It's a shame the boys didn't want to stay with her, but Matty is loving all the attention from her Mum. She sees the boys at least once a week but they've gone kind of bratty these days. I think Gerald just gives them money to shut them up and Evelyn isn't in his league financially. She wouldn't pay them off anyway. As a teacher, she believes in discipline, not bribery.'
'It's never good to buy a child's affection or good behaviour,' Granddad tuts, 'she has the right approach.
'Yeah, for sure, she's given the boys Latin names due to the fact they've turned into complete little shits in her absence. Bratticus Maximus and Painicus Arsicus,' I giggle.
Granddad lets out a booming laugh that startles both cats.
'I'm loving this new Evelyn, she's very funny,' he wipes his eyes with the back of his hand. 'She always was amusing with her older-than-her-years, dry wit. She just lost herself for a while by being around Gerald. She kind of moulded herself to fit into the role of his wife instead of him accepting who she was. Why do some people try to change their partners? Surely the way they are is what attracted you to them in the first place.' Granddad takes my plate away and I shrug my reply. I had tried to change Will, I suppose, but that was for health reasons; drinking as much as he did isn't healthy for

anyone.

I head off upstairs to get ready. I love shopping in Kingston; all the same stores that central London has but without the risk of losing an eye in the crowds. Granddad rarely ventures further than Richmond or the lotty unless I'm around but he always has a great time when he does. We catch the bus opposite the house and I admire all the mock Tudor homes on our journey. Now these are more in an affordable range but not quite as grand as Richmond Hill. Tomorrow, I will try out my new paints; it's something I've never felt too confident in doing, it just seems a bit too much like proper art for me to be comfortable with, but I've promised Granddad, so I'll give it a try. Stepping into the art supply shop is like entering a different world for me. I feel like a kid in a sweet shop as I lovingly stroke the brushes and admire the easels. The tranquility of the atmosphere calms me; now this is a job I could see myself really loving. Not some crazy call centre atmosphere. Granddad was right; I hadn't really thought about if I love the job that I do, I was just flattered by the fact that somebody had told me that I did it well. The rather bohemian owner of the shop takes my questions very seriously; as if I could indeed be the next Monet. All around the shop he has displayed his own artwork, with prices ranging from £250 for a small one up to £1500 for a large mural type painting of Richmond deer park. The quality of his work is so high that it makes me feel like a fraud for even wanting to try. He assures me that he started off exactly the same way as I did, with sketches, and once I get used to it, I will be fine. He sells around two paintings per month but has an exhibition planned for a city centre gallery in a few months. People like supporting local artists, he had encouraged. I feel a little buzz in my stomach at the thought of being classed as a local.

Granddad and I move on to the Bentall shopping centre to begin my search for a winter wardrobe. He persuades me to try on a bright red, wool coat that I wouldn't have even looked twice at. I tend to stick to 'safe' colours, black with a splash of bold detail, maybe, but Granddad comments on how striking it looks against my dark hair, and the new me decides to go for it. I buy two new jumpers, some skinny jeans, a skirt and a dress for Christmas nights out. I'm starting to feel a little nervous about my blow-out until Granddad reminds me about my sales from my sketches and we decide I just have to have a new pair of boots and some sparkly heels too. There's nothing like a spending spree that you can actually afford to make you feel good about yourself. I can kiss goodbye to all my art sale money with today's purchases but Granddad assures me that I've earned it so I deserve to spend it. He refuses my offer of a new coat for himself, due to the fact he has five but still favours the same battered, wax jacket that Nanny bought him years ago. He relents over a new pair of wellies for the lotty, as his have a hole in them. I sneak in a pair of thermal gloves and a hat, for his Christmas present, when his back is turned, and then we head off for lunch in O'Neills. Just being in an Irish pub makes my mind wander to thoughts of Conor. I find myself wondering if he goes along to his girlfriend's gigs. He could be so nearby right now and I wouldn't know it. It would have made my trip compete to have a catch-up night out with him. We take our seats in a booth by the window and Granddad notices my expression.

'Not quite as grand as your young friend's old pub, but not far off it,' he casts a critical eye around the premises.

'I've always loved this place, we've had some fun days out in here, Granddad,' I expertly deflect the conversation from talk of Conor, marveling at how my Grandfather seems to have the ability of mind-reading, at times.

'Did you ever think of contacting him after you broke up with Will? I thought you two made quite a nice pair.'

'I couldn't, Will went into my phone and deleted all my call history and Conor's number. I called the pub but he had already gone back to Dublin. Anyway, he has a girlfriend now and she's in one of the biggest bands in the UK.'
'Does he now? Oh that's right, I'd forgotten that controlling idiot had ruined any chance of that.' Granddad gives me an amused expression, 'and how did you happen upon this information about his girlfriend?'
'Oh, it was in the Metro. He's an author now, he's better suited to a high profile partner these days.'
'I see,' Granddad looks thoughtful for a second before snapping out of his reverie and picking up the menu. 'Right, let's see what delights they have in here since we were last in.'
I head to the bar for Granddad's real ale and a white wine for me. He let that conversation go surprisingly quickly, but with no way of contacting Conor there isn't much I can do; even he can see that. We order our usual of Irish stew and soda bread and chat excitedly about Christmas. I've already thought about coming down to spend it with Granddad; he would often come up to Edinburgh but he hated leaving the boys now they were old and frail. I voice my wishes to Granddad and he beams at me.
'Of course I'd love you to be here. Will Tasha be fine on her own?'
'Oh, she's already told me she's going to Ralph and Mima's, Christmas Eve to Boxing Day. Evelyn is at Mum and Dad's but I'd rather poke myself in the eye with a shitty stick than see Mum tanked up on gin and complaining about Dad's inferior cooking. So, I guess you'll be stuck with me.'
'And what about a permanent move? Will you talk to Tasha about it when you get back? Two weeks' notice you have to give?' I nod my agreement. I'd been most surprised that it wasn't the standard one month but that's what was in my contract. 'Well there you are then; you could come for Christmas and not go home.' I inhale deeply, it's a huge risk

but so very appealing. I give my Grandfather a worried glance.
'Live a little, Ivy. Life is too short to do something you don't love. All those years your Nanny and I saved for our little cottage, we could have done it before we really did. I won't get that time back with her now. Don't have regrets, me love.'
He's right, I know he is. If this art buyer wants more and has suggested I do an exhibition, I could live quite happily on a few sales a month. It's just the insecurity of it all that unnerves me, there is no guarantee of an income.
'OK, I will chat to Tash as soon as I get back. Work won't be happy, though. They've just promoted me again and I haven't even started my new job yet.'
'Who cares? Will you ever see any of them again? Team Leaders are ten a penny to the likes of them. We are talking about real creative talent and your happiness here. This buyer will be round again to discuss with you what else he wants from you, before you go back. Work on your other 'Fundon' one and see if you can have a painting to show him too. He's really keen.'
'I will do, Granddad, I'm planning on starting early tomorrow morning. I should be able to get it done if I work flat out. How exciting that someone loves my work. What's he like, this buyer?'
'He seems a good guy, youngish, but then fifty seems young to me, these days. A bit "luvvy." Wouldn't know if he's good looking or not. Men can't tell that sort of thing. He's a friendly enough chap; I think you'll like him.' Granddad mops his soda bread in his gravy and I contemplate what my first painting should be of. Local sights, maybe? The river would be a good start but so would the bustling Richmond Quadrant. I could take a few pictures to work from; maybe head down there to catch the early evening light. That's always when it feels most festive to me; just as the shops are closing always gives me that last minute Christmas Eve feel.

Granddad gets off the bus with all our bags while I stay on to Richmond. I have a good enough camera on my phone to be able to print off pictures to work with. I'm excited at the thought of painting; the colours really do come alive compared to sketches. The thought of captivating my favourite ever place, forever in my work, warms me. I could even aim for a spring collection if I'm doing this as a full-time job. How nice to start the year with an ambition like that. I jump off the bus and cross over to where the Christmas tree stands. I try a few angles before finding the perfect one. People with brightly coloured carrier bags scurry by, as the light begins to fade from the sky. The people are clear as day in the picture but the tree lights have an ethereal haze around them from my flash, if I can translate this on to a painting it will look fantastic. I take a few more shots before jumping back on the bus and heading for home. A quiet night in with Granddad and an early night is just what I need before beginning my new project and the new chapter of my life.

Chapter Twenty-Two

The next few days pass in a flurry of frustration. My first two attempts at the painting of Richmond Quadrant were scrapped with an angry shout that woke Granddad from his nap. He appeared, tousled and confused, in the doorway to see what the problem was. He didn't think it looked so bad but I'm a perfectionist. The microscopic smudge may not be visible to Granddad but it was all I could see as I tried to paint on. By attempt three, I'd started to get the hang of it, but wasn't quite happy enough with the result. I abandoned the idea in favour of my sketch, of Boris on the London Eye, which had taken just over two hours. Granddad had laughed when he saw it, which gave me the impetus to give the painting a go again. By just after lunch, I was ready to try once more. After a deep breath and the scrapping of yet another, I finally had a painting that I was reasonably happy with. I placed it in the summer house, out of reach of curious paws and decided to call it a day. The next morning I had headed out to take more photographs. The snow whirled around me as I walked along through Petersham, Terrace Gardens dramatic landscape would make the perfect scene for a painting. The barren trees stark blackness against the snowy hill, the little café in the middle which although closed, would come alive if I painted a warm yellow glow in the window. At the top of the hill stands an army of eye-wateringly expensive homes that I'm sure Granddad said one of the Rolling Stones used to live in. I had sighed at the thought of having a view like that to look out on; not just the gardens themselves but just beyond the underpass, where the river Thames snakes by. I had taken a few more snaps before heading back for home through the now heavy snow. Thankfully I had my new, warm coat on with my hat and gloves. Granddad had taken one look at the sky and dug out Nanny's old wellies from the back of the wardrobe. I was grateful for them as I crunched my way through the snow, back along the riverside path. Tomorrow, the art buyer will be here. Nervous anticipation fills my stomach at the thought of having to show this stranger my offerings. I have no idea if my paintings will cut it in the competitive world of art. I already know that he loves my sketches; luckily I have the opportunity to see firsthand what he thinks before I do something stupid like pack in a job that could also be promising, in a less risky way. I stand back and cast a critical eye over my latest effort. It's not too bad for a first attempt. I contemplate trying again but I'm running out of time. This bigger one has taken all day; I haven't got the hours left tomorrow and I really don't think I can do this all night too. I call for Granddad to come and take a look. 'Do not touch another thing, it's perfect the way it is. Simple, yet striking, less is definitely more with this one. I just know the buyer is going to love this, Ivy. Richmond is quite close to his heart, he told me that last week. '

'Yes, I think you're right, actually. I'm only going to mess it up if I add anything more, let's quit while we're ahead, shall we?' Granddad helps me to carry my painting through to the summer house. He stands back to admire both paintings together.

'You know, if I thought I could afford these, I'd tell this guy to sod off,' he laughs, 'but you need to make the big time, young lady, so I'm willing to let these pass.' I give my Grandfather a squeeze and we walk back into the house together. I lay on the rug in front of the fire like I used to do when I was younger. Dave reluctantly budges over a bit to accommodate me and I put my arm around his small body, inhaling his warm, kitty smell. This is exactly how I used to lie; same rug, same cat, same position. I must have dozed off because the next thing I know, Granddad is waking me to come through for his legendary roast beef with all the trimmings. If only I could find a man like him, I'd never have another thing to complain about in my life.

Friday morning arrives; my stomach flips over with the realisation that today is the day. I had the most amazing dream in which I was graciously greeting people at the opening of my exhibition. I wore a long, sparkling black, designer dress, with my hair in some technically styled up-do. I had glanced at myself in the dark window as my guests arrived and saw although my make-up was minimal; I had a shock of scarlet lipstick to highlight my look. It's never occurred to me to be brave enough to try a bold red, and I make a mental note to pick some up when I'm next in town. I wander towards the stairs, in my housecoat and slippers but as I pass Granddad's door, I see that he's still in bed. It's unheard of for him to sleep in any later than six; a fallback from his old market trader days when he would be up to catch the early morning commuters. I creep to his door and peek into his room. He lies perfectly still on his side, facing away from me and a chill fills my heart. No! Please be all right Granddad. I shake him gently; his skin has a waxy, pallor to it that terrifies me.
'Granddad, Granddad! Wake up!' I shake him harder and he looks up at me sleepily.
'I'm not dead, Ivy, he gives a throaty laugh, but it turns into a coughing fit. 'I'm just not feeling too good. I think I'm coming down with a bloody cold.'
'Oh, thank God,' I gasp in relief; I thought you were a goner there.' He sits up with difficulty.
'You don't get rid of me that easily, you know. One day this house will be yours, but not quite yet.' I stare at him sadly. He's often joked that since I'm the only one who visits him that the Back-Arse of Beyond would be mine one day. Much as I love this home it could never be the same without him.
I'm not after your house, Granddad, I only want you. Now stay put and I'll fetch you a cup of tea and some paracetamol.'

I walk quickly downstairs, my heart still in my throat. That really scared me; losing my Granddad is my biggest fear. Any of my family dying terrifies me but because of his age, he's always been a particular worry to me. Saying that, Ginny had been right up there with the rest of them and the worst had happened to her while she was still so young. I put the kettle on and feed the cats. Archie asks to go out but the second I open the door and a brisk wind blows his whiskers back, he has a change of heart. A fresh blanket of snow has covered the garden over night; untouched other than a few bird footprints around the seed feeder and Nanny's fountain. It looks Christmas card perfect and I decide that once the buyer has been, I will make a start on painting this very scene, for Granddad. Something that he can keep and hang above his mantle, this view is far too precious to sell. I walk back upstairs with tea, toast and paracetamol for Granddad. He has propped himself up on two pillows and is watching the breakfast news.

'Here you go, Granddad. I'm going to pop for a quick shower and then I'm going to run you a nice, warm bubble bath to soothe your old bones.' He takes a mock swipe at me and I duck away laughing.

'Thank you, nurse Efferson. I think I'll give the allotment a miss today. Has it been snowing again overnight?'

'Yes, it has, and you're going nowhere. I'm on the cooking today so you can just stay put until your nose gets the better of you and you come downstairs to see what the buyer says.'

'You know me too well, Missy,' Granddad mumbles through his cough.

'Right, enjoy your breakfast, I'll go fetch the paper, I just heard the letterbox. Then I'll leave you in peace for a while.'

I stand under the hot water enjoying the soothing calm wash over me. The relief when Granddad woke up, to throw an insult my way, had been palpable. The complete shock when we lost both Nanny and Ginny had been overwhelming. I never ever want to feel that way again but, with sadness, I recognise that the reality is that I will. This is why I treasure these moments with the people that I love; I know they, or I, won't be around forever and you just never know when it could strike. I could quite easily drive myself crazy by indulging in thoughts such as these. I climb out of the bath and wrap myself in a warm, fluffy towel from the radiator; I huddle under it for a few moments, allowing the heat to seep into my skin. A nice, cosy day at home is just what I feel like today. The art buyer will be here just after lunchtime. I can take some time to set out my work, maybe make some home-baked cookies and get the house looking all festive and even more welcoming. I wash out the tub and run a bath for Granddad. He won't stay in bed for long; he's a stubborn, old bugger. The only thing I will be able to convince him to do is to have a whiskey toddy to help stave off the chills. Tonight is dominoes night but I will try my best to get him to stay home.

By the time I've finished making my trademark, chocolate orange cookies; Granddad is downstairs in his good clothes ready to greet our guest. I glance nervously at the clock, its ten minutes to one. I have never been one for having faith in my abilities; I'm convinced this guy is going to turn up with a dog in a high-vis sash and carrying a white stick. My Granddad probably sold him it based on how wonderful he said it was, and that alone. I pace around the living room until my Grandfather complains that I'm wearing out the carpet and finds an old, Christmassy movie to pass the last hour. He claims to be feeling better now and does have a bit more colour about him. If he's not better by tomorrow, I'm making an appointment for him at the surgery. At ten to two, I put the kettle on; I nervously tap my fingers on the work top and freeze as I hear the doorbell.
'You get that, Ivy, love. That'll be your guest. I smooth down

my new skirt and jumper, fussing with my hair all the way to the door. I see the imposing figure on the other side of the glass and with a deep breath, pull open the door. I stare in shock at the person in front of me; I can't quite believe my eyes.

'Hello, you must be Ivy,' smiles the man, holding out a hand for me to shake. My head reels in disbelief before I finally manage to stammer out my words.

'Oh my God! What the hell are you doing here?'

Chapter Twenty-Three

'I'm your mystery collector, you know I'm a big fan of your sketches, Ivy,' Conor gives me his familiar lopsided grin, 'aren't you pleased to see me?' Of course I'm over the moon to see him but I'm in complete shock, mixed with a tiny hint of disappointment, if I'm being totally honest. I really thought this could be a serious buyer. Conor liking my art, whilst flattering, isn't quite the same as some big-shot art dealer who wants to plan an exhibition for me. I can't believe that Granddad managed to keep this secret from me; he must have been beyond excited after I said I couldn't get in touch with him and he knew he had planned for him to be here.
'Of course I'm delighted to see you. I tried to get in touch but my ex deleted your number and all my call history, by the time I thought about calling the Inebriated Leprechaun, you'd already gone. Oh, and I'm reading your book! It's scaring the shite out of me, you git.' I give Conor a light slap on his arm before pulling him into a hug. He laughs at my sudden outburst.
'Yes, Granddad told me about you losing my number. I didn't want to get in touch as I thought it may mess things up with your ex. But I hear you broke up with him months ago.'
'Yes, he's an idiot, I don't know why I thought we could make it work the second time around, but I guess we had to try because of the…' I stop abruptly, for some reason I can't bring myself to tell Conor about the baby yet. He notices my discomfort and changes the subject.
'So, can I see these works of art then or have I had a wasted trip?' I feel suddenly self-conscious about showing Conor my work, but I walk through to the front room and he follows.
'Hello there, son. What a surprise to see you here,' Granddad gives a throaty laugh.
'You old bugger, you knew all along,' I shake my head at my Grandfather, who gives me a rather sheepish look.

'Well, the boy has started collecting art for his nice new home he's planning on buying. I met him in Richmond a couple of weeks back when he was on his way to some gig. He asked if you'd carried on with your sketching but I told him you were too busy being a big-shot in the city.'
'Hardly,' I throw Conor a self-deprecating glance,' I'm only a Team Leader. Anyway, come through, Conor. You coming along, Granddad?'
'No, no, you young things go ahead. I'll get a brew going for us.'
'These are amazing, Ivy. I absolutely love that one of Terrace Garden. I used to hang out there sometimes in the summer, if the riverside got too busy. I'd find a little nook to hide in with my laptop. Apart from the occasional squirrel jumping around me, or the odd kid saying 'what'cha doing, Mister,' it was actually very tranquil.'
'I've always loved the gardens,' I smile nostalgically, 'we would have picnics there in the summer and go sledging in the winter.' I tilt my head to view the scene from a different angle. Conor spots the latest 'Fundon' Boris Johnson and David Cameron sketches and gives me a wry smile.
'You remembered,' he raises his eyebrows at me, 'that first day I met you, this is what I suggested. Right, how much for the lot? The two paintings and the two sketches.'
'Conor, you don't have to do this, it's a really nice thought but they're just not good enough to be on show.'
'Of course they are, Ivy. I am a serious buyer and I do think you have the potential to host an exhibition. Just because you know me doesn't mean you should value my opinion any less. I didn't even know you would be here until a few days ago. This is not some elaborate attempt to get you to like me.'
'I didn't say it was!' how dare he think that I assume he's buying my work to keep in favour with me, 'I don't *need* you to like me. I just don't need any pity sales from you. I don't need to do this at all, actually, I have a perfectly good job back

in Edinburgh.'
'Wow, Ivy, harsh! It's not a pity sale; I'm not trying to worm my way back into your life. I met your Granddad and saw a way of getting some good, quality art for my new home. Jaysus, and I thought pop stars were mardy.'
'Yes, that's another thing. Shouldn't you have your girlfriend here to choose with you, I mean I'm assuming she's going to have to look at them on a daily basis too.' We both stop abruptly as a loud clatter from the kitchen startles us. Granddad! We both run for the back door at the same time as the cats come tearing outside. A large puddle of tea seeps its way towards us and that's when I see him, my Granddad, lying face down on the floor by the kitchen table.

'He's breathing, Ivy, and he has a pulse. Where is that *fucking* ambulance?'
'It's OK, Granddad, we're going to get you to hospital in no time.' I stroke his calloused, rough hand. Thank God for Conor being the nominated first aider at the pub. I wouldn't have had a clue what to do. After checking Granddad's airway and pulse, he had lain down his cardigan to protect Granddad's head and elevated his legs over the waste paper basket to get more blood pumping to his heart. Conor paces anxiously between checking Granddad's pulse and respirations. In the distance we hear a siren and give a synchronised exhale in relief.
'I knew he shouldn't be living alone,' I shake my head angrily; 'I should never have left him last time.'
Conor throws me a sympathetic glance before jumping to his feet to show the paramedics where to find us.
'Hello, there, love. Is this your Granddad then? What's his name?'
'Yes, he is, his name is George Efferson. He had a bit of a cold and a cough this morning but he's been fine for weeks after his antibiotics. What's wrong with him?' I plead.

'Well that's what we're going to find out, try not to worry,' the older of the two males smiles at me reassuringly. 'I think we'll take him into Kingston to get checked over, his heart rate is a bit fast; tachycardia is always best checked out. You want to come in the ambulance with Granddad?' I nod mutely.
'I'll follow on behind, Ivy. I'll see you at the hospital.' Conor gives my arm a gentle squeeze, 'he will be fine, don't worry.' I throw a wad of kitchen roll on the floor to soak up the tea, as the paramedics put my Granddad on the stretcher.
'Mind you don't slip,' I urge, 'he was making tea and it's all over the floor.' I run outside to find Granddad's beloved boys, who are cowering together under the rhubarb patch.
'Come on, kitties,' I soothe, scooping one under each arm and carrying them into the front room. I set them down on the sofa and give them a head rub each. Granddad is in the ambulance now, so I quickly lock up and jump in the back.
I sit by Granddad in the ambulance as he drifts in and out of consciousness. I chat away, reassuring him when he's awake and let him rest when he dozes off. Finally, we arrive at Kingston hospital and Conor runs over to the back of the ambulance. We follow quickly behind as Granddad is wheeled into the Accident and Emergency department. He is taken straight through and a nurse stops us at the swinging, plastic doors.
'Just take a seat over there, dear, we're just going to run a few tests on your Granddad and will let you know of his progress as soon as we can. There's a coffee machine just through those double doors there.' Conor and I take a seat in the waiting area, mindlessly watching a silent Sky news on the TV on the wall.
'He will be fine, Ivy. He's tough as old boots, that one. Anyway, while I have you trapped, you still need to give me figure for all your art work.'
'Two and a half grand,' I shoot him a sidelong glance, I do appreciate his distraction techniques, even if all I can think

about is Granddad. Conor lets out a low whistle.
'So you had priced it all up then, you stubborn wench. Done deal! By the way, thank you for the sympathy purchase of my book. I just need another hundred thousand, or so, of those and I may make it into the best sellers list.' Point taken, I didn't buy his book for any other reason than I wanted to read it. Maybe, just maybe, he was buying my work because he genuinely wanted to look at it.
'I'm only joking, it's not worth all that, just give me a hundred quid.'
'Ivy, do me a favour, if you ever do have an exhibition, don't stand next to the prospective buyers telling them how shit you think it is and how there's a slight smudge over on that one. You have to sell your art to people; tell them what your inspiration was behind it. Self-deprecating bullshit does not a salesperson make. Is that all you want to achieve career-wise? The front end of a cow instead of the back?' I give him a gentle punch.
'No, anyway, I'm something big in the city, according to Granddad, but I'm moving back. I had almost decided but now I'm sure. Tash will manage, she will have to. My Granddad needs me now. Oh no, you wouldn't have heard! My best friend Ginny drowned on holiday in October. It's just been the most awful time since I saw you last. And now this,' I indicate to the plastic doors of the resus unit.
'Oh, I'm so sorry, Ivy, I know how close you were to her, were you with her on holiday?'
'No, just her and Tasha, her girlfriend. I flew out as soon as I heard and that's when they discovered her body in Rhodes harbour. It was just the most awful time,' I shake my head sadly at the memory. 'But at the very least, she got the funeral she wanted, we always told her she was being maudlin by telling us what she wanted but it proved rather comforting to know her last wishes in the end. She got everything she asked for apart from Elton John writing a song for her.' The giggles

start as I remember Ginny's serious face as she had begun to sing the lyrics she had envisaged; 'Goodbye lezzer Gin…' Conor crumples over in two as he tries to stifle his laughter. And of course, just like in the fertility clinic, this is the point when the nurse chooses to appear to tell us how Granddad is.
'You can see him now, dear,' she pats my shoulder and I realise she thinks we are extremely distressed with our red faces and streaming eyes. I follow her through guiltily.
'Ivy,' Granddad smiles as soon as he sees me, 'this one here seems to think I'm a bloody pin cushion. They want to do a chest X-ray on me so I'm being punted up to the wards.'
'Yes, we've had enough of your cheek here, Mr. Efferson. He caused us a bit of concern, you know. He told us his name was Bert and we thought he'd banged his head in the fall. Granddad is going to have a few tests, as he said, Ivy. We will keep him in for a day or two, it could be that his infection hasn't been properly cleared up but we will know more tomorrow.'
'Shall I come up too, Granddad?'
'No, love, it's teatime, you go have a catch up with your young friend here and I'll see you tomorrow. Save me some of those chocolate orange cookies, they're my favourite.' I kiss my Granddad's rough old cheek.
'You sure you don't want me to come back tonight?'
'No, I need a snooze and then they've probably got all sorts of punishing tests to try out on me. I'll see you tomorrow.' I hate leaving Granddad here but I feel better knowing that he's going to be thoroughly checked over. It's always been a struggle to get him to the doctors; now they have him, he can expect a full MOT.

We arrive back to Granddad's house and I pop in to check on Archie and Dave. They snooze oblivious on the couch. I mop up the spillage from the floor and tidy away the cups.
'I need a drink, I don't know about you, Conor.'

'Let's go and have tea out and a few drinks, just for old time's sake. The hospital has your mobile number, they'll call if there's any news. '
'Yeah, OK, Inebriated leprechaun?'
'Well, if we must, although I hear the food is shit since the old manager left. But since they're putting me up in the spare room at the moment I suppose I should really pay my keep.'
We head out to Conor's car and drive through Petersham, to the riverside. Conor pulls into a driveway off Richmond Green.
'One of my old punters houses, he's in his seventies and got rid of his car now. He said I could park here instead of paying the astronomical fees to park around here.'
'You are shameless, Byrne, preying on elderly people for free parking.'
'Hey, he had many a free pint from me during our lock-ins, it's payback time.' We walk down towards the river and immediately I'm filled with that familiar wonder of how beautiful Richmond is. At least now my mind is made up I can focus on thinking of what to say to work and to Tasha. I reckon Mum will have more to say about me quitting work than my boss will, but I made the mistake of going back once, I don't intend on making it a second time. We walk into the bar and I immediately notice two seats, right in front of the roaring fire. I walk quickly across the room and mark my territory with my coat and bag. Two men on their way over with their pints, give me a withering look. I pretend not to notice and Conor gives me a sly grin.
'Done like a true Londoner,' he laughs. We order some food and drinks and I really enjoy catching up with my friend. We talk about his books and how he was sorry not to get in touch when he was in Edinburgh. He is shocked to discover that I was living on Lothian Road at that time and he was out there for pizza with his agent. Then it's my turn to be shocked when I discover it was my favourite one, right under the flat.

'All this time we could have been catching up and we didn't,' I shake my head in disbelief. 'So, what's your girlfriend up to tonight?'
'Who? Oh I take it you mean Marissa? She never was my girlfriend. Sure, we went on a few dates but I got a bit uncomfortable when she started talking to the press about me. She's one high maintenance chick.'
'So, you weren't in Richmond to see her gig in Twickenham, then?' Conor laughs.
'No! I'm in Richmond because I'm about to do book signings around London. I did see a gig but it was an old, Dublin mate, doing an acoustic set. I figured I'd cash in a favour from the brewery for working my ass off for years and crash for a few nights in one of the staff rooms. Luckily, one of my old buddies in Head Office has been promoted and he sorted something out for me.'
'So, you broke it off with Marissa? I'm betting she's not used to that kind of treatment from a mere mortal. Oh, sorry, but you're not just a mere mortal now, are you, Mr. published author?'
'I'm just me, and I just got lucky. No, she was well pissed at me. Said I was a nobody just using her to further my career. She forgets that she asked me out and insisted on being seen out and about on our dates. She's a fame whore, I want the money but stuff the limelight.'
So, Conor is single, is he? Why does this give me a warm feeling inside? Perhaps it's just the wine. He voices this aloud; what is it with people knowing what I'm thinking?
'Hey look at that, I'm single and you're single, just like last time. But hey, don't worry, I know your life is far too complicated and you don't want a relationship.
'Oh, do shut up. Go and fetch me another drink.'

At nine o'clock, I head outside to call the hospital. Granddad has had his chest X-ray, a few more tests and is settled in for the night. He didn't eat much dinner but he wasn't too keen on the food. He was feeling much better and on a strong course of new antibiotics, they're not convinced it's an infection but he's on them as a precaution. I feel relieved hearing this and head back in to finish up my drink. Conor asks if he can visit tomorrow to pick up his paintings and calls me on my mobile so I can store his number again. Just like before, he walks me up to the bus stop by the poppy factory and waits with me until it arrives. I get home to the darkened house and a note from the lady next door; she had seen the ambulance and wished Granddad well. If there was anything she could do, please call. Who says Londoners have no sense of community. I place her note on the kitchen table; feed the cats and head upstairs to bed, with Granddad's two boys trailing behind me.

Chapter Twenty-Four

Conor appears just after lunchtime the next day, offering to give me a lift to the hospital and to pick up his paintings on the way back. I agree, it will be good to have the company and I want to take Granddad in some fish and chips since he's not eating. With a lift to the hospital they'll stay nice and hot. I have no idea if I'm allowed to take in food but as he's in his own side room, I'm planning on sneaking in with them well wrapped up. We arrive just before two and scurry past the nursing station as quickly as we can. Luckily, nobody is there at the moment and we manage to find Granddad's room before we're spotted. He's sitting up in bed watching TV when we go in, he looks delighted to see us and even more so when I hastily unwrap his lunch.

'Here, hide this under your blanket. The nurses may not allow this but I know you don't like the hospital food.' Granddad gives a raspy chuckle and lifts his blanket for me to put his lunch under. He tucks in immediately and I pour him a glass of the Lucozade that I've brought in.

'You're a bad girl, Ivy Efferson. Did you have a nice evening then,' a curious smile plays on his lips.

'Yes, we did, thanks. We went to Conor's old pub. The food is so much better under the new management. ' Conor elbows me and narrows his eyes.

'Want a chip, son? I'll never eat all this.'

'Oh go on then, George, if only to stop you from being busted.'

'How are the boys?' Granddad enquires.

'Oh they're fine. Archie slept with me, as usual and Dave took advantage of the fact that you weren't at home and spread right over your bed horizontally. They've been fed and watered but they can tell something's not quite right in their world. Granddad rips off a piece of fish and puts it quickly in his mouth whilst glancing guiltily at the door.

'So, do they know what's wrong with you yet?'
'I've had the Oncology doctor down this morning. Seems there's a shadow on my lung in the X-ray.'
'Oncology! Oh Granddad, there must be some mistake,' I look from Granddad to Conor in horror. 'What can they do? Can they treat it?'
'Oh, I don't know, love. I'm an old man; I'm not messing about with that radioactive therapy or whatever it's called. I never was going to live forever, Ivy.'
'But Granddad, you have to try everything. They can probably do a combination of chemotherapy and radiotherapy. You've got years in you yet.' Conor squeezes my hand.
'Wait and see what tests come back, Ivy. It may not be what you think, and Granddad wants to enjoy his naughty lunch, don't you, George.'
'That I do, son, anyway, they reckon there's no need to keep me beyond another day or so. I'll be back home in no time. I'm worried about my allotment.'
'Don't you dare!' I scold, 'I'm going to contact work and tell them I need to stay here. I can send for my clothes and stuff, I don't need to go back.'
'You go and get your things, Ivy. Speak to work by all means but you need to speak to Tasha face to face and make sure your Dad knows I'm fine. I spoke to him last night and he sounded worried, said he would come down but I don't need all that fuss.'
'I could always stay over to help you out at home, George,' Conor offers, 'I'm bordering on alcoholism living in that pub anyway. I could check in on your allotment too or at least give you a lift over to see what's going on.'
'Yes, that's a great idea, Granddad. I'd feel so much better leaving if I knew Conor was there with you.' Granddad rolls up his chip paper and hands it back to me to hide in my handbag.

'Well, I don't think I need a babysitter but if it would help the lad out, I don't see why not.'
'It's settled then,' I beam, 'I'll go home tomorrow and wrap things up in Edinburgh. I'll be back down in a few days, in time for Conor to start his signings.' Granddad nods his agreement and Conor smiles his relief at me. He's cute, I'm noticing it more and more now. There's nothing as attractive as an attentive man and he's really pulling out all the stops for Granddad and I. I'm so happy to be back in touch with him. We all turn as the door opens and in walks the nurse.
'Right, Mr. Efferson, time for your meds. Is that...is that chips I smell?' All three of us shrug in unison, with innocent smiles.
The next morning, Conor drives me up to Kings Cross to catch my train. He's heading back to Richmond via Dukes Meadow, to check on the allotment, before heading on to Kingston hospital to collect Granddad. I'm still really worried about him but I feel so much better leaving him in my friend's competent hands. I text Tasha to let her know I'll be in at teatime. It's Thursday so this is her early finish day. I called Dad to tell him about the Oncologist visiting. Dad agrees it's a good idea for me to move down, he could see I wasn't enjoying my job to the fullest and after Ginny's death; he just wanted to see me do what makes me happy. Life is too short to do otherwise, we've seen that now. Dad will drive me down himself as he really wants to see his father. It's been over a year and I can tell he feels a little guilty about this, especially now Granddad's health is worsening. I sit on the train and watch the scenery fly by. I haven't had a reply from the text I sent Tash, but I'm taking that as a good sign that she's coping just fine.

I arrive into Haymarket station just before four; perfect timing as I can head straight into work to see Steve before he finishes at five. I do feel rather apprehensive as I buzz myself in with my pass. They're not going to be happy but I'm just going to have to be as honest as I can. I had hoped to tell my parents face to face too but because of the Oncology referral, I decided I wanted to say to Dad as soon as I could. I take the lift up to the seventh floor and walk through the office, waving to my team who I'm pleased to see are all hard at work. Steve's secretary calls through to say I'm here and I can go straight through, I take a deep breath and give two sharp knocks on the door.

'Come in,' he shouts.'

'Hi Steve, sorry to drop in on you unannounced like this but I just need a quick word. '

'I have no problem with staff who love their work so much that they even come in on their holidays,' he laughs. Oh dear, now I feel guilty. I take a seat opposite him and decide to come straight out with it.

'Thing is, Steve, my Granddad collapsed the other day and now has a referral to Oncology. He really isn't managing too well on his own anymore and I really want to be there for him.'

'I see,' Steve nods slowly, 'and this is your Grandfather in London, I take it.'

'Yes, he has no other family nearby. I really need to do this, Steve. I'm really sorry; I know I was just about to take up another new role too. I do feel like I'm letting you down.'

'I understand, Ivy. You're a real family person, I can tell. So you'll just work out your months' notice and move down then?'

'Oh, a month? I thought it was two weeks' notice I had to give,' panic fills my heart; I can't possibly leave Granddad for that long.

'Ahh, now it was under the terms of your original contract but the senior role is one month. Think yourself lucky, I have to give three.' Steve gives me a knowing look, 'You need to go sooner, don't you?' I give an apologetic nod. 'Well, I can't stop you from walking out, of course, but I must warn you, they'll never re-employ you if you do and you won't be allowed to use us as a reference, either.' I give a deep sigh. What if I can't live off my art? There will be a big gap in my CV without this job. But then, I could say I took time out to follow my new career path and care for Granddad. To be completely honest I don't know that I'd choose this line of work again anyway. I'd maybe take a bar job, or some other kind of evening work, so I can combine it with my art in the days and still have money. The image of my Granddad lying face down on the hard floor tiles fills my head, there's no competition.

'Steve,' I begin, assertively, 'I'm very sorry, but I quit, effective as of today.' Steve smiles, knowing he is beaten.

'In that case, Ivy, I am very sorry to see you go and I wish you every success in your future.' Steve puts his hand out for me to shake but then changes his mind and comes around the desk to give me a hug.

'I hope your Granddad gets well soon, Ivy. Take care.' I rush quickly from the office, waving goodbye to my team, for the last time; I'd stay to explain but I won't get all of them off the phone at the same time and I'd really rather get home to see Tasha. I skip out into the setting sun, feeling free and relieved. Now, Tasha, the last one to face. I turn into Lothian Road and head for the flat.

'Tasha, Tash? Are you home?' I can hear music coming from the front room and walk quickly down the hall before I can lose my nerve. 'Tasha, I… Oh, Evelyn, hi! What are you doing here?'

'Ivy, I thought you in Richmond?' Evelyn throws a confused glance at Tasha, who has just appeared at the kitchen door with two plates of food.

'I text Tasha yesterday, didn't you get it?'

'No, I didn't get any text from you, Ivy.' Tash puts the plates down and checks her phone. I take mine from my bag and tap

the message icon.
'Oh shit, it never sent, I'm sorry Tash, I've only just noticed this. Oh my God, are you two having a date? I'm *so* sorry!' I stammer in shock. My sister and friend look at each other and laugh.
'Not exactly,' Evelyn smiles, 'Tasha isn't ready for a new relationship but we are friends. We're just enjoying each other's company…a couple of nights a week.'
'OK, well that makes what I have to say a little easier. I just quit my job and I'm moving down to Richmond to care for Granddad. He collapsed yesterday as you probably know, but now they've found a shadow on his lung. I'm really scared that he has cancer, I need to be with him.'
'Oh, Ivy, I'm so sorry to hear that. Yes, of course you should be there,' Tash pulls me into a hug.
'Oh poor Granddad, Ivy, I'll come down to see him as soon as I can. I thought his chest infection had come back, I feel terrible that I wasn't even too worried.'
'That's OK, Evelyn, that's what Conor and I thought too.'
'*Conor*?' they shout in unison.
'Er, well we kind of met up again, Granddad shamelessly made him buy some of my art.'
Evelyn gives me a sly look, 'Oh get you, Florence Nightingale, it's not going to be all hand on brow down there then.'
'Oh do fuck off, dear,' I laugh. 'Anyhoo, I'm off to see Mum and Dad now, do you want me to stay out until late?' I smirk.
'No, not necessary thank you. Mind the door doesn't hit your arse on the way out,' my sister shouts after me. 'Oh, and you're in for a big surprise at their house.' I skip downstairs wondering what that's supposed to mean.

'Dad, what do you mean Mum's in rehab? I stare at my father in disbelief.
'Just what I said, Ivy, I told her either she sobers up or I'm filing for divorce,' Dad shrugs and pours me a cup of tea from

the pot. I sit down heavily on the kitchen chair.
'Jeez, I can only imagine how pissed at you she is right now,' I swirl my spoon absentmindedly around my cup.
'She was fine, actually. She admitted that it was creeping earlier and earlier in the day and she really needed to get it under control. We can't see her this week, though; she has therapy sessions and withdrawal to go through first. They sent home her perfume with me, she wasn't happy about that, wouldn't even let her have her mouthwash in there.' I shake my head to waken myself from this bizarre dream. What a head-fuck of a year, I'm having. Perhaps I've just gone mad and none of this is even true.
'So, what time do you want to leave tomorrow? Any time is good for me.'
'As early as possible, Dad, I can't wait to get home to Granddad.'
'I'm amazed you didn't do all this years ago, you know. You always loved Richmond so much so that I thought you'd be off like a shot as soon as you could make your own decisions,' Dad frowns.
'I should have really, life got in the way, I suppose. I just kind of settled for what I had.'
'You should never 'settle,' Ivy. You should always make your life extraordinary. It's not a dress rehearsal.'
'Now where was that advice when I needed it,' I throw my father a cross look.
'You never bloody ask my opinion, young lady; I'm a fountain of knowledge, I'll have you know.'
'Oh yeah, and you're so happy with lil' old gin drinker Babs, are you?'
'I'll be happier when she's clean but yes, I am actually. It's all just a bit of banter with your mother and I.'
'Hmmm,' I mutter under my breath, unconvinced. 'Anyway, I'll best make tracks, shall I take the car so I can load up and come and get you tomorrow?'

'Yes, that's fine, although I don't mind giving you a hand in the morning.'
'No, that's fine; I'll get packed up tonight and come over for you about ten.' I pick up Dad's car keys and kiss him on the cheek. 'Thanks for this, Dad. I'm sorry I won't see Mum before I go but at least this way she can't nag me to stay.' I head home for my last evening with Tasha but in my head, I've already started my new life in Richmond.

Chapter Twenty-Five

Dad and I arrive into London at half past six the next evening. I had lost patience in a service station on the M6 and demanded that I take over the driving. Dad's insistence at sticking to the slow lane and driving no more than sixty, had finally tipped me over the edge. He had reluctantly agreed and we had made good progress from then on. I can barely contain my excitement as Dad, Conor and I carry the cases and boxes up to my room. The cats have a good sniff around all these new items with an unfamiliar scent on them. Once we are unloaded, Dad and I freshen up before we all head out to the local pub. I had suggested it may be better to stay in, since Granddad was not long out of hospital but was shot down with his words,

'I may be dead soon; let me enjoy myself before I go.' If I have any say in this at all, and the worst is confirmed, Granddad with be having all treatment possible to cure him. I can be a force to be reckoned with too, when it suits me. We pull on our coats and all traipse the short distance to Granddad's local.

'So, Conor, when are you telling Ivy your news?' Granddad gives my friend a mischievous look.

Conor looks slightly uncomfortable and takes a long sip of his pint before answering.

'Well, I do have good news actually, Ivy. I showed some of your work to a gallery manager friend of mine and he thought it was fantastic. They're having an exhibition in March and he wants to show off some of your paintings.' I stare at Conor in disbelief. I don't know if I want to punch him or hug him right at this moment.

'He actually *liked* it?'

'He actually *loved* it! He wants some more local stuff and the 'Fundon' ones in paintings. He was really excited about those.'

'That must have been the exhibition that guy from the art shop was on about, Granddad. Do you remember? He said he was taking part, oh I hope he doesn't think I'm barging in there because he told me about it.'
'Nothing wrong with a bit of healthy competition, Ivy,' Granddad dismisses my concerns with a wave of his hand.
'And…' Granddad prompts Conor to continue.
'Oh, yes, and I made the bestsellers list with my first book. They've re-signed me for another three book deal.'
'Conor, that's fantastic,' I shout. He laughs and puts his hand over my mouth.
'Shush, I don't need the whole pub to know. It's a pretty hefty advance this time so I'm looking at buying a property. I first thought Dublin but the Edinburgh agency has just opened a London branch, so it makes more sense to stay here.'
I raise my wine in a toast and the others follow suit.
'Cheers, to both of you,' Dad announces. 'I'm so proud of you, Ivy, and even though it's not my place to be, I'm proud of you too, son.' Conor smiles warmly at my father before heading to the bar for refills for us all.
'Now that's a lad I'd be happy to see you with, lass. Not just because he has ambition but there's something in the way he looks at you.' Granddad nods his head.
'I've seen that look before, son. It's the same puppy dog eyes that you used to give Barbara, many moons ago, before the eye-rolling began.' I can't hold in my laughter, I know exactly what Granddad means.
'Oh, and you weren't all pathetic over Mum, were you, Dad? You never embarrassed us kids by sneaking little kisses when you thought we weren't looking,' Dad banters back. Granddad tuts and shakes his head as Conor takes a seat back at the table.
'So, I could do with some advice on house hunting, Ivy. You fancy helping me?'
'Yeah, sure, just say when and I'll be there.'

'And if you fancy it, do you want to come up to Oxford Street for the first signing? I could do with some moral support.' I glance at Granddad.
'I'll be fine, the lad needs you there. I'll get you to come to the hospital with me tomorrow, though. All my results are back and I have to go in to discuss them.'
'I'll take you, Dad,' my father pats Granddad's rough old hand.
'That would be good, son. We don't like to put upon these young ones, do we? You know what it's like to be old and a burden.' Dad frowns at Granddad's comment.
'You're not a burden, Granddad, not at all. I wouldn't mind going with you, but if you want Dad there instead then that's fine. If he's driving then you probably should have left an hour ago, though.' Dad chortles into his pint and I give him a sarcastic smile. I'm secretly relieved that he will go instead. I don't know how to prepare myself for any possible bad news and I won't be much use to Granddad if I'm a sobbing heap on the floor.

The next morning I awaken early with a sinking feeling in my stomach. I glance at the clock; it's just after nine. Granddad's appointment is at ten. I jump quickly out of bed and wander downstairs in Nanny's housecoat and slippers. Christmas carols float out of the front room and the tree lights twinkle gently as if dancing in time to the music. I walk past Granddad's boys who are stretched out in front of the crackling fire and into the kitchen to find my family. There's an amicable silence in the kitchen as Dad finishes off a fry-up whilst reading the newspaper. Granddad potters around the cooker in Nanny's floral pinny. I lean against the door frame and smile at the sight of my two favourite men, enjoying each other's company. Granddad looks around, sensing me watching.
'Oh, there she is. You ready for your breakfast? It's all ready

in the oven.'
'Yes, please, Granddad.' I take a seat at the table and Dad looks up from his paper, with a smile.
'Good morning, love. We are just about to head off. I remember how the parking was at Kingston hospital and want to leave plenty time.' I doubt I'll be able to manage much of my breakfast; I'm so nervous about Granddad's results. Granddad puts the plate down in front of me then puts on his coat and bonnet.
'Right, son, let's go see what this lot know.' I watch through the frosty kitchen window as they walk down the path. My stomach flips over several times and I take a deep breath. All will be fine. I pick a little at my breakfast and put the remainder of my bacon into the cat's bowls, Archie runs through at the sound of my plate scraping. I glance at the clock; they should be back by twelve, maybe a warm bath will calm me down.

I hear the familiar sound of my Granddad's clapped out Volvo an hour and a half later. I immediately stop my unpacking and run downstairs. I stare at my father's ashen face and know the diagnosis. I hold my breath and wait for Granddad to start talking.
'It's lung cancer, Ivy, secondary cancer. I also have it in my liver.' I stare at my Grandfather in shock before running to hug him.
'Shush now, I'll be fine. We spoke about chemo and radio therapy and I said I'll think about it. Me and your Dad are off for a bar lunch in Richmond. I intend to cram in as much as I can, so get your coat, love.' I scrub away at my eyes in my bedroom; I somewhat resemble a panda. So this is it. The worst has happened again. Why doesn't it matter how much I try and stay positive, I get the same result time and time again. My poor Granddad; he must be terrified. I redo my eye make-up and pull my brush through my hair. It's not fair

to ruin what time Granddad may have left by being miserable. I should be taking a leaf out of his book and staying positive to enjoy the time he has. I can be with him every day for the rest of his life now, and for that, I'm so grateful. I text Conor to let him know about Granddad's results and to ask if he wants to meet us for lunch in half an hour. He replies immediately saying he is shocked and sorry to hear the news and if it's appropriate for him to be there, then he'd love to come along. I know it will be fine as Granddad had already suggested it; I think he wanted a distraction for me. We take the bus to the Inebriated Leprechaun and take our seats in a booth by the window. I glance outside; the river is like a scene from a Christmas card. Being here with my family, in spite of our shocking news, is perfect. This is the stuff memories are made of. Nanny was right with her favourite phrase, what's for you won't go past you. I've always looked so much into the future that I forget to enjoy the present. We aren't guaranteed the future, but we do have today. There is a little evidence of forced joviality in the beginning, but by the second drink we are sharing our memories of the years gone by. I always have enjoyed my Grandfather's tales of his life, but now it's like I'm hearing them for the first time, like I need to absorb every detail. One day I'll wish he was here to repeat some particular funny story that I can't quite recall. I tell Conor that I always dreamed of living here when I was little. Because Scotland had different school holidays, we were often down in the summer holidays whilst the English kids were still in class. I'd look enviously at the children coming out of Vineyard School, in their little gingham dresses. Traipsing over for an impromptu art class in Terrace Gardens or sitting with their Mums or Nannies eating ice cream after school. Edinburgh seemed grey and busy to me; ironic really, as that's usually the perception people have of London. But Richmond is leafy and green, with big, open spaces and seems to catch all the best of the summer weather. After lunch, Granddad looks

tired and drawn, Dad suggests taking him home to rest but Conor has a naughty twinkle in his eye.
'Ivy, I need to borrow you for an hour or so. I need a second opinion on a house I want to look at.' Granddad and Dad exchange a look.
'Sure, if that's fine with the others.'
'Yes, you go ahead. We're travelling in style and taking a cab home today, aren't we Dad,' my father smiles.
Conor and I walk through the gardens, laughing as we cling to each other on the icy path.
'Let's go buy a sledge and come back later, Ivy. I bet you haven't done that in years.'
'I can't go sledging, we're far too old, Conor,' I smile.
'So what? We could still show the kids a thing or two, I'm betting.'
'I'll think about it. Where is this place, anyway?'
'Here.' Conor stops in his tracks and points to the smaller of the grand, hilltop houses.'
'Are you serious? Even with a huge advance you couldn't afford this, could you?'
'Don't be fucking stupid, of course I can't afford this. But I do need something to aspire to and the estate agent doesn't know we can't afford it.'
'We?' I raise my eyebrows mockingly.
'Yes, *we*. Conor Byrne, the bestselling author and his talented artist girlfriend. Oh come on, Ivy, it'll be fun.' The estate agent pulls up alongside us, jumping out of the car to shake our hands and gushing about how he has just downloaded Conor's new book for his kindle. I had no choice but go along with it. I wander in awe from room to room; even the view I had imagined isn't a patch on this one; I can see for miles, right over to Twickenham and beyond. This property porn has made me so envious of how some people live. Conor may one day afford something like this but I never will. I gasp as we walk into a beautifully decorated nursery; complete with

old fashioned rocking horse. I run my hand along the well-crafted baby crib and can't help but give a wistful sigh.
'Oh-er mate, best watch out; looks like someone's getting broody,' the estate agent gives a jolly laugh. I was born broody, but still, what a cheeky bugger. I glance at Conor and luckily he's taking it in good form. 'So what do you think? Will you be putting in an offer?' the estate agent can't help rubbing his hands with glee.
'We still have a few to see; Richmond Green and a couple in Barnes. We'll let you know.' After more hand shaking at the door, we finally part company and head into Richmond town centre.
'That was mean, Byrne. I'll never afford a place like that in a million years.'
'I plan to,' Conor shrugs, 'my agent has organized a few chat shows and stuff for me, I have a new deal signed and anyway, you have an exhibition to organise, paint as many as you can and the sales will come, trust me.'

After an afternoon of revisiting our childhoods, sledging down the steep slopes of Terrace Gardens, Conor finally drives me home, soaked and shaking with the cold. We'd ignored all the grumpy looking parents, watching us scornfully as they stood, bundled up in gloves and hats. Only the children they were with laughed, squealed and had any kind of fun. Rather than feel silly in front of the other adults, I actually felt sorry for them. Sometimes we get so caught up in the minutiae of our lives, work and paying the bills that we do forget to stop and smell the roses. I like that about Conor; he brings out the fun side of me, left to my own devices I can tend to be rather serious. Ginny was very like him too in that way. Maybe that's why Conor and I get on so well. He's not afraid to laugh at life and go after what he wants; it's a good way to live. We pull up outside Granddad's door.
'Now go paint, Efferson. Let's see who can make their half of

the money for a house on the hill first. I shall pop by tomorrow to see Granddad and view your progress on the painting that you *will* be up at seven to start.' He gives me a blink-and-you'd-miss-it, kiss on the lips and I watch in shock as he zooms off into the early evening half-light; feeling like I've just been hit by a tornado. That's exactly how I'd describe Conor, a whirlwind; so full of energy and excitement that you just can't help being pulled along with him.

Chapter Twenty-Six

I fidget nervously in the entrance to the gallery, glancing at my reflection in the window and fiddling with my rather complicated up-do. My floor length, black, sparkling gown that left me little change from a grand, clings to me in all the wrong places. I should have got a twelve but the sales assistant had insisted that this size had looked better. Unfortunately, that was three weeks ago when the stress of having a complete collection, coupled with worry over Granddad's health had rendered me nauseous and virtually unable to eat. Now, three and a half months after Christmas, with Granddad's chemotherapy finished for the time being and a full complement of art to show, I had made up for it, and some.

'You look lovely, stop fussing. I love that red lipstick on you, it looks *hot.*'

'Not now, Conor, I'm shiting myself here,' I tut.

'Oh, you're all class,' he laughs, 'and me? How do I look?'

'Really smart, very hipster in your slightly too skinny suit and pointy boots. What time is it?'

'Ten to seven. They'll be letting the hordes in soon. Have you seen the queue? There must be fifteen people out there.'

'Oh shut up, I counted twenty-six. Just 'cos you had over five hundred at your first book signing. I prefer to have a small, select group of pity buyers, you clearly had Sir Bob Geldof and Midge Ure organise it for you, a full on pity benefit event.

Conor chuckles and pours us a glass of champagne each; we clink glasses. I down mine like a shot and Conor rolls his eyes.

'Right, that's it until you're schmoozing with your fans, and don't forget, you don't know me; I'll bump those prices right up by pretending I want to buy.'

'Don't you dare,' I hiss, 'you're my boyfriend; don't see this as an excuse to chat up women. What time is it? '

'Women who aren't barking mad, making me trail round every store in London, looking for a dress she saw in a dream, you mean. Bring 'em to Papa. And it's three minutes past your last enquiry about the time.'

'It was a premonition, not a dream; and besides, I don't remember you being in it, nipping my head.'

'That's fine, I can leave. I have better things to do with my time anyway…'

'No! You can't leave me, I need you here.'

'Oh you *need* me, do you? I thought little Miss independent needed no man? Conor smiles sarcastically. There's a loud clunk as the gallery manager slides the bolt on the door. I stare at Conor in horror before grabbing his champagne glass and downing that too.

'It's squeaky bum time, Ivy, are you ready?'

'No!' I fix a welcoming smile to my face and brace myself for the walk to the door.

An hour later and I'm feeling much less anxious. I've already sold three from my collection of twenty; two large ones of the riverside from different angles and a small one of a doe with her fawn, in Richmond Deer Park. Conor placed the sold stickers under them with great care and pride. I'm chatting to a lawyer from Chiswick when I first see them and I do a double take, as does my sister, when she sees me.

'Please excuse me, I need to greet my new guests,' I say politely to the gentleman before running, most ungraciously, the full length of the room.

'Evelyn, Tasha! I can't believe you're here. I didn't actually expect you to accept my invite.'

'Who the fuck made you over, Ivy? Is Gok Wan here?' Evelyn looks around urgently, smoothing down her hair.

'I'll take that as a compliment, shall I?' I smile before moving on to Tasha. 'How are you, love?'

'I'm good, thanks, Ivy, although I am wondering if I picked

the wrong sister,' she laughs at Evelyn's frown. 'Look who else is here, Ivy,' Tasha smiles. I turn back to the door where Dad is pushing Granddad up the ramp, in his wheelchair, with Mum following closely behind.

'Oh, Granddad, you're here! Thank you all for coming; I'll feel so much better with my family here. I thought you had plans this weekend, Mum and Dad?' I pull them into a group hug.

'We did. This!' Mum gives me an incredulous look. I embrace my Granddad as he stands, with difficulty, from his chair.

'Let me be your personal guide,' I link my arm with his and my family follow on behind, making approving noises over their champagne, or in Mum's case, a sparkling water.

'I love that one, Ivy,' Evelyn points to 'Terrace Gardens in spring.' It's one of my own favourites with its watery sunshine and blossom.

'Well Evelyn, it's yours for three fifty. I thought you may like that one; it reminds me of our childhood; Easter break holidays is what I think when I look at it.'

'What do you think, Tash? I can't spend all my divorce settlement by myself; and the colours would go with the newly decorated living room in the Bitchelor pad…'

'I love it, Ev. Conor, we need a sold sticker over here.'

'This is my favourite,' Granddad smiles nostalgically at one of him and Nanny sitting on their deck chairs in the garden. Nanny with her sewing and Granddad with his newspaper, a jug of lemonade sits on the table and the cats lay at their feet.

'Oh, look at the sign; it's not for sale, what a shame. I could have blown some of your inheritance on it,' Granddad gives a raspy cough through his laughter.

'Oh, I displayed that just for viewing purposes, it already has a home.'

'Oh well, not to worry. Get a photo of it, Evelyn, on that fancy, new phone thingy of yours.'

'You won't need one, Granddad; its new home is the Back-Arse of Beyond in Richmond.' My Grandfather's face crumples as he looks at me. 'It's for my favourite man in the world, but don't tell Dad and Conor I said that,' I whisper.

I manage to sell a total of seven paintings and one donation to a very good home. I would have been delighted to even have sold one. There were a lot of I- told-you-so moments that weekend, from Granddad and Conor; for the first time ever I believe that I could potentially consider myself an artist. I had the most amazing time with my family; a pub lunch on the river, on the Saturday and a Sunday lunch at Granddad's which rolled back the years for all of us. I was sorry to see them leave on Monday morning. Tash and Evelyn had even called in sick for the occasion. Granddad's painting has pride of place over the mantle in the living room. Now he can see Nanny every day until they are reunited, which I'm hoping will not be for a long time yet. He's far from well but has responded fairly promisingly to his treatment. The doctors say he will never be cured, it is terminal, but they can try to buy him some time and manage his pain, which is at least something.

I wave off my family with Granddad and Conor by my side. What a fantastic weekend, not just because of my successful exhibition but seeing Granddad's face when I told him the painting was his and having the surprise of everyone traipsing down from Edinburgh. I glance down as my phone buzzes in my pocket.
'Hello? Yes, this is she. You do? Oh, Ok. Can you give me five minutes please? I'm just around the corner. Thanks, bye.'
I help Granddad back to his chair in the back garden. Dave jumps into his lap and settles down for a snooze. 'Conor, can you stay with Grampy for a minute, please? I just need to pop out.'

'Yeah, sure thing; tea and dominoes, George?' My Grandfather gives an approving nod and I turn back down the path.

'I can't be! I stare at Dr. Cameron in shock, 'I mean, I've been really stressed, what with Granddad's health and my exhibition, but I had a urine infection, I'm sure of it. I was told the results were back and to pop in, just five minutes ago.'
The doctor stares at me with the declining patience of someone who has seen this before.
'Ivy, we sent your sample off to the lab and I can confirm you are eight weeks pregnant,' she pauses, giving me a withering gaze. 'Go on then, this is the part where you tell me you've done loads of partying,' she prompts.
'Oh my God, but I have! Well not loads, just weekends, but enough to know I wouldn't have, had I known.'
'And what did I tell you before?'
'I know, I know, it's really common and it feeds from the yolk sac. Do I get a scan?' I give the doctor my biggest smile. 'I do have history of miscarriage, I'd feel so much better for one.'
'Yes, pop up on the bed and we'll take a look, then.'
Oh, but I really want my boyfriend with me for the scan this time; it's a different one,' I add sheepishly. 'He's just around the corner, I'll be really quick. Five minutes, tops!'
'I have five other patients out there, Ivy. Come back in an hour, I'll squeeze you in before I have my lunch,' Dr. Cameron gives an exasperated sigh.
'Thank you,' I squeak, and off down the corridor. I'll fetch both Granddad and Conor; just in case this is the only chance Granddad gets to see my baby. Although the thought makes me shudder, I want him there, just in case. I swing open the garden gate and run into the house.
'Hey, you two, don't get too comfy, we're going out soon.' Conor and Granddad look up from their dominoes.

'Where to? We've just got into this, I'm winning,' Conor complains.
'You'll see, it's a surprise.' I skip into the house to fetch myself a tea. So, you think you're the masters of surprise, do you? With your mystery buyers and your organising of exhibitions. Well, more power to you both, to steal Conor's phrase. Just you wait and see. Ivy Eff is better at surprises than any of you!

Epilogue

The July sun beats down on my back; it feels so much hotter than last year, but then, I didn't have this huge bump to contend with then. I sit in the garden of the Back-Arse of Beyond and work on my sketch. This one is for baby's room. We don't yet know if we're having a boy or a girl but we'll find out later today at our twenty week scan. It's been almost a month since Granddad went home to Nanny and I miss him so much. He went peacefully and for that I'm thankful. I'd been sat by his bed, in his own home, when I knew. His eyes opened and he looked up into the corner of the room, smiling and listening intently.
'What is it Granddad, is she there? Is it time?' He had glanced at me, then. His eyes were slightly glazed over but for some reason he seemed more alive than he had in years. He gave a slow nod and reached up to pull down his oxygen mask.
'Hi Nanny,' I whispered into the silence. My Granddad's voice croaks a little as he speaks but I can hear him clearly enough.
'Goodbye, Ivy,' he murmurs, before turning back to the corner of the ceiling. It was peaceful, beautiful almost. I kissed his rough, old cheek,
'Goodbye, Granddad.'

The package I received in the post this morning, had both surprised and delighted me. The huge sentimental value held within had brought back so many happy memories. I smile over at Conor as he sits in Granddad's old deckchair, eagerly typing away at his latest creation. Archie and Dave lazily sun themselves by his feet.
'It's finished, come and see.' We look at it together and he gives my shoulder a gentle squeeze.
'Baby will love it, I'm sure. It's really good, Ivy.'

‘Thanks,’ I smile, ‘I think so too.’ I’ve learned how to sing my own praises these days, no more self-deprecating Ivy Efferson. That won’t buy our house on the hill, and I intend to make my share before Byrne can.

You know what the nicest thing is about this sketch? It’s that even though our baby will outgrow these tiny, red trainers, our son or daughter will always have a reminder of just how important they were to their Auntie Ginny. Because even though the ones we love may move on, as Ralph once told me. Nobody is ever ‘lost.’

Louise Burness was born in 1971 and raised in the Scottish town of Arbroath. She spent several years living in Edinburgh and Fife, travelling around Australia and South East Asia and eight years living in West London. She currently lives in Arbroath and writes full-time. Louise has also written chick-lit, 'Crappily Ever After' and two children's books, 'Under the Sun,' and 'Rock upon a time.'